Praise for Bianca D'Arc's
Border Lair

"*Border Lair* is part of a complex series but can be read as a standalone, with sympathetic characters and well-imagined warfare. [...] I enjoyed this exciting tale and will be looking out for more of her work."

~ *Fresh Fiction*

"...I was enraptured by D'Arc's world. Bringing together dragons, war and love, D'Arc is readily able to transport readers to another time, giving them an escape that they will sure to remember."

~ *Under the Covers Book Blog*

"*Border Lair* keeps the suspense going, not only about the war with Skithdron but Jared's emotional turmoil. [...] I am looking forward to reading the next book in this series."

~ *Literary Nymphs Reviews*

"With her usual flair, Bianca pens an amazing story of heroism, loss, love, and renewal. Weaving together the lives of three unique people and making it believable is an enviable talent and I cannot wait until the next books are out."

~ *Fallen Angel Reviews*

Look for these titles by
Bianca D'Arc

Now Available:

Dragon Knights
Maiden Flight
Border Lair
The Ice Dragon
Prince of Spies
Wings of Change
FireDrake
Dragon Storm
Keeper of the Flame
The Dragon Healer
Master at Arms

Resonance Mates
Hara's Legacy
Davin's Quest
Jaci's Experiment
Grady's Awakening

Tales of the Were
Lords of the Were
Inferno

Brotherhood of Blood
One & Only
Rare Vintage
Phantom Desires
Sweeter Than Wine
Forever Valentine
Wolf Hills
Wolf Quest

Gifts of the Ancients
Warrior's Heart

String of Fate
Cat's Cradle

StarLords
Hidden Talent

Print Anthologies
Caught by Cupid
I Dream of Dragons Vol. 1
Brotherhood of Blood

Border Lair

Bianca D'Arc

SAMHAIN
PUBLISHING

Samhain Publishing, Ltd.
11821 Mason Montgomery Road, 4B
Cincinnati, OH 45249
www.samhainpublishing.com

Border Lair
Copyright © 2013 by Bianca D'Arc
Print ISBN: 978-1-61921-548-1
Digital ISBN: 978-1-61921-395-1

Editing by Amy Sherwood
Cover by Angela Waters

This book has been previously published and revised from its original release.

First Samhain Publishing, Ltd. electronic publication: September 2012
First Samhain Publishing, Ltd. print publication: October 2013

Dedication

This is for all those who have experienced loss and somehow learned to go on. When I first created Jared and wrote his catharsis, I was afraid I'd gone too far. I thought maybe I'd crossed a line.

Thanks to so many wonderful readers who reached out to tell me that Jared's story somehow helped them deal with their own grief. Because of your response and my subsequent journey through devastating loss in my own life, I know that Jared represents something many of us must deal with in our everyday lives.

Hopefully he will continue to inspire and aid those who are facing their own heartache. That wasn't quite what I had intended when I first wrote this book, but somehow, that's what's happened and I'm thankful for it. They say the Mother of All works in mysterious ways...

Prologue

The feminine moan of pleasure was music to Lord Darian's ears as he brought Varla to yet another peak with his tongue. She was greedy, but then, being the king of Skithdron's current favorite had to leave her cold. The lecherous bastard had become king after killing his own father—or so Lord Darian suspected—and didn't give a rat's ass about anyone's pleasure but his own.

"Are you ready for me now, Varla?" Darian looked down toward the woman under him with little feeling as he rammed his cock into her.

"More than ready, my lord!"

The bitch was panting and practically tearing his skin off with those long red painted claws of hers. He moved her hands, grasping them tightly and holding them forcibly above her head, away from his skin. He'd be damned if he would wear her bloody marks. He was here for one reason alone.

Well, maybe two reasons, he admitted with a mental shrug. Getting his rocks off was part of the deal and a good excuse to bed a willing wench, but the more important reason was that this particular wench could grant him access to places in the palace he otherwise would not have. If he were seen coming from her chambers, so close to the king's apartments, it would be more natural if he was her fuck for the night. If not for her, the guards would question his presence in the palace. If not for her, Lord Venerai would have him run out of the place completely, denying him his right as a noble of Skithdron to serve at court.

Venerai was a viper. Climbing to the top of the pile of Lucan's sycophants by any means necessary, Venerai wanted all possible competition for the King's favor out of his way. That included Darian, though he had been more in favor with Lucan's father, King Goran, than with the current king.

But Darian was of royal blood, a distant fifth in line for the throne, and Venerai saw him as a threat. He went so far as to have Darian followed by an inept spy or two—spies Darian liked to send on wild goose chases, much to Venerai's disgust.

Darian would tire Varla out, then go on his real mission of the night. He suspected some awful things were about to transpire, but he had to have proof before he gave up his birthright. If he was going to forsake his country, his lands, his title, and risk his very life, he had to be damned sure of his information.

He rammed the wench harder as determination fed his strength. This final round ought to do her in, and then he could go on his little reconnaissance mission. First he had to fuck her into oblivion though, and that was proving harder than he'd thought. Not only was she insatiable, but he just wasn't interested enough in her to make it really worth his while. Oh, she was a sweet release to his aching balls, but she failed to meet the strange yearning that had been building inside him for years now.

He really didn't know what he was looking for, but all the women in his life to this point were definitely not it. There was not one he would regret leaving behind if it became necessary to leave his homeland. Not one he would consider asking to go with him. Not one he could love.

That was just a shame. How did a man pass thirty-seven winters without finding one single woman he could care for at least enough to make some small commitment? He didn't even have a steady mistress.

Was there something wrong with him? He was past the age where most men settled down with one woman and started reproducing, but he'd never found a woman he wanted to birth his heirs. He'd never found a woman he wanted so much he would pray to the gods his seed took root in her womb. He couldn't imagine ever finding such a woman among the many he'd tried on for size, but oh, how he had enjoyed the search.

Varla was a hot fuck and she writhed on his cock in a way that had him fighting to control his release, but she was just a means to an end. She had already been claimed by the ruthless bastard who now sat on the stolen throne of Skithdron. Darian might enjoy the pleasure of her body, but he felt nothing for the cold woman inside.

And he knew she felt nothing for him. Even as she came for the seventh time that night under his skillful thrusts, he knew she cared more for the sexual release than for the man who gave it to her. After all, she had already sold her soul to the devil.

After finally exhausting the voracious creature, Darian made his way to the king's study. Using all his skill and stealth, he found the grim proof he had been searching for—and dreading. He was not surprised to find his old adversary, Lord Venerai, was right in the thick of the evil plot. Darian's course now was clear.

In that moment, Lord Darian of Skithdron became a traitor. At least that's how King Lucan and his followers would see his actions. Still, Darian knew sitting by and doing nothing while a mad king herded deadly, venomous skiths toward innocent villagers would be a crime he could not live with on his soul.

What the king had planned next was even worse, and his ultimate goal was completely insane.

But King Lucan was so far gone in his madness, his plan just might succeed. Someone had to warn Draconia. The peaceful land to the west had been a good neighbor to Skithdron for many generations, but it was all coming to ruin now with one crazy tyrant. Darian now knew beyond the shadow of a doubt, Lucan sought power through demented magics that drove him ever closer to the edge of sanity.

Lucan had to be stopped and Darian was the only one to do it. For one thing, Darian had no immediate family against whom Lucan could retaliate. For another, as the former ambassador to Draconia, he had once had contacts in high places. If he could just get across the border and then across the lines of battle to the Draconian side, he might have a shot at getting his message through to the people—and dragons—who needed to hear it most.

Chapter One

Adora opened her eyes slowly. Her head tilted to the side as she lay on her stomach. She could just make out the huge form of Sir Jared, hovering over her, as he had for the past few days. His ruggedly handsome face carried a stark, broad scar down one cheek and onto his neck. The ragged mark of his warrior profession disappeared below the neckline of his shirt, making her curious to see just how far down it went on his broad, muscular chest.

"How are you feeling?" His voice was husky with disuse and she guessed it was late in the night.

"Jared, you should really seek your own bed. Sitting up with me does neither of us any good."

The knight favored her with a small smile as he poured a cup of water from the pitcher on the bedside table. Hearing the splash of water suddenly made her thirsty as her tongue moved around in her cottony mouth.

"Humor me, Adora. Besides, Kelzy wouldn't let me leave, even if I wanted to try." His gaze shifted to the wide archway, neatly blocked by the blue-green dragon's huge head. Kelzy blinked at them sleepily—even the massive dragon showed weariness in the vigil she'd kept at Adora's side for the past few days.

Jared sat on the side of the bed with a gentleness she found astounding in such a powerful knight. He was so big and muscular, so able to fight and destroy, but she had learned over the past days his magnificent warrior's body housed a gentle soul.

Because of the deep, slashing wounds that reached around from her back to one side, she had to lie on her stomach or the uninjured side and found it difficult to use one of her arms. Levering herself off the bed even to drink a glass of water was almost impossible to accomplish alone. Jared lent her his strength every time she needed to rise and use the bathroom or as now, take a drink of water.

He slipped one hand under her torso from the uninjured side, his forearm settling intimately between her breasts as he spread his hand against the opposite shoulder. This odd position allowed her to use her one good arm to push herself upward while he held her securely, in case her strength gave out. As it was, her arm trembled as he held the cup of water to her parched lips. She wasn't entirely sure whether her trembling weakness was from the injury or the mere proximity of the dashing knight.

It had been years since she'd been touched so intimately by a man, and never by a man such as this. Jared took her breath away. A warm gust of air settled over her from the direction of the dragon in the doorway. Adora swiveled her head to look at Kelzy, but the motion caused her healing wounds to pull and she gasped. Jared reacted instantly, sliding both hands up her torso, supporting her, guiding her gently back to lie on her stomach.

"Easy now." Jared's voice was warm and soft near her ear. It made Adora feel safe and protected. She tried not to think about the hand resting between her breasts as he lowered her slowly to the bed, nor the way he slid his rough palm out from between the sheets and her body, his strong fingers grazing the swollen sides of her breasts.

"Can you help me turn to lie on my side? My neck hurts a bit from sleeping in this position."

"So you admit you do need me here after all?" He chuckled and it warmed her heart.

Jared was always so serious that it was good to hear him laugh as he put his big hands on her once more. He handled her as if she were a priceless treasure but with a strength that would not be denied. Never had such a masterful man been so close to her. Her long-dead husband's touch had been quite different. Jared was strong and sure, yet showed obvious care in the way he used his strength.

Adora liked the way he touched her. She liked him, if she was being honest with herself. Jared was a man among men, otherwise the dragon who had been like her surrogate mother would never have chosen him as her partner. Not only the dragoness, Kelzy, but King Roland himself entrusted a great deal to this man, for Adora had learned Jared was a general in the king's fighting forces. Jared and Kelzy were the leaders of this new Lair filled with dozens of knights and fighting dragons.

"I admit nothing." She enjoyed challenging him and smiled as Jared paused, his hands around her, his face very near.

"Adora..."

She felt his grip tighten on her and saw his face lower. She hadn't been kissed in far too many years, but still remembered the signs. She knew she could turn away—his approach was slow enough to give her time to call a halt if she wished—but she wanted his kiss. Suddenly, she wanted nothing more desperately in the world.

The moment his lips touched hers she knew why. His kiss was everything. Soft and gentle at first, firming to hard, demanding, male. Oh, so male, and so missed. She had missed this in her years of widowhood. She had missed a man's strong hands molding her body while his lips and tongue plundered her mouth.

After the first few blissful moments, Jared's kiss turned molten and hungry. Powered by a lust that fired through his veins, he seemed to ignite as their lips came together for the very first time.

"Adora." He broke off the kiss but buried his hungry mouth at her throat, nibbling at her soft skin.

"Jared," she whispered. His nipping teeth were just powerful enough that she knew he would leave a mark on her tender skin. The thought excited her. Never had a man been so hot for her, or she for him.

"Interesting as this development is," Kelzy's dryly amused voice sounded through both of their minds, bringing them back to earth with a thud, *"Adora is still hurt, Jared. Leave off before one of her wounds reopens."*

"Sweet Mother of All." Jared released her slowly. His blue eyes smoldered with something like shock laced with a bit of anger and frustration as he looked down at her. "Did I hurt you, Adora?"

She shook her head slightly, but his hand traced down her throat to the tender spot he had bitten, and their eyes locked and held. She suspected he had bruised her on purpose and she would wear his mark for a few days.

"Nothing significant." She tried to put his mind at ease about the love bite, but his expression went cold, and she realized her words might have sounded different than she meant them. She tried to find something to say that would fix her error, but Jared was already on his way out the door. He was gone before she could speak and she found herself lying on her side, staring at the dragon in her doorway with mixed feelings. "I didn't mean that the way it sounded."

"I know, my dear. Jared is a hard man. His emotions are held close inside. In fact, I'm amazed he even let go enough to kiss you. He's not a knight to court the ladies. Let him be for a

while. He has much in his past that he needs to come to terms with if he is to ever reclaim that portion of his life."

After long moments thinking on the dragon's words and that startling kiss, Adora finally slept.

The next day Adora woke to an empty chamber for the first time since she'd been hurt. Her back was on fire with pain as she slowly remembered the events that had confined her to the bed for the past few days. She'd come under attack by huge, venom-spitting skiths while walking back to her forest home. Her little house in the woods was destroyed now, infested and torn apart by the giant, slithering creatures their Skithdronian enemies had driven across the border.

Adora had only escaped their snapping jaws by climbing the tallest tree she could find. She'd known she was going to die, clinging to the top of a tree, her specially treated leather clothing smoking from the spray of acidic skith venom that had hit her from the waist down.

A scream had sounded through her mind as she prayed to the Mother of All that her end would be fast and as painless as possible. Then Adora had sought the mind of the dragoness who had practically raised her. Her mind had sent out a call— much stronger than she realized—to Lady Kelzy, and miraculously, the dragon had heard. Kelzy had summoned her knight, Sir Jared, and two other fighting dragons and knights, and raced to her rescue. It was Kelzy who had plucked her out of the tree with wickedly sharp claws.

And for that brave action, Kelzy was in torment now, Adora knew. The dragoness blamed herself for the scratches she had unwillingly inflicted on Adora's back with the razor-sharp talons. Adora also knew the daring mid-air grab was the only way she could have been rescued from that tree without putting all of them in even more danger from the multitude of crazed skiths twining around its base.

Skiths were afraid of dragon fire, but had their own weapons and could fell a dragon with alarming ease. Lady Rohtina, the young golden dragon, had in fact been mortally wounded while providing cover for Kelzy's daring swoop. Thank the Mother of All, Rohtina had been healed of her grave wounds. She had managed to limp back to the Lair, at which point Adora's daughter, Belora, had been able to heal her. It had been a very close call though. One that drove home to all that war with Skithdron was coming fast, and this sudden invasion by venomous skiths was only the first wave.

Adora sank back with a sigh as the cuts on her back protested. They had scabbed over for the most part but were still very painful. Kelzy's apologetic and remorseful clucking almost made it hurt more. Adora told the dragon over and over that she was not to blame, but Kelzy would hear none of it. She was wracked with guilt over hurting her "baby" even it if had been the only way to save her life.

Kelzy's knight partner kept careful watch over her too. Sir Jared had barely left her alone, forever checking her wounds or seeking to make her more comfortable. Jared wasn't a chatty sort of man, but his steady, unsmiling presence had been oddly comforting. He was so solid and had such a pure heart. He had been hurt deeply—Adora knew with a certainty stemming from her own healing gift and intuitive nature—but he was a good honest man, though one who did not make friends easily.

He was also more ruggedly handsome than any man Adora had ever seen. Appearing only slightly older than she, he had short dark brown hair gone silver at his temples and striking, deep ocean blue eyes. He kept himself neat at all times and commanded great respect from all the other knights as well as the dragons who lived in this new Lair.

Adora knew his bond with Kelzy kept Jared from aging as a normal man would. When dragons bonded with their knights, and by extension with their knights' chosen mate, the dragon magic worked to slow the humans' aging process considerably. Jared had partnered with Kelzy more than a decade ago and he probably hadn't aged much since, though his penetrating gaze reflected the wisdom of his years.

Adora dozed through most of the day, only waking when Jared came to bring her meals. He was distant today after their passionate encounter the night before, and he made no reference to it, only staring long and hard at the purple love bite on her neck when he'd first seen her. Other than the leap of fire in his eyes when he saw his mark upon her skin, he had shown no emotion at all. Adora quickly gave up on the idea of trying to explain her hasty words of the night before. She was too tired anyway and in too much pain to sort it out now. She fell into a deep sleep that night without further complications from Jared.

Chapter Two

The black dragon winged in under cover of darkness. No one saw him land except the few sentries posted to stand guard and lend assistance to any who should need it. Black dragons were rare. In fact, only the royal line could boast the starkly gleaming, tar-colored scales that characterized this dragon, so it was understandable word of his presence in the Lair spread quickly.

The tall man who emerged from the shadows a few moments later—dressed all in black, with the same gleaming dark light in his hazel eyes as that of the dragon—strode forward confidently though he'd never visited this Lair before. The sentries bowed to him, as was his due, and received a regal nod in return.

He was not the king, but he was damn close. Prince Nico preferred to leave the political intrigues to his older brother while he engaged in more...stealthy pursuits. As spymaster for the king, he was aptly suited to the task at hand. Nico had not arrived at this new Border Lair by accident. No, he was on a mission of the highest importance to the royal family. His mission would either bring rare royal blood back into the fold or expose an imposter.

The Prince of Spies. That's what the dragons laughingly called him and it was an apt title. He prided himself on his ability to get in and out of places with none the wiser to his presence, but the trip to this out-of-the-way Lair was official business.

"Greetings, Lady Kelzy. What news do you have for me?"
Nico sent the message to the mind of the blue-green dragon
whose glistening body was spread out in the wallow before him.
He'd known the layout of the new Lair even before he left the
palace and had made it his business to know where the leaders
of this particular Lair lived. Kelzy's head rose in surprise,
swiveling on the long, sinuous neck to face him. Her
aquamarine eyes glinted with happiness.

*"Nico! You're here already. I should have known you'd hear
about the events of the last few days before we could send
official word."*

Prince Nico loved the easy manner of this particular
dragon. She had taught him a great deal as a youngster and
guarded him when he was still too young to protect himself. In
a way, she had been like a second mother to him and his
brothers, though she was just one of many dragons who served
the royal family directly.

Her knight partner, though, was one of Nico's favorite
people in the world. Sir Jared had taught him to fight and how
to protect himself. He had also trained the young prince in the
arts that helped him become not only a spy and reluctant
politician, but a true diplomat when it was needed.

Prior to the tragedy that had taken his wife and child from
him, Sir Jared Armand had been one of the old king's most
trusted counselors. That one horrible event had taken the spark
from Jared's eyes and sent him into self-imposed exile in the
mountains. It was there Kelzy found him and finally claimed the
man as her knight partner. The soul-deep bond between dragon
and knight gave Jared renewed purpose, though he was still
alone and would probably never marry again. The first time had
undoubtedly been much too painful to bear.

Nico bowed in respect to the motherly dragon and smiled as
she moved closer to him.

"It's true then, what I've heard? You've found a mother and daughter who possess the royal gifts?"

Kelzy's large head bobbed in eagerness. *"Both Adora and her daughter, Belora, are true healers. Belora healed a mortal wound to Rohtina, the dragon partner of Lars, one of Belora's mates."*

"How did Rohtina come by her injuries?"

"You mean you don't already know?" Kelzy's eyes snapped in humor at the Prince of Spies.

"Actually, I can guess. Skiths, right?" He fairly spit the name of the huge, snake-like creatures that gave the neighboring kingdom its name. The king of Skithdron was using the skiths on the border—herding them and coaxing them across the border to destroy villages and towns in preparation for a large-scale invasion. The man was mad, Nico suspected. It was said King Lucan had spent too much time tampering with magics better left alone. Rumor had it dark magics had changed him and warped his mind.

Skiths were killing machines that slaughtered everything in their path. The only thing they were even remotely afraid of was fire, and luckily, the dragons had that in quantity.

"The skiths attacked Adora. Jared and I had to snatch her from a tree. Rohtina and my son, Kelvan, engaged the skiths below. That's how Rohtina was so badly injured. She got too close to the skiths and nearly paid with her life."

"Where is the woman now?"

Kelzy's great head rotated to the doorway where she had been resting when he came in. The suite was arranged, like most sets of rooms in any Lair, around the central, heated oval sand pit that was the dragon's wallow. All the rooms flowed around the wallow with archways large enough for the dragons to lay their heads in if they so desired. In this way, the dragons and their human families could be together in all things.

"She lives with you?"

"She is like a daughter to me. When my last knight died, I went into the forest to grieve and recover. I met little Adora there. She was only a toddler when she first found my cave. I returned her to her family, but none of them could hear me."

"But she could?"

Kelzy nodded slowly. They both knew the ability to hear dragons was passed from generation to generation. If neither of the people who claimed to be Adora's true parents could hear the dragon as the child could, they were not her birth family.

"She spent most of her time with me until she was just coming into her teen years. That's when your parents were killed and your brother, Roland, took the throne. I moved back to the palace then to aid Roland in his new duties, but it became clear to me over time that he needed wise counsel. When things had settled and Roland was steadier in his role as king, I set off on my quest, in search of Jared. I remembered him from when he'd served your father. He'd always impressed me as a strong warrior and never failed to give your father good counsel. I hoped he could be convinced to do the same for your brother. It took a while to find him, but when I did..."

"You chose him as your new knight partner." Nico finished her sentence with a respectful nod.

Kelzy's eyes dimmed with remembered sadness. *"I lost track of Adora, I'm shamed to say. I went back to look for her years later, but she was long gone. Her family had moved and no one knew where they went."*

"And you just found her again, after all these years?"

"Actually, my son, Kelvan, found her daughter. The girl was poaching in the forest and they argued over a stag. When she met my son's partner, Gareth, he knew he'd found his mate. We celebrated their joining shortly after. When Kelvan met Adora that first day, she talked of the dragon she knew in her youth

23

and from her description, he knew she was talking about me. He convinced her to come here for a visit and we were reunited." The dragon's jeweled eyes sparkled with remembered happiness. *"But Adora is a dedicated healer and wanted to return to her hut in the forest so she could tend her patients in the nearby village. When the skiths overran the village, they nearly got her too."*

"You said she climbed a tree to get away from them? She sounds like a brave woman."

"Brave and ingenious! Jared gave her some treated leather before we left her in the forest and she fashioned it into the most remarkable garments. I asked Jared to give her some of my shed scales and she sewed them between layers of leather in her boots and in strategic spots on her clothes. She got sprayed pretty thoroughly with skith venom, but not a scratch on her."

"Then why is she recuperating? How did she get hurt?"

"That was my doing. I had to snatch her out of the tree and I clipped her with my talons." Kelzy seemed very upset by the incident. *"I hurt my own girl! How could I have been so clumsy?"*

"It happens to the best of us, Lady Kelz. It's hard to be perfectly accurate all the time, much less under combat conditions, with such sharp talons. Don't be so hard on yourself."

"You're a good boy, Nico."

The prince laughed outright. *"Only you would have the nerve to call me that, Lady Kelz."*

At that moment, Jared emerged from the doorway Kelzy had indicated was Adora's room, surprising Nico. The older knight looked worn and tired, but there was a light in his eyes that had been missing for many, many years.

"Nico, my boy! When did you get here?"

A smile spilt the older man's face as he moved forward to catch Nico in a fierce hug. Jared was one of the few people in the world who would dare approach Nico and his siblings with such familiarity, but he was also one of the few people in the world who Nico actually loved as if he were part of his own family. Jared had been there for him after his parents' deaths, and for that he would forever love the slightly older, wiser man.

"I just got here a few minutes ago. Kelzy was filling me in on the history of your guest."

"Adora." The way Jared spoke the woman's name sent up warning signals in Nico's mind. There was something between them, he realized with a start, though he never thought Jared would heal enough to let another woman into his life, even just a little.

"You think she's of royal blood?"

Jared nodded. "I can't see any other explanation for what's happened. Her daughter definitely has the wizard gift. She healed a dragon's mortal wounds in front of half the Lair. They're all treading on eggshells around her now from what I hear." Jared chuckled, offering Nico a drought of mulled wine from the sideboard. "You'll stay with us, won't you?"

Nico took the goblet and smiled. "I'd enjoy that. If I'm here long enough."

"Adora stirs." Kelzy sent her thoughts to both men. Jared instantly moved to the archway, a look of touching concern on his weathered face. Nico suspected the older knight was already half in love with the mysterious woman who could very well be a lost member of the royal family.

"Perhaps I can help?"

Nico didn't make the offer lightly. The royal line was said to be among the last of the wizard blood in this realm, and each of them had some healing talent. Nico didn't use his often, but it was there. He could do small healings, but his true magic was something far different. Still, if he could help this woman who clearly meant so much to two beings he valued so highly, he would do what he could.

Kelzy's glowing eyes pinned him. *"Would you? Oh, Nico, I'd be forever grateful! We don't have another true healer in this Lair. Her daughter's gift only works on dragons, not humans."*

Nico knew the dragon didn't bother stating the obvious—that Kelzy's own magical healing ability, known as the Dragon's Breath, could not heal wounds made by dragons or that Adora's own healing skills were useless on her own wounds. It was a quirk of magic that healers generally couldn't heal themselves.

The prince followed Jared into the small guest room, noting instantly the unusual tenderness with which the older knight stilled the thrashing body of a small woman mostly hidden under the covers. Nico moved closer to stand on the other side of the bed as Kelzy's head filled the doorway, watching all closely. The dragon hovered over the woman as if she was truly her own dragonet, and Nico had to hide a smile at Kelzy's completely un-dragonish behavior. That was one of the many things he loved about this particular dragon. She never let anyone—be they dragon or human, prince or pauper—dictate her actions. Kelzy was her own dragon, through and through.

Nico could see the woman more clearly now and she was exquisite. Only a little older than him, she looked somewhere near thirty winters or so. Though if she had a grown daughter, she must be a bit older than that. Still, she was a beauty. Her flowing hair was auburn in the dim light of the room and her features could almost be described as fragile, though what he could see of her bare arms were lithely muscled. She had not lived a life of leisure, but she looked every inch the fair damsel. And she was most definitely in distress.

Jared soothed the woman and drew her onto her stomach, pulling the blanket away from her loose bandages. Three angry red, parallel furrows were partially covered by light swaths of linen across her back.

"Adora, wake up." Jared spoke softly near her ear and her head shifted sideways toward the knight.

Nico saw her eyes open and was stunned by the deep green reflected there. Most of the royal line had green eyes. His own hazel color was the exception rather than the rule.

"Adora, we have a guest. He has a bit of healing skill and is willing to try and help you." She looked as if she would have objected, but Jared placed a finger over her pouty lips, stilling her words. "Just lie still and let us do this for you. You haven't slept well and it pains Kelzy to see you hurting. Think of her before you object."

Nico sensed the resignation in the woman as she turned her tired green eyes to the doorway.

"For you, Mama Kelzy."

Nico was amazed by the mental communication all three of them heard in their minds. Unskilled, but powerful, this small woman showed yet another of the gifts of the royal line. While knights could certainly communicate with dragons in such a way, it was a rare female human who could even hear dragons, much less send their own thoughts. All royals could do it, of course, but such a gift was rarer than emeralds among regular folk.

The woman settled down with a sigh, her magnificent green eyes closing as she trusted the men to do what they would. It was clear she had no doubts that Kelzy and Jared would protect her. She trusted them, which was undoubtedly why she didn't question his presence. That and her own pain and fatigue conspired to make his job easier. Willing patients were always preferable to those who were in too much pain to lie quietly. Nico's healing talent was small when compared to some of his kin, so it was important he be able to focus without too much distraction.

Jared stripped away the bandages with a gentle hand, and Nico was surprised by just how badly this little woman was injured. She had borne her injuries without much complaint from what he'd just seen and that was remarkable in his

27

experience. He'd seen these kinds of wounds before and they weren't pleasant. The gouges were deep. Neat and clean, but very deep. Without help, they would take weeks to heal and scar badly, but he thought he could at least speed up the process, to help limit the scarring and take away the worst of the pain.

Focusing his energies, Nico reached out and touched the woman with just his fingertips. Then the strangest thing happened. A flare of light filled the small chamber as his energies met and reacted to hers. There was a moment of resistance, then a moment of pure bliss as the woman's magic welcomed his, aiding him in the healing and directing his meager skill with all the knowledge and power of a highly skilled healer.

Nico found himself wielding the strong healing power with ease. The serious wounds were no challenge to the incredible energy that echoed through him. When he sat back after a few minutes, all of them were smiling and Adora's back was whole and unblemished.

"Merciful Mother." Nico stared at her back in amazement. "That's never happened before."

"Your energies recognized each other. They meshed so you could work together." Kelzy spoke softly to all of them. *"This cements it then. Adora has royal blood. This just proved it."*

Adora shifted in the bed, clutching the blanket to her nakedness as she looked at the strange man at her side.

"Who are you?"

The rogue smiled and bowed, winking at her. "My name is Nico."

"The Prince of Spies," Kelzy supplied with a dragonish cough of laughter. *"We'll have to track down exactly where you come from, Adora, but this boy is probably a distant cousin of*

yours. Don't let the fact that he's a prince stop you from boxing his ears if he gets too fresh."

"Prince Nicolas?" Adora's eyes widened even more as she realized the prince had just healed her and was even now watching her lounge, half-naked, in bed. Could this day get any stranger?

"I'll leave you to dress, milady. We have much to discuss as soon as you're ready."

The prince winked at her again and walked easily out the door, past Kelzy's bulky head, leaving Adora alone once again with Jared. She looked up at him, seeking answers.

"Did the *prince* just heal my back?"

Jared chuckled but nodded solemnly, his eyes twinkling. "Nico is an old friend, Adora. I've known him since he was just a boy. He's still a bit of a rascal, but a good lad. He came to see if you were what you claim to be."

"I don't claim to be anything!"

Jared shook his head. "That was a bad choice of words on my part. I should have said what you *appear* to be."

"Why?" A knot of fear settled in her stomach and unreasonable anger battled with panic just below the surface. "Just what do I appear to be?"

Jared eyed her bare shoulders, making her all too aware she was naked under the blanket. He stepped back and seemed to force his gaze to meet hers.

"Royalty, milady."

"You've got to be kidding."

He twisted his lips wryly. "I'm afraid not. Your daughter healed Rohtina's wounds. Healing dragons—now that's a gift reserved to those of royal blood alone, Adora, and you bespeak dragons as easily as a knight. Kelzy heard you call her when you were hiding in that tree. Even I couldn't reach her over such a distance, and we're bonded."

"It was an emergency. Sometimes people can do amazing things when faced with a life or death situation."

"That may be the case for others, Adora, but I believe you'll find no ready explanation for the way your magic sparked off the prince's just now. I think the magics recognized each other and that allowed him to use your knowledge and his gift to do a more thorough healing than that lad has ever been able to do before. He's not a strong healer. The most I expected was for him to be able to speed your healing a bit and maybe take some of the pain. Kelzy will back me on this."

Adora shot her gaze to the dragon whose head still filled her doorway. *"What Jared says is true. Nico has never been a strong healer. His talents lie elsewhere."*

She stared at them both, speechless for a moment. Flopping her hands down on the blanket, she shook her head.

"I can't deal with this right now. I've got to get dressed. There's a *prince* waiting out there for me to make my *royal* appearance, for heavens' sake! Go away, Jared, and let me dress. I'll deal with all of this once I have some clothes on."

Jared moved toward the archway. "Your leggings were ruined, but I found a few things that might fit and put them in the wardrobe for you."

"Thank you, Jared." Her voice went soft as emotion threatened to overwhelm her. "Once again, your thoughtfulness is very much appreciated."

He just shrugged and left, but Kelzy stayed in the doorway as Adora stood. She walked to the mirror along one wall and examined her back as best she could in the polished metal by the wardrobe. Her skin looked healthy and pink, without a scar in sight. Amazing.

Adora pulled on her own soft leather shirt, needing something familiar to help her deal with the upheaval in her life. She had to search in the wardrobe for leggings that would fit. There was a selection of both skirts and pants in the small cupboard.

Jared must have scrounged clothing from some of the younger boys who lived in the Lair to find leggings that would fit her small frame, and it was these she took from the closet. Adora was used to the feel of soft leather against her skin after having worn the unconventional outfit she'd made for a few weeks.

She needed comfort now. She couldn't worry about style. The reassuring feel of Kelzy's shed scales sewn into the layers of her tight-fitting top made her feel good. Adora only hoped her odd clothing wouldn't offend the prince. He was royalty after all.

More importantly, what would Jared think of the form-fitting outfit? He'd given her the costly leather in the first place, way back when she'd stubbornly refused to leave her home in the woods. That such a gruff man would think of her comfort and safety still touched her deep inside. He'd surprised her with the gift, and the precious dragon scales that rightly should've been for his use as Kelzy's partner. Adora felt bad the outfit she'd spent so much time and effort to make was half destroyed now, but the leather top and matching leggings had undoubtedly saved her life when the skiths attacked. Only the specially treated leather and the few precious dragon scales had stood between her and their poisonous venom. She'd felt special wearing those clothes, because the leather and the scales had been a gift from the complex man who waited even now outside her door.

Would he be shocked by her appearance? Would he think her beautiful? It had been so long since Adora had cared what a man thought of her looks. The very idea of it made her heart speed and her palms sweat like a young, untried girl.

31

"You're beautiful, Adora. You were always a pretty child, but you've grown into a gorgeous woman, no matter what you're wearing."

"So now you're a mind reader?" Adora raised one eyebrow, turning toward the dragon hovering in her doorway.

"We females always tend to worry about how we look to an attractive male."

"Kelzy! The prince is young enough to be my son."

"Is not. Besides, who said I was talking about the prince? It's Jared I had in mind. And so did you."

Adora plucked up her courage and strode into the main room, finding the men at the edge of the dragon's wallow. Jared had installed a soft couch and chairs for human visitors' comfort. Being the one in charge of the Lair, Jared probably entertained knights who had to speak to him in privacy about one thing or another, she reasoned. Kelzy had told her all about Jared, and she knew the crafty dragon was doing all she could to promote a match between her and the slightly older knight.

For her part, Adora thought Jared was an amazing man, but wasn't quite sure she could handle *any* man in her life. Though if she had to choose just one, it would probably be Jared. Still, she knew he'd been hurt badly by the death of his wife and child. It was Jared who always backed off when they seemed to be getting close and she respected his right to do so. She wouldn't force herself on any man, even if they did live together at this point because of their close—but separate—ties to Kelzy. Kelzy wanted them both living with her and it was usually unwise not to give a dragoness what she wanted.

Adora squared her shoulders and strode with a confidence she didn't feel to where the men sat. Both had goblets of mulled wine in their hands and were talking easily. Her soft footsteps went unheard as Kelzy moved her great body in the sands, so both men started when she appeared before them. With a lithe grace, she curtsied deeply to the prince in the formal manner.

"Your majesty," she spoke demurely, "I humbly thank you for your healing skill."

The prince surprised her, standing to take her hand in his. He raised her easily to stand beside him.

"Then you feel better?"

"Much better, your majesty."

The prince sighed theatrically. "If you insist on calling me 'your majesty' then I'll have to call you 'milady' and we'll waste all our time on extra words that mean nothing in the grand scheme of things. It's all so tiresome." He sniffed with regal disdain, making Jared laugh out loud. "Please, call me Nico and I'll call you Adora, all right? After all, we're kin."

She gasped. "You can't know that for certain."

"Oh, I think it's safe to say that you have the blood of Draneth the Wise in your veins somewhere. Our magics would not have meshed in such an agreeable way had you not."

Adora swayed on her feet and Nico's strong arm steadied her, guiding her to sit on the couch. Settling her there, he pressed a full goblet into her trembling hand.

"It's impossible."

"No, I'm afraid it's not. I did some research before I left the castle, and it seems there are quite a few members of the various royal lines unaccounted for through the years. The most likely scenario is that you are the Princess Amelia Jane, who was stolen from her home the same night the rest of her family was killed. The baby princess was never found, though the rest of her family was left where they were slain."

Adora found herself reaching out for Jared, needing his strength as the prince relayed the sad facts.

"There was some talk at the time about a maidservant who'd gone missing as well, and many of the chroniclers believed the maid took the baby to safety, but she was never seen again." Nico sat next to them on the long couch, taking her other hand in his. "You would be about the right age to be little Amelia Jane, I think, though you look much younger than your thirty-eight winters."

Adora gasped. "How did you know my age?" Her eyes sought his, her confusion plain, then understanding dawned. "Oh, sweet Mother! The princess you mentioned. She would be thirty-eight?"

Nico nodded. "This year."

Adora felt a tear slide down her cheek, followed by another and another. Kelzy growled, crooning in her dragonish way as she had when Adora had been just a child, but it was Jared who pulled her close against his broad chest, comforting her with his warm strength.

"Do you have anything from your childhood, Adora? Anything that might tie you to your past?"

She sniffled, cuddling against Jared as if she belonged there. Turning slightly, she looked up at the handsome prince.

"Only one thing. It's not much." With shaking fingers, she reached into the front of her shirt, separating the seams she'd sewn between the layers, reaching for something only she knew was there, just under her heart. "I didn't even realize what it was until recently when Kelzy gave me her shed scales. My mother gave it to me when I got married. She said it was an ancient and valuable good luck talisman that I should keep with me wherever I lived. She told me to keep it a secret, instructing me to hide it under my mattress and to never let anyone see it. One day, she said, I'd need it. I guess that day has come." She pulled out a gleaming black panel that was wafer thin and resilient as only true dragon scale could be. Nico went silent as she handed the evidence of her heritage to him. "But I've never seen a black dragon scale before."

Jared's arms tightened around her. Adora's breath caught in her throat as the prince turned the gleaming black scale over in his hands, studying it with an odd sort of knowledge. Kelzy's head loomed up over his shoulder, then suddenly, Nico spun to hold the deep black scale up to the dragon.

"Anybody you know?" Nico held up the scale like an offering as Kelzy reached out her long tongue, licking the black scale delicately with just the tip.

"Not your direct line." Kelzy was more serious than Adora had ever seen her. *"I think it likely to be from the line of Kent, but we need a dragon who knew one of them personally. I think Sandor served Prince Fileas when he was just a dragonet. He arrived at this Lair recently. I'll call him."*

While they waited for one of the older male dragons to make his way to them, Adora moved away from Jared's tempting strength. She sat up straight on the couch and tried to gather her scattered emotions. She felt shaky, but she knew Jared was there should she need him. It was a reassuring feeling.

"I never would have guessed you were over thirty, Adora." She felt Jared's hand stroking her hair softly and turned to look into his amazingly gentle eyes.

"I have a grown daughter, Jared. And I had twins before her."

"You must have been a child bride." Jared's teasing lightened her heart.

"Twins?" The prince turned back to her. "Where are they now?"

"I don't know. They were stolen from me when they were just little girls."

After the revelations of the last moments, it was devastating to think about the little girls she'd lost so cruelly. Adora gripped the cushions of the couch until her knuckles turned white. Jared must have seen her distress. He pried one hand up from its death grip on the couch and grasped it firmly between his own rough fingers. His silent encouragement meant the world to her in that moment.

"Girls?" The prince ran a rough hand through his hair. "Merciful Mother."

"What?" Adora's gaze went from the prince to Jared to Kelzy.

It was Jared who finally answered. "Royals, probably because of the wizard blood, have more twin sets than is usual. Twin girls are a rarity, though. Few girl children are born to any of the royal lines, and only very rarely in pairs."

"Sandor approaches."

A large, battle-scarred dragon with coppery brown coloring entered the archway leading to Kelzy's suite. He started in surprise when he saw the prince and bowed his great head in respect.

"How can I serve you, my prince?" The newcomer's voice boomed with resonance through the minds of all present.

Nico walked up to the huge copper dragon and held out the black scale. "Do you recognize this? Can you tell us who it may have belonged to?"

This new dragon repeated Kelzy's odd licking gesture and then his garnet eyes opened wide. *"Fileas! This scale belonged to Prince Fileas."*

Adora was confused. "Fileas was a dragon?"

Nico turned back to her, his hazel eyes shining. "Yes, he was. As am I."

Jared stood at Adora's back, his presence reassuring as a black mist began to form in front of their eyes. Between one moment and the next the prince was gone and a sleek black dragon stood in his place. He was somewhat smaller than the other dragons, but obviously built for speed. He also had sparkling tourmaline eyes—eerily like the hazel gaze of Prince Nico.

"The only black dragons are of the royal line. We alone have the ability to shift our shape from human to dragon, and it is that dual nature that solidifies this land's ties with dragons and humans alike."

"Prince Nico?"

"It's him, Adora," Jared assured her. She walked up to the prince and reached out hesitantly, but the black dragon moved forward into her touch with his sleek black-scaled head.

"Incredible." Her voice was a breath of a whisper. "You're dragon and human? Half and half?"

The dragon lifted one shoulder as if to shrug. *"That's one way of looking at it. But Adora, if you are the daughter of Fileas as we believe, then half of you is dragon too."*

"Don't be ridiculous."

Kelzy claimed her attention. *"Think about it, child. Why did you seek me out when you were just a baby? How did you even know where to find me? My lair was well hidden. None of the humans in the area knew I was even there until you toddled off to find me."*

"I can't shift into dragon form and fly away with you, Mama Kelzy." Her sarcastic tone was laced with shock and a bit of fear.

The very idea of Prince Nico being able to shift into dragon form tantalized her, though Adora knew in her heart it was impossible for her. Surely if that kind of power existed inside her, it would have made itself known long before now. Sure, she had a little healing talent, but most of the healing she did relied on skills learned through hard work and trial and error, not dragon magic. Or any other kind of magic at all, for that matter.

The black dragon moved closer. *"Royal females generally can't shift, but they are usually healers of great skill and ability. Their dragon magic manifests itself in the healing arts—the Dragon's Breath made human, if you will. I understand your daughter is a dragon healer."*

The prince stepped back from her and the black mist swirled, leaving him human again, clothed all in black leather, before her. That was some powerful magic indeed.

"Sweet Mother! Belora." Adora's legs gave out and she found herself hoisted back onto the couch, wrapped securely in Jared's strong arms.

"She healed Rohtina," he reminded her gently.

At this point, the huge copper dragon craned his neck forward to lay his great head at Adora's feet. A rare tear sparkled in his deep garnet eyes. His tongue flicked out to touch the back of her hand and she started.

"You are Fileas' daughter. You're little Amelia Jane. Thank the Mother that you've finally found your way home to us." The tear leaked out of his eye and tumbled onto her hand, a sparkling magical gem showing the great extent of emotion he was feeling. *"I served your father when I was just a youngster. I was away when the attack came, on a quest issued by your sire, but if I'd been there, I would have given my life for his. He was a great man. You have his eyes, though you have your mother's smile and her beautiful hair. I stand by my pledge to your sire and I will serve you and your line all my days, if you will have me."*

Adora was moved to tears by the dragon's solemn pledge. She reached forward and touched his long snout, rubbing gently and feeling the magic inside her tingle in a way it never had before.

"*You're hurt,*" she thought, surprised when the dragon answered her.

"*An old wound, my princess. Nothing to worry over.*"

"*Wait.*" Adora felt the healing energy gather and suddenly overflow from her into the dragon, shining light all around them as her energy came alive as never before. She looked at the dragon's left foreleg and the awkward angle at which it was held. It had been broken sometime in the recent past and set badly.

He hid it well, but Sandor was in a great deal of pain that communicated itself to her when she touched him. Sometimes it was like that for her with human patients, but never had Adora felt such a response with a dragon. Then again, the only dragon she'd ever known before now was Kelzy and she'd always been quite healthy.

As they all watched, the magic flowed, and Sandor's leg straightened out, the lines of pain just visible around the dragon's eyes easing. Adora pulled away and felt the residual high of the magic already beginning to fade in her body. It felt much like it did when she did a complex human healing, but with so much more energy. It was very nearly overwhelming.

Adora sank back and Jared was there for her.

"Do you really have any more doubts about who you are, Adora? You're my cousin," the prince said, kneeling at her side. "You're Princess Amelia Jane of the House of Kent."

"That's not my name."

"It was." Nico shook his head. "But you never knew it, did you? You'll be Princess Adora from now on, of the House of Kent. Welcome back to the family, cousin."

Adora tried to focus but was fast losing energy. It was a phenomenon she knew well. She had overextended herself in healing Sandor, but it was worth it to know he was whole again and no longer in pain. She just needed sleep to recover.

"Thank you, my princess," Sandor said gravely in her mind. *"I'm only sorry you tired yourself so on my behalf."*

"I'm fine. I just need sleep."

Jared lifted her into his arms as she leaned back against him, cuddling close to his warmth. He felt so good. It was heaven to rely on his strength for just this short moment.

"I'll seek you out when you wake, princess. I have no knight partner at present, but I would be your guardian as I was your father's before you."

"That's nice," she mumbled. "You're such a pretty copper color."

The dragon's voice rumbled comfortingly through her mind as she drifted into unconsciousness. *"I match the lights in your hair, as I matched your mother's."*

Jared found himself again tucking Adora into the bed in the guest chamber that was now hers. Kelzy wanted her adopted human daughter close and Jared found himself wanting to keep Adora close for entirely different reasons. If he wasn't very careful, he could easily lose his heart to such an amazing woman. But his heart was too badly damaged to take such a chance again.

He realized, despite his best intentions, he had spent a great deal of time in Adora's room in the past few days, tucking the covers around this small, puzzling woman. No, he thought ruefully, make that this small, puzzling *princess*.

He could still hardly believe Adora was lost royalty. True, she was not in direct line for the throne. In fact, her family line was quite remote from the ruling line—only very distant cousins at best—but the fact they had bred true and the males of the House of Kent could shift to dragon form made them all princes and princesses of the realm. It was a closely guarded secret—and something of a legend now to the people of this land—that their kings were descended from dragons.

Few now knew how true the legend really was. Not only were they part dragon, but the males actually could *become* dragons when they chose. It was a very useful ability and one that allowed them to rule wisely over both human and dragon kind, giving them personal insight into both races.

Jared had been a knight for quite a few years, but before Kelzy partnered with him, he had served as an advisor in old King Jon's household. He knew the royal secret and had seen them shift back and forth from human to dragon many times. Each time though, it was still a bit of a shock. He could only imagine what Adora must have thought seeing the roguish Prince Nico shift not five feet from her.

Of the brothers, Nico was Jared's favorite, though he'd be damned if he'd ever let that scamp know it. Nico had been the wild child—the one who constantly needed supervision—and more often than not, it fell to Jared to get the young prince out of whatever scrape he found himself in at the time. Over the years, Nico had come to respect Jared's advice almost as a son would—or younger brother, at least. Jared looked at Nico now and thought sadly of what might have been had his family not been torn apart by tragedy.

For years it had been hard to be in Nico's presence, but now after time and distance from the horrific deaths of his family, Jared found he had missed Nico's peculiar brand of deviltry. He thought of the prince as he had thought of his son, with an almost fatherly regard and a fondness deeper than most.

"She's quite a woman." Nico's voice drifted quietly from the archway as Jared straightened and moved out of the small room.

"You haven't met her daughter yet. She's just like her mother, only younger."

"Too bad she's already mated." Nico's eyes flashed with humor.

"You've got to be kidding me, Nico. You, interested in a woman of substance? What? Have you gone through all the whores in the kingdom already?"

Nico laughed, but Jared noted the slight echo of hurt in his eyes with some amazement. Could it be the rascal really was starting to think about settling down?

They went back to the sitting area and saw that Sandor had not left. The big copper dragon sat quietly with Kelzy, apparently deep in conversation, all but ignoring the humans. Jared was taken aback by how cozy the two dragons looked together, sharing the comparatively small wallow. It drove home the fact that Kelzy had lived a long and full life before choosing him as her knight partner. He'd never asked her about her past though, having been too wrapped up in his own misery in those days just after they bonded. Afterwards, he'd been too busy working towards the safety of the kingdom with war clearly on the way. Jared made a mental note to talk more to his dragon partner about her own life, just as soon as he found the time.

It was important to him that he give as well as take from this relationship and it suddenly struck him that Kelzy had been giving and giving to him for years. As far as he was concerned, she was the only reason he wasn't already dead. Since she'd come into his life, bonding with him on a soul deep level, he had a reason to live. Before that, in the dark times when his family was ripped from him, he had wanted nothing more than to join them in death. It was Kelzy who had given him a reason to go on. Kelzy had given him hope, companionship and a kind of love he hadn't ever expected.

"I won't dignify that little dig with a reply," Nico laughed, bringing him back to the conversation at hand with a jolt.

The prince was pouring more wine. He drank too much, Jared thought, but he knew that was just a symptom of unhappiness. Nico needed a wife.

"Nevertheless, I want to meet my younger cousin at the first opportunity." Nico turned to the dragons, lounging in the warm sands of Kelzy's wallow. *"Lady Kelzy, on the way in I saw your son and a very pretty gold taking off for the moon. Do you think they're back by now?"* His snicker was echoed by dragonish coughs of smoky laughter from the occupants of the wallow.

"Are you asking if the human part of the family is recovered enough to speak with you? If so, I would say yes. They've been mated for a while now and are beginning to slow down and savor their moments a bit more."

"Good. I'm going to pay them a call."

"I'll warn them so they at least have a chance to dress." Kelzy sent after the prince who was already on his way out.

"Aw, Lady Kelz, you take the fun out of everything."

Jared went to check on Adora and found her tossing restlessly. She looked so fragile, so small, and so alone in the big bed. His heart went out to her as she moved in troubled sleep and he found his feet taking him closer, despite his intentions to stay away from her. Sitting on the side of the bed, Jared took her restless hands in his own, speaking softly.

"Hush now, Adora. Everything is fine. You are warm and safe, as is your daughter. I won't let anything happen to you. Be at peace."

Kelzy puffed warm air over them from the doorway, offering her own sort of comfort to the girl she had practically raised. He smiled over at the dragon. Her head lay in the archway, her neck stretching out from the heated sand pit that was her favorite place to rest. From that central wallow, she could crane her neck to reach just about any room in the roughly circular

43

suite, ensuring that she was part of every facet of her chosen humans' lives.

Rather than intrusive, Jared had always found Kelzy's interest in his doings comforting. She was a friend, a companion, and a sounding board who lived, breathed, and cared deeply for him. He didn't question the bond between them. It was deep and it was real. It had formed that fateful day when Kelzy had found him.

Jared had been on the raw edge of despair for a long time after the loss of his wife and young son. The pain of losing them had almost driven him mad, but Kelzy's magical appearance in his life somehow made it just a bit easier to go on. Kelzy had found him deep in the mountains, hiding away from people and dragons alike.

Jared discovered only later that Kelzy had gone deliberately looking for him. Returning from a time of self-imposed exile while she mourned the loss of her previous knight, Kelzy had come back only after the old king and his wife were slain. Answering the call of her kind, Kelzy went back to the palace to find the king and queen dead and the youngster Roland being crowned king—without the benefit of one of the crown's top advisors. Kelzy had been one of the top-ranking dragons, well acquainted with the palace, the royal family and their advisors. She and Jared had always had a friendly relationship, if a bit distant in times past. But when she found him years later, so near the end of his sanity, only her claiming of him gave him reason to go on.

It was Kelzy who had broken the terrible news of the king's and queen's deaths. It was Kelzy who had talked Jared into returning to the palace, assuring him that young Roland would need him, that his country needed him, that *she* needed him.

There was no greater guilt a man could feel than failing to protect his family, failing to be there when they needed him. Failing to help the young king—a young man he had known all his life—was something Jared could not allow on top of all the other tragedies in his life.

Kelzy had given Jared reason to live back then and he never regretted her interference. He loved her. But she was the last being he would love, he vowed. Loving came with too high a cost and he refused to hurt that way ever again.

He couldn't love Adora, no matter how much he might crave her. She was light in the darkness, a gentle balm to his injured soul. Just having her in his home made him happy, but he refused to allow her into his heart. He refused to let the gentle feelings welling up inside him show. He couldn't give her the false hope that somehow they could be together. It would not be fair to her, and he didn't want to leave himself open for that kind of pain ever again.

For she would leave him eventually. It would hurt bad enough as it was, without letting the bond between them get any deeper. Still, he couldn't help but savor these few moments he had with her. He would not let himself love her, but he couldn't help caring deeply for the lost little woman who had shown him her bravery, her courage, her care for his best friend Kelzy and all the dragons he held dear, and her very human vulnerability. She was a rare treasure and he could appreciate her beauty—both inner and outer—from a safe distance. He hoped.

"Jared?" Her voice touched him as she blinked her wide green eyes sleepily. He turned from his contemplations to the woman whose hands he still held lightly within his own.

"I didn't mean to wake you, Adora." He tried to keep his voice low. "You were restless and I came in to make sure you were all right."

"I was dreaming. It was a nightmare." Her sleepy eyes grew frightened and huge as she remembered the vision that had disturbed her slumber. "You were falling. Jared, you were falling off Kelzy's back and you had an arrow through your

45

Bianca D'Arc

chest. There was a lot of blood and you were so high." Her voice broke as real fear shivered through her small body.

He had no choice then but to pull her into his arms and comfort the trembling woman. She was so beautiful and so vulnerable in that moment. He couldn't bear to see this strong woman so afraid. Especially on his behalf. Especially when it wasn't even real.

"Ssh, Adora. It was only a dream. I'm here and I'm fine. Kelzy would never drop me. You know that." He rocked her as she clung to him, his voice crooning to her.

"It seemed so real. Jared, what if it's an omen? What if—?" She broke off on a sob and clung to him.

He rubbed her back with one hand, his frozen heart cracking open at her distress. Without thought, he brought his head down to rest against her, cuddling into her warm neck, inhaling her delicious scent. He kissed her, placing soft little nibbles on her neck, just under her jaw and near the delicate shell of her ear. The shivers of fright changed to something more enticing. Biting gently on her earlobe, Jared felt her soft, sexy sigh as she relaxed into his embrace.

"Don't be afraid, Adora." His whisper sent warm, moist air into her ear and she gasped. "It's only a dream."

"Jared."

Her gasping moan brought him closer to her lips, his arms shifting, drawing her nearer to his hard body. He wanted her desperately.

Giving in to desire, he brought his mouth to hers, sipping at her sweetness, drowning in her enticing flavor. This was what he wanted. This! He wanted her.

Aligning their bodies, he laid her back on the bed, tearing away the covers that tried to get between them. He lowered his weight onto her carefully, his mouth following hers, surprised a little by her passion, but meeting it with an equal fervor. She

46

was with him every step of the way, her little hands clawing at his shirt with a strength and enthusiasm he had not expected. It was devastating and all too enticing.

Impatiently, he ripped at the ties of his shirt, breaking their kiss only to tug the garment over his head and throw it across the room. It landed somewhere near Kelzy's head. Jared looked up enough to see the jeweled dragon eyes blink open with surprise, then narrow in seeming satisfaction as Kelzy noted what the humans were up to. Jared was too far gone to care what conclusions his dragon partner jumped to though, turning back to whip off Adora's thin nightgown.

When her lustrous skin was bare, he moved back to enjoy the sight of her generous breasts, her soft skin, and her womanly form. Something was driving him to take her and make her his own. No matter how he fought it, the drive was there, pushing him beyond control.

"Adora," he gasped as she raised her hand to caress his chest, following the line of his scar.

It flowed down from his face, over his pectoral muscle and past one hard male nipple, down onto his stomach and lower, beneath the waistline of his leggings. He stopped her when she would have delved beneath and brought her soft hand to his lips, holding her gaze.

"You are so beautiful." He put her hand on his shoulder, then pulled her soft body against his, meeting her halfway to the mattress. She was wonderfully warm beneath him. She was not shy or hesitant, but he could tell she hadn't done this in a very long time. Just the idea was entrancing.

Slowly, he rubbed his chest against her breasts, enjoying the way her eyes lit up and her body twitched in passion. He did it again, liking the drag of her hard nipples over his skin. Lightly, she traced the muscles on his arms and he felt himself weaken. She could easily turn him into her slave with just her touch alone.

47

He brought his hands to her breasts, pulling back only slightly to fondle and stroke her taut peaks. Her little gasping breaths fired his blood and when he took her in his mouth and sucked, she bucked and moaned. He suckled her strongly, gauging her reaction by the way she moved in his arms. It had been so long since he'd had a soft woman writhing in pleasure beneath him. So long since he even cared who the woman pleasuring him was.

But he cared about Adora. No matter how hard he tried, he couldn't stop himself from caring at least a little. It was dangerous, he knew, but it couldn't be helped.

Firmly, he moved back from her, enjoying the view of her rosy nipples, still wet from his tongue and one of them holding the faint imprint of his teeth. He liked that.

Perhaps a bit too much. Alarms went off through his brain.

When she reached for him, he pulled back, but saw the need in her beautiful eyes and knew he couldn't leave her like this.

Gently, Jared pushed her back on the bed, lowering himself between her soft thighs. He wouldn't go any further than this, but he owed her something. He wouldn't leave her unfulfilled and needy. He would bring her pleasure and lull her back to sleep, then seek his solitary bedchamber. Even if it killed him.

And it probably would.

Sighing, knowing this was the one time he would allow himself to feel her feminine response, Jared lowered his head to her slightly rounded stomach, biting gently. Adora giggled and he pushed lower. The giggle turned to a gasp and then a moan as Jared brought his fingers and tongue to her secret folds. Gently, he probed, learning her body. He'd never wanted so badly to bring his partner pleasure before, never cared more for the woman's response than at this very moment. Adora was special.

Too special for the likes of him.

Jared parted her nether lips, blowing a current of air over her distended clit. She sighed as her body trembled, hips moving in an uncontrollable rhythm. Covering her clit with his lips, Jared tongued her lightly at first, then more steadily as her temperature rose.

She moaned, her body thrumming against his lips as he took her higher. She tasted of warm honey and sweet woman, creaming for him. Delving inside with his fingers, Jared curled just the tips, looking for that magical spot that would take her over the edge.

Adora cried out when she came, a sob of relief offered up to the night as he rode her through a glorious climax. Clenching around his fingers, Jared nearly died at the thought of how she would feel clenching just the same way around his cock. How he wanted to experience that. How he wanted to take her and make her his own.

But he couldn't. It wouldn't be right.

Adora deserved a whole man—one who could love her with a whole and unscarred heart. She didn't deserve a broken down, second-hand knight with ice in his veins instead of blood. He would not let her make such a sacrifice, but he would enjoy the few stolen moments this night gave him. Jared licked her again, lapping up every last bit of her excitement and taking it within himself.

He would never taste such ambrosia again.

After a while, she settled down and he found the strength to move away from her tempting thighs. He kissed his way up her soft body, pausing for a long tender time at her full breasts. Then he found her lips with his own and kissed her delicately, as if he never would taste her again.

And he never would. He kept that thought foremost in his mind. Adora deserved better than the likes of him. Kissing her long and sweet, Jared cuddled her close as her sleepy eyes closed and her breathing returned to normal.

"Go to sleep, Adora."

"But what about—?" Her voice was already dreamy with satisfaction and the sound of it sent tingles down his spine, straight to his hard cock. But he wouldn't trespass further. She was too good for him.

He stroked her hair tenderly. "It was just a dream, Adora. Sleep now and have no fear."

As he smoothed his hands over her soft body and shining auburn hair, he could feel her drifting closer to the edge of peaceful oblivion. He felt good that he'd been able to soothe her, but knew she would be hurt when he turned cold on her in the morning light. Still, it had to be done.

Rising regretfully, Jared watched her sleep for a moment more before finally steeling himself enough to leave her side. Kelzy was there, of course, partially blocking the door, staring at him with her wise blue topaz eyes.

"It's for the best," he said, knowing she would understand.

"I disagree, but you must be the judge of your readiness to commit to a woman, not I."

"You're damn right about that, Kelz." The dragon sounded like she was humoring him, but he couldn't be sure. He was frustrated and angry that things couldn't be different. But they just couldn't.

Jared stalked past the dragon and made his way to the bathing chamber. Kelzy followed, watching as he tore off his pants, releasing his straining erection.

"Adora would have welcomed that," she said, flicking out her long, thin tongue toward his cock, but not touching. *"She hasn't had a man between her legs since her husband died. I think she's lonely."*

"Lonely is no reason to climb in bed with me. She deserves better."

Kelzy shot a lick of flame toward the stone basin that was filling with water to heat it for him.

"Again, I disagree. You're just what she needs, Jared. A man who will put her needs above his own, but I won't nag you."

"Could've fooled me." He laughed without humor. *"Now, can I have a little privacy to bathe?"*

"And jerk off? Certainly." The dragon left him with a broad-eyed wink.

Chapter Three

Young Belora stretched, luxuriating in the feel of two strong male bodies, one on either side of her in the warm bed. She would never take for granted the love she had found with her two mates, Lars and Gareth. Nor would she ever take for granted the pleasure bond each of her knights shared with her when their dragon partners soared to the stars in a mating flight. When the dragons mated, the residual energy washed over their human counterparts in a wave of pleasure unlike anything she had ever known before.

Gareth was Kelvan's knight and Lars was partnered with the dragon's mate, Rohtina. Belora was wife to both men in the tradition of the Lair, since there were so few females able to live and communicate with dragons. That Belora was also able to heal dragons was a relatively new discovery and one that still had her puzzled.

The knights insisted she must be of royal blood, but she had been raised simply in the forest. Belora had never been rich, but had always been happy with her mother and the simple life they led. Her mother, Adora, was a powerful healer and they made their living off the land and from the herbal remedies they had traded with the people in the small village near their home. The place had been overrun by the first wave of the enemy invasion. Venomous skiths had decimated the village and destroyed the women's tiny house in the forest.

Belora's mates had helped rescue her mother from the skiths. For that she would be forever grateful. When the dragoness, Rohtina, was mortally wounded, Belora's own latent healing ability seemed to come to life. Never before had she tried to heal a dragon, and suddenly all the power she had ever wanted was hers to command.

She'd used the magic to heal the beautiful golden Rohtina and discovered she was pregnant with a dragonet at the same time. It was a double miracle as far as Belora was concerned. She was so happy. Life couldn't get much better.

"Uh, sorry to wake you all." Kelvan's voice sounded through all three human minds with some degree of urgency. *"But you'll very shortly have a visitor."*

"Tell them to go away." Gareth threw a pillow out of the bedchamber toward the general direction of the dragons' wallow.

"I can't." Kelvan sounded rather pained this time. *"You have to get up and get dressed."*

"Who is it?" Lars asked, raising up on one elbow and scratching at his muscular chest.

"And what's the bloody rush? It's not even dawn," Gareth grumbled while Belora giggled.

She climbed over Lars, pausing to kiss him good morning before she headed first for the wardrobe and then small bathroom next to their bedchamber. She was just too happy to be grumpy in the morning. Her mates had made her the happiest woman in the world—repeatedly—last night. Humming a light tune, she dressed and moved into the small kitchen area to heat water for the tea she liked to drink in the morning.

The small fire she used for heating water had gone out, but with a quick look at the dragons, she got their help in lighting it once more. They were handy to have around, she thought with a grin, when one needed a light. She was still chuckling when Gareth came into the room, stretching and yawning. He grabbed her in a fierce hug, kissing the breath out of her as was his custom first thing in the morning.

Lars was just a bit more conservative. He stumbled in—still a little bleary eyed, but his usual calm, quiet self. She knew well by now that still waters ran very deep indeed when it came to Lars. His steadiness warmed her as she set mugs of the strong tea she blended especially for them in front of her mates.

Belora noticed some activity out near the entrance to their suite and saw the dragons bowing their heads to a newcomer dressed all in black leather. He was a striking man, and more than a little scary. He moved with such self-possession, as did all the knights, but this was something more. This man prowled. It was as if there was a caged beast inside him, just waiting to be let out. She shook her head, smiling at her fanciful imagination as she nodded to Lars and Gareth.

"Looks like our guest is here. Do you know him?"

Both men turned and their eyes widened before they stood hastily. They bowed in respect as the man approached and he took it as his due while Belora stood dumbfounded.

"Your majesty." Gareth spoke for them all. "Welcome to our home."

"What do you know? Gareth and Lars, together again, I see. The Mother of All must have been sleeping on the job to allow this sort of pairing." The man's hazel eyes flashed, obviously teasing, and the knights relaxed in his presence.

Belora was intrigued.

"Congratulations on your wedding." The black-clad man stepped forward, offering his hand in warrior fashion, indicating he thought of her men more as contemporaries than underlings.

She liked that and found herself liking the tall man with the dancing hazel eyes almost immediately.

Both of her knights shook the man's hand with broad smiles, thanking him for his good wishes. They turned to her.

Her mouth went dry for no reason she could discern. Again, Gareth spoke for them all.

"This is our mate, Belora. Sweetheart, this is Prince Nico."

Belatedly, she remembered to curtsy, but the prince's next words nearly threw her off balance.

"It's a pleasure to meet you, cousin."

"Cousin?" Lars was startled into speaking, his turquoise eyes wide with the shock they all felt.

Nico nodded. "Shall we sit? I have much to say and I'd like a chance to get to know your mate a bit better as well."

"By all means." Gareth gave the prince his own chair, pulling over another for himself and one for Belora. She brought the teapot and another cup, setting it before the prince, all the while marveling that a prince should be sitting to morning tea with her, of all things.

"I met your mother just a short while ago," the prince began. "I'm convinced that she is the daughter of Prince Fileas of Kent who was killed along with his entire family by our enemies many years ago. The only survivor of the massacre was his youngest daughter, the Princess Amelia Jane, who disappeared that day and was never seen again. Until now."

"Bright stars!" Belora's whisper reached the men, making them smile.

"I believe your mother is Princess Amelia Jane, though she will be known now as Princess Adora of Kent. That makes you Princess Belora of Kent and distant cousin to the royal line." The prince leaned back, apparently enjoying the stunned stares of the people around him. "And that makes you two..." He eyed the knights. "Prince Consorts."

"Holy shit." Lars and Gareth spoke at the same moment, clearly stunned.

Belora was overwhelmed. Her mind seized and her stomach revolted. Jumping up so quickly her chair crashed to the floor behind her, she ran for the bathroom.

She had never been so sick in her life, grasping the seat of the commode for dear life as her stomach emptied itself over and over. Dimly, she realized the bathroom was crowded with her mates and—horrors—the prince. Gareth wiped her brow with a cool wet cloth, which felt very good, while Lars held her, tying her hair back with a stray piece of leather. That done, he rubbed her spine gently. The prince watched with a pitying look, but there was a light in his hazel eyes that was more than calculating. He made her feel a little uncomfortable as he moved forward to squat down next to her.

"May I?" he asked both her and her mates as he stretched his hand near to her forehead. She nodded hesitantly, uncertain of what he intended, but one didn't say no to a prince, after all.

He touched her head and suddenly the knots in her stomach eased. She realized he was using his own healing energy to still her rebellious stomach. His touch soothed and within moments she felt much better, though still a bit too shaky to stand on her own. Lars helped her up, holding her against his chest as she faced the smiling prince. He had the most luminous look in his eyes as he regarded her.

"Congratulations, cousin." His words were low, filled with emotion. "You carry twin boys and they will both be black dragons."

"Praise the Mother," Gareth whispered. He swayed for just a moment, seeking the stone wall for support.

Kelvan and Rohtina raised their heads in the archway and trumpeted their joy, nearly deafening all the humans present. Lars squeezed her close, his face buried in her neck as he kissed her.

"I don't understand." Belora looked up at the prince from within Lars' strong hold.

The prince laughed gently. "I know. Forgive me, cousin. This is just such a momentous thing. There are so few of us left. Every birth is a miracle to our line. Black dragons even more so."

"I still don't get it. Why are you calling them black dragons? I know that's the symbol of the king, but what has it to do with my...oh, sweet Mother, did you say I was pregnant?" Nico nodded and she felt tears gather in her eyes. "You felt them? Twins?"

"Yes, cousin. Two strong, healthy boys. One from each of your mates."

"Sweet Mother of All!" She turned in Lars' arms and hugged him hard, then reached for Gareth who still appeared stunned by the news. She embraced them both and her smile stretched from ear to ear.

"I take it the news is both happy and unexpected." The prince spoke once their rejoicing had died down a bit.

"Rohtina's pregnant too," Belora said, tears of joy nearly overcoming her.

"Then double congratulations are in order." The prince turned to the dragons and placed one hand, as if in benediction, on the young female dragon's head.

"Thank you for telling me! And for making me feel better too. My own small healing gift never works on myself."

The prince shook his head with a smile. "Such is the pity for most healers. But I understand your power is better suited to dragons anyway, which is a wonderful thing."

"Yes." She moved out of her mates' arms to face the strange prince. "We discovered it only a few days ago."

"So your mother told me."

"Oh! Mama's going to be so happy! And Kelzy!"

"All the dragons in this Lair will undoubtedly be happy to hear the news that your sons will soon be joining them."

Belora was puzzled by his wording. "Joining the dragons?"

"It's a gift of the royal blood we share, Belora. We are both human and dragon. That's why the females of our line can heal dragons when few other human healers can do so effectively. The males of our line take that one step further."

"How?" She was afraid to breathe.

The prince stepped back from her toward the dragons. Kelvan and Rohtina welcomed him with respect and a kind of deference she had never seen them display before.

"We *are* dragons."

So saying, the prince faded for a moment, a thick black mist swirling around his body. Belora recognized the tug of powerful magic on her senses. A moment later, a compact but still huge black dragon stood outside the archway between the other two dragons. The prince was nowhere to be seen. Or rather, he was there—incredibly—but in dragon form.

"Sweet Mother of All!" Belora strode forward, entranced by the gleaming black dragon. He was somewhat smaller than the other dragons, but he looked just as lethal, just as beautiful. She reached out to him and he craned his neck forward into her touch, allowing her to feel the shiny black scale of his neck and face.

"Do you understand now, cousin?"

Belora gasped as she felt the presence of the prince within the striking black dragon with the tourmaline eyes. No, that wasn't quite right. The prince wasn't inside the dragon, the prince *was* the dragon, and the dragon was the prince. It was simply amazing.

"My babies—?"

"*Your sons will be as I am, able to shift from human to dragon at will. I show you this so you will be prepared when they are ready. They'll probably begin to shift shortly after they learn to walk. They'll start flying around the same time Rohtina's dragonet will, I think, so they can all learn together. The Mother certainly knows what She's doing, doesn't She?*"

"I can't believe it."

"*Believe it. Your sons will bring hope to the dragons here in this Lair, which will shortly become key in our battle with Skithdron, if I'm not mistaken. Just their presence will bring renewed hope for our land to the dragon population and the knights as well. I tell you this from my own experience. I've felt the power and the responsibility that comes with being of two worlds.*"

"Is it hard? I mean, it's such a responsibility. I was raised simply. You can call me a princess all you want, but I'm still just a peasant really. I always will be."

"*Then you might understand what it's like to live in two worlds as well, for you are a princess and apparently a peasant too. And to answer your question, no, it's not hard at all. It's the most amazing blessing of my life and I thank the Mother every day for allowing me such gifts. She was wise when She allowed the last of the wizards to form the pact between the dragons of our land and our ancestor, Draneth the Wise. He was the first black dragon, forged by magic and his own wizard blood, but each of us since has been truly of both races. It's how we can understand the needs of both humans and dragons and continue to guide both races in harmony and cooperation. It's a gift, Belora, a precious one.*"

His words touched her so deeply she felt a tear trickle down her cheek. The prince moved back and the black mist swirled once more, leaving him clad in black leather, human once again.

"Whatever doubt remained is now gone. You carry royal black dragons in your womb. There can be no doubt you are of the royal line." The prince moved forward, kissing her on both cheeks. "Welcome back, cousin, to our family. It's a happy day to have found you and your mother once again."

This time, she did cry—her emotions all over the place with the shocking news of her bloodlines and her pregnancy. Gareth and Lars came up behind her, their supportive arms around her, there for her.

"There's one other thing I have to discuss with you, Belora, if you think you're up to it." The prince looked uncertain for a moment in the face of her turbulent emotions and she smiled to reassure him.

"Anything, Prince Nico. You've given me such happy news."

They walked back toward the kitchen area and sat down once more. Nico reached out a finger to each cold cup of tea and warmed them with his inner fire. Apparently he didn't have to be in dragon form to call on his fire. She would have to remember that for when her boys started to experiment with their own abilities.

"I don't mean to bring up bad memories, but I need to know everything you can remember about your sisters."

Belora gasped at the sudden change of topic. She had not expected it but realized it made sense that the prince would want to account for all the members of her line. The kidnapping of her sisters suddenly took on an even more sinister light in her mind. Had the kidnappers known their true identities? Is that why they had been targeted? She shivered and Lars and Gareth were there, putting one arm each around her at shoulders and waist, silent and supportive. Stars! How she loved them.

"As I told my mates, all I remember is that we were in a big town, at a market. My mother could tell you where exactly. A bunch of men rushed us. Big men. I remember one had a jagged scar on his face and was missing the two little fingers on his left hand. He hit my mother and the others grabbed my sisters. They were very strong and no one would help us. The scarred man tried to grab me, but my mother held me tight and started running. She ran and ran. They pursued us but didn't catch her." Gareth and Lars moved their chairs closer. "My mother and I went back later and tried to find my sisters, but they were long gone. We left that day and never went back. We walked and walked, through forest mostly, and when we came upon the cottage, we watched it for a few days before my mother would approach."

"Sounds like your mother was taking wise precautions." The prince's voice held respect and admiration, which warmed Belora's heart.

"We didn't have any money or much to trade except my mother's healing skills. No one claimed ownership of the cottage when my mother asked in the village and they welcomed the idea of having a healer move in nearby. Some of them helped Mama in the early days, bringing her food and household items to trade for her herbal remedies. That's how we've lived for the past decade and more."

"How old were your sisters when they were taken?"

"I was about five, so I guess they were about ten."

"Then they'd be in their early twenties now."

"Yes, I think so."

The prince stood. "Thank you, cousin. I want you to know that I'll do everything in my power to find your sisters."

Nico went back to speak at length with Adora while Belora and her new family celebrated the two pregnancies—both human and dragon. Adora, after she woke, was able to fill in the blank spaces in what Belora remembered about the day her sisters were snatched.

It was a cold trail, over ten years old, but Nico was a man who prided himself on his ability to learn things that others could not. He wasn't known as the Prince of Spies for nothing. He now had a place to start at least, knowing the town from which the children had been snatched. He would start there.

The black dragon winged away from the new Lair under cover of darkness, off on his quest.

Everything was not as it seemed in the royal palace of Skithdron. While on the outside, things looked much as they had during old King Gorin's time, on the inside, an evil pestilence roamed freely through the new king's chambers. Lord Venerai knew his friend and sometime lover, King Lucan, dabbled in magics not of this land—perhaps not of this world— and paid a high price for such power, but Venerai understood. He too, would do anything for power.

When Venerai received the royal summons to present himself in the king's private bedchamber, he prepared himself for a night of serving the young king's rather rapacious desires. But he found quite a different evening awaited upon entering the king's chambers. For one thing, Lucan was not as he had seen him last. Lucan greeted Venerai with inhuman, slitted eyes that reminded him of the reptilian gaze of a skith. Then, as Lucan shrugged off his robe, Venerai saw the changes that had been made to Lucan's once soft and pampered skin. Gone was the almost boyish pudginess, replaced by a sleek, *scaled,* lithe musculature that was startling to say the least.

Lucan's skin had an earthy cast and it rippled like a snake—like a skith—in the candlelight. Venerai didn't know what to make of it and for once in his life of political intrigues and power struggles was at a total loss for words. The young king noted all with his new eyes and laughed, but Venerai didn't care. Lucan was dangerous now. Let him laugh. As long as King Lucan wasn't ordering his death, Venerai was pleased to serve as the king's fool.

As Lucan approached, appearing to slither more than walk, Venerai held himself still. He started to notice changes in the room since the last time he'd been summoned to pleasure the king. Desperately trying to hide his reactions, Venerai knew one misstep here could easily get him killed.

A ragged girl cowered near the foot of Lucan's bed, bound to its ornate golden post with a golden chain. She was dressed scantily, but dressed nonetheless. Venerai assumed she was not there for the king's pleasure, but for some other purpose he could only guess at. The girl watched Lucan's back with hate-filled, startlingly green eyes that were huge in her gaunt face.

Venerai also noted the large trapdoor that had been installed near the ornamental golden fountain at one end of the grand room. It opened and Venerai tried to hold his reaction back as three giant skiths slithered into the room, making their way to Lucan's side as if seeking their master.

Skiths were native to Skithdron, and gave the land its name. They lived in the rock formations that littered the land, menacing all living creatures. Most active at night, skiths would eat anything that moved and seemed to rejoice in ripping people's heads from their bodies. Skiths were truly evil creatures, with acid venom that could burn through just about anything. Only the stone walls that surrounded every village kept the people of Skithdron safe from the predatory creatures.

They slithered like snakes and had slitted eyes, but they were as large as dragons, though of course they couldn't fly, or even climb very well. Solitary creatures, Venerai knew Lucan had found a way to herd them before his armies. Just how he'd learned to control the creatures was a subject of much conjecture and Venerai almost feared he was about to find out the secret of Lucan's power.

The power itself was tantalizing to Venerai. The hideous creatures were not.

Lucan welcomed the deadly skiths with outstretched arms as they twined around him like puppies. Venerai had never seen the like. It was a moment before Lucan turned back to him, his pet skiths standing tall, extending upward from the floor on their sinuous bodies, backing Lucan with their immense size and fearsome presence.

"You have pleased us greatly, Lord Venerai. You have always been a faithful servant."

Venerai bowed low, nearly scraping the floor, and dropped his gaze as the king demanded of his subjects. "Thank you, your highness."

"In recognition of your service to us, we have decided to raise you higher in our esteem."

Venerai's heart stilled with a mixture of fear and anticipation. Power was what he wanted, but what price was too high?

"Come forward, Lord Venerai, and join with us. We promise it won't hurt...much."

Venerai stumbled forward as the king laughed.

Chapter Four

War came on a quiet day. The wild skith raids on border villages had diminished in the days just before Skithdron launched the entirety of their first wave. Venomous skiths were herded before the army, bringing utter destruction to anything in their path. Somehow the generals were able to direct the creatures, bringing their army up behind. They destroyed three villages completely before enough dragons raced to the incursion to put up a decent defense against the unprecedented swarm of skiths.

Flames flew everywhere as Jared arrived on the scene, swooping in on Kelzy's back to lead the dragons and knights in their forays against the lethal creatures. But the skiths weren't the only thing to worry about—as if they weren't bad enough by themselves. The army of men and horses just behind the skiths was armed with crossbows that could shoot small but dangerous arrows at the dragons. A lucky hit to the eye or some of the rare sensitive places on a dragon's body could do enough damage to take them out of the fighting. The knights, too, were vulnerable to the arrows, so the danger was real, as all the knights knew full well.

They flew higher to avoid arrows as best they could, but in order to effectively fight, they had to make low flame runs. Though he hated to give the order, Jared knew the dragons' flame would be effective against the bowmen as well. Jared watched grimly as the new assault started to have some effect.

Suddenly, Jared saw a familiar banner as it dipped and rose once more with an additional white flag of surrender on its pinnacle. The lone rider made a break for the Draconian side, across the field of devastation, riding for the nearest dragon and knight—Kelvan and Gareth.

"Kelzy, can you see? Is that—? Sweet Mother! Is that Lord Darian?"

"It is. The crazy loon. He doesn't see the skiths turning to chomp on him."

"We have to do something. He's flying a white flag."

"I see it, Jared." Kelzy made a swooping dive toward the man on horseback, who was almost entirely surrounded by venomous skiths, but another dragon got there before her. This copper dragon had no rider on his back and was acrobatic enough to scoop the man right off his horse a moment before the skiths reached it. The skiths feasted on the poor beast, rending the horse limb from limb with their razor sharp fangs.

"Sandor! Good flying." Jared heard his dragon partner call to her friend. *"Will you take him to the Lair while we finish here? Don't let him out of your sight."*

The copper dragon gave a smoky snort that clearly said he would never do such a ridiculous thing and winged for the Lair, the man clasped tight in his sharp claws. All in all, Jared was glad the other dragon had made the save. He knew Kelzy might have balked at snatching a human, since the last time she had done it the guilt of inadvertently hurting Adora had bothered her for days and days. He didn't want to live through that again right now, though he was planning some drills with inanimate objects to sharpen her skills and build her confidence in snatching and grabbing targets as soon as they had a free moment. A fighting dragon needed to train constantly and keep all their skills as sharp as their talons.

When Jared and Kelzy landed at the Lair, they found a scene of chaos. Several knights shoved the Skithdronian man around, sneering and shouting angrily at him, though he did little to defend himself from them. Jared called for order and the knights grudgingly moved away, staring down the stranger with hatred in their eyes.

"What in the hells do you think you're doing? Acting like a bunch of children in a schoolyard!" Jared admonished the knights, most of whom were on the young side. Few had seen real fighting before. "This man came to us under a flag of surrender. You young hotheads should at least wait to hear what he risked his life and forfeited his country to tell us!" He noted a few eyes clouding with chagrin, but some were still defiantly angry.

"It's probably a trap, General," one of the younger knights yelled from the other side of the crowd now gathered on the wide landing ledge. "How do we know he's not some kind of spy sent to mislead us?"

"I know because I know this man. I've known him for years and have called him friend for just as long." Jared moved to stand beside the Skithdronian lord. Darian was a little worse for wear after the way he'd been greeted by the knights, and Jared was disgusted. Knights were supposed to behave better than this. "I lead this Lair until the king says otherwise and I trust this man. So you all had better just calm yourselves."

A dead silence fell then as the younger knights simmered. They didn't have to like his orders. They just had to follow them. He was the leader here and their job was to follow. Simple as that.

"Now, if you'll all get back to your duties, I'll talk to our guest and learn what news he gave up his home, his lands, and his title to bring us."

There was muttering and shuffling of feet but the knights dispersed, leaving a few curious dragons who were being tended by their knights for less serious wounds sustained fighting the skiths. Many were being doused with water to remove small spots of the venomous skith spray from their tough hides. It was best to do that here on the ledge where provisions had been made to remove the contaminated water safely, before the dragons moved into other parts of the Lair and spread the noxious stuff around too much.

Jared turned to the man at his side, looking him up and down before reaching out a hand in welcome. Absently, he noticed Adora hovering near one of the injured dragons some yards distant, a strange look on her face as she watched them. She'd avoided him since that night he'd brought her to climax with his mouth and fingers, just as he had avoided her.

"I'm sorry for their behavior, Lord Darian. They're young and inexperienced with real war."

The other man sighed as they shook hands. "Would that I were the same, but I've seen too much in my years, Jared. I don't blame them."

Jared growled. "I do. I command here and their ill behavior reflects poorly on my leadership. I apologize."

"No problem. I didn't expect to be welcomed with open arms, but I had to come. I thank the gods that I got through and that you're here, of all people, to hear what I have to say."

Both men's expressions grew grim. Jared realized many ears were craning to hear what they would say to each other.

"Come with me where we can talk privately. I'll also ask our healer if she will see to your wounds." He looked over at Adora and with a slight motion of his head asked her help. She waved a hand and nodded in agreement, and he knew without words that she would join them as soon as she finished her work with the badly injured dragon. He could count on the fact that she was a truly dedicated healer to bridge the icy gap that had grown between them since the night he had lost control of his senses.

Jared winced as he watched his old friend limp down the corridor with him. Kelzy followed behind with Sandor. The break from his own people, the skith attack, being snatched up by Sandor and flown here in the dragon's fist, and the beating from the young knights, had left Darian with a pronounced limp and assorted cuts and bruises. But true to his character, he didn't complain. Jared respected the man. Always had. Of all the Skithdronians he had met as counselor to the old king, this was the man he'd dealt with the most, and the most successfully.

Darian winced with every step but couldn't complain. He was alive and luckier than he had a right to be. He'd hoped to get to someone in power who might believe him and take his message higher, but he never expected to see his old friend, Lord Jared, riding atop a dragon. When Darian had lived near the palace, serving as the newly appointed ambassador from Skithdron to the old king's court, he and Jared had formed a close friendship. As a bachelor, he was often invited to spend holidays with Jared and his family.

Darian knew the new Skithdronian king had been behind the attack on Jared's family but didn't know how in the world he would ever break such news to his old friend. Besides, that was in the past and Lucan had gotten his wish—Lord Jared, the keenest of the old king's advisors, had been a broken man after the deaths of his young wife and child. He had left the old King's service and retreated into obscurity for a long time. In fact, Darian would bet none in Skithdron yet realized just who commanded the dragons on this part of the border.

Jared led him to a large chamber that had at its center a massive oval pit filled with sand. The dragons who followed close behind made for the sand pit and sank into it with what Darian would have sworn were dragonish sighs of enjoyment. They rolled slightly in the abrasive sand, which seemed to brighten their iridescent scales to a glossy shine even as he watched.

"Be welcome in our home, Lord Darian. As you can see, everything is designed around Lady Kelzy's comfort here." The other man gestured toward the beautiful blue-green dragon he had been riding.

Darian knew enough about dragons to make as deep a bow as he could manage toward the large heads that watched him carefully.

"Thank you for your hospitality, Lady Kelzy." He turned to the copper dragon then. "And thank you, sir, for your timely rescue."

"You're welcome. Though I've yet to decide if you were worth risking my neck for."

Darian's eyes widened as he heard the booming voice echo through his mind. It could only belong to the huge copper dragon whose garnet eyes twinkled down on him with a sly sort of merriment. Tentatively, Darian sought the way to the dragon's mind with his own thoughts.

"I can only hope that after you hear what I have to say, you'll be convinced."

The dragon gave a smoky chuckle and turned back to the sand and his grooming. Apparently neither Jared nor the female dragon was aware of the silent communication that had just taken place between Darian and the big copper.

"Sir Sandor," Jared spoke again as he led Darian to a long couch, "is an old friend of Kelzy's. He's newly arrived to our Lair and without a knight at present." Darian sat with only a small grunt of pain but Jared grimaced when he looked at him. "Our most gifted healer will see to your wounds as soon as possible."

"Don't worry about me, Lord Jared. There are things I need to tell you. Things you need to hear—"

He stopped speaking as the most beautiful woman he had ever seen walked through the main archway. She spared a smile for the dragons and it lit her entire face. Even from a distance he could see the glint of deep green in her wide eyes and it drew him in. She was a goddess come to earth and he would gladly worship at her feet, if she would let him.

The very idea of it shocked Darian right down to his toes. He'd long ago given up on finding a woman to share his life. No woman had ever evoked such a violent or immediate response in him. Darian knew deep inside, just from looking at her, this was a woman he could spend the rest of his life with.

As simple and startling as that, Darian knew he was looking at his destiny. Never one for overly romantic thoughts, Darian was laid low by the seductive sway of the woman's hips, the gentle glide of her dainty feet across the stone walkway.

The woman turned her head, spotting them, and it was as if his prayers had been answered when she made her way directly to the couch where he sat. As she drew closer, he could see she was no young maiden, yet there was a freshness about her that made her appear innocent and much younger than the wisdom in her startlingly beautiful eyes betrayed.

Jared stood stiffly and Darian noted the longing that entered the other man's eyes as he gazed on the beauty who approached. Darian realized Jared was not unaffected by the woman's grace. The knight wanted her, it was plain to see, but Darian questioned whether Jared—after the devastating losses in his life—would ever act on it. Darian's eyes were drawn back to the stunning woman and he noted more than a flicker of interest as she looked at him. But the dewy admiration in her eyes was for Jared alone as she passed him.

There was something there, on both sides, but he knew Jared was probably too wounded emotionally to be a good match for this delicate flower. If Darian could, he would have her—take her and cherish her in the way she deserved to be cherished. He knew in his heart he would be better for her than pining away after Jared—a man who might never be heart-whole again. Darian would make her forget the impossible longing for Jared that showed in her every movement. Darian would teach her the delights she'd find in his arms and the love he would give freely, if she would but accept it.

"Princess Adora of the House of Kent." Jared made formal introductions, but Darian could see from the woman's start of surprise that she wasn't comfortable about something. "May I present Lord Darian Vordekrais of Skithdron, former ambassador to our land during old King Jon's reign."

The woman stopped in front of him and smiled, nearly taking his breath away.

"I'm not big on formality, milord. I'm a healer and would help you if I could. May I?"

"Princess Adora, you may do whatever you wish with me. I'm yours to command."

The woman blushed so prettily at his daring words he almost wished he could spend the rest of the day making her smile, but he had come here for a reason. He had to get his message out and Jared was just the man to use his information.

She directed him to lie back on the couch, pulling a wicked-looking knife from her waist and setting to work cutting her way through the ruined leather boot and leggings that contained and constricted his swollen foot, ankle, and leg. She was efficient and so gentle he felt little pain.

Darian shook himself, focusing on his task. No matter the distraction of the woman tending his wounds, Darian knew he had to deliver his message. He'd given up his home and country to deliver his warnings, and they had to be heard as soon as possible.

"Jared, you've got to get word to your king. Lucan has gone completely 'round the bend."

The knight dragged a chair closer and sat, leaning forward to catch every word. Darian also noted the dragons had craned their necks over near them and listened intently as well.

"I've heard rumors about him, Darian, but nothing concrete."

"Jared." He grabbed the man's wrist, trying desperately to make his old friend understand the urgency of his news. "I've seen it with my own eyes. Lucan has sunk into dark magics that have twisted him into something not quite human. He keeps skiths as pets and trains them. They are far smarter than I ever gave them credit for being. Jared, the ones he trains go out and teach the others. They're learning to hunt in packs, in orderly groups, to work together. What you've seen so far on this side of the border is nothing. Lucan had them test and train on some of our own villages. Every human and animal for leagues around the villages of Vorkrais, Hemdan, Pennrin and Sokolaff are now gone. Skith food."

The woman gasped, drawing his eyes. She was white with fear and Darian regretted immediately putting such a look on her lovely face. He let go of Jared's wrist and—almost without realizing he was doing it—moved to cup her cheek, offering what comfort he could from such dire news.

"I'm sorry, Princess, to have distressed you. I should have waited to speak."

"No." She surprised him by reaching up and taking his hand in her own. He felt a spark between them and his gaze was glued to hers as she spoke. "Jared needs to hear what you have to say. I thank you for your selfless act in coming here, breaking with your people and subjecting yourself to the Lair's questionable hospitality." She made a face at his swollen and bruised leg. "It's just that I was chased by skiths not too long ago and almost didn't make it."

His hand tightened on hers. "Thank the gods you got away. I hate to think of what could have happened to you." Darian fought back the amazing attraction that flowed between him and this woman. He had a mission to complete. He had to impart his information. Only then could he concentrate on the gorgeous woman who ministered so tenderly to his wounds. "Jared, Lucan has found a way to communicate with the skiths and I believe he's made some kind of bargain with them."

"Sweet Mother of All!" Jared rocked back in his chair.

"As you probably know, wild skiths are solitary creatures. They hunt and live alone, usually in wilderness areas. They aren't much trouble unless you blunder into their territory or they try to take up residence near a village or something. But Lucan, he's organized them. They're working together, fighting together, living and hunting together. I've never seen the like. He's formed an army of the creatures, and they're coming this way. They will kill every man, woman, and child in Draconia, sweeping through your lands with the help of the human army Lucan has at his command, until they take it all." His voice rose with the passion of his words. "Jared, Lucan doesn't want to just conquer your land, he wants to destroy it utterly. He plans to kill every last human and dragon and allow the skiths to breed and multiply to numbers we have never before seen."

"That's insane." Adora's shocked whisper brought his eyes back to hers.

"Sadly, you're right. Lucan has gotten involved in sinister magics that have warped his mind. It is said he drinks skith venom and bathes in blood. He's consulted a foreign witch who some say managed somehow to allow him to communicate with the skiths. They say that's how he's been able to convince them to do things they never have before. He can control them."

Jared's scarred face was very grim. "I can't thank you enough for risking your life to come here and tell me this. You have my guarantee of sanctuary and a place in my House for as long as you need it."

Darian realized it was a generous offer and more than he had expected when he set out on his dangerous quest. To have the protection of Lord Jared's ancient and distinguished House meant quite a bit in this land or any other, for that matter.

"I am deeply honored, Lord Jared, and thank you."

He hissed then, involuntarily, when the woman shifted his injured leg. All eyes moved down to appraise the damage she had revealed by removing the boot and cutting his legging up to mid-thigh.

"You won't be running anytime soon, but slow walking with a stick to help support you is allowable. I'll do what I can with poultices and what healing energy I can spare." She shook her head sadly. "I'm sorry to tell you I must save most of my energy for the dragons."

He was shocked. "You heal dragons?"

The princess nodded, her gentle hands already ministering to his painful leg. He waited patiently, amazed at the tingle of her healing gift when she put out a tiny bit of energy to mend his abused muscles. With that little head start, he knew his healing time would decrease significantly.

She swayed just a bit when she stood and it was Jared who caught her, betraying his concern over the small woman. He steered her to a chamber in the suite, disappearing inside with her for a few minutes while Darian fought off sleep. There was more he had to tell Jared, but he hadn't the heart to speak the worst of his news before the tender creature who had done her best to heal him.

When Jared returned, his expression was thoughtful.

"Tell me the rest."

Darian chuckled wryly. "You know me too well, old friend." He settled back against the arm of the couch. "Lucan has been

75

sending envoys to that heathen Salomar in the north. They are working together to develop weapons that will take down dragons. I saw some drawings of one briefly, but it was too fast for me to get much detail. What I did see, though, gave me nightmares." He sat up, his eyes narrowed. "I've since learned that Lucan is sending massive shipments of diamond blades from the mines in the south to Salomar. I fear the worst."

Both men knew that a diamond blade was just about the only thing that could slice through dragon scale as if it were butter. Jared sat heavily in the chair at his friend's side.

"This is bad, Darian. Very bad."

"I know. It's why I came. You have to warn your dragons, Jared. I believe the human army will try to use their new weapons to drop the dragons from the sky and let the skiths do the rest. I wouldn't wish that sort of death on even my worst enemy, and I've never considered the dragons of your land or any of your people to be my enemies or the enemies of Skithdron. It's Lucan who's started this war and as far as I'm concerned he is the real enemy here."

Jared stayed by Darian's side, talking quietly and thinking through the dire news until the other man fell into a restless sleep. Adora had been more worn out than he liked her to be in healing the dragons who had come under attack that day. She had dropped off into an exhausted sleep moments after he'd put her to bed and would sleep for many hours yet.

He covered Darian with a blanket where he lay on the couch. He didn't have the heart to wake the injured man just to move him to a bedroom. Tomorrow was soon enough.

Jared wanted to seek his own bed, but he feared sleep would not come so easily to him. Not after what he had just learned. He stood, stretched, and walked over to the edge of the dragon's wallow. Kelzy and Sandor lay side by side in the large tub of heated sand, each looking at him with troubled jewel eyes.

"You heard?"

"We did." It was Kelzy who answered into the minds of all three.

"We must send word to the king right away, but we need more information if we're to train against this new threat."

Sandor elevated his head so that he was on a level with Jared's eyes. *"Though I have no knight partner at present, I wish to stay in this Lair and train with your ranks, Sir Jared. Kelzy and I have worked well together in the past. I would do so again, if you agree."*

"You're most welcome to stay, Sir Sandor. Right now, I think we need all the help we can get. Thank you for volunteering."

Sandor settled back down beside Kelzy as if he meant to stay right there in her wallow with her, but Jared didn't question it. His mind was too preoccupied with more desperate concerns than where a new dragon chose to sleep. If Kelzy didn't throw him out then who was Jared to say anything?

On his way to his own chamber, he stopped to look in on Adora. He almost wished he could talk to her about these troubling developments, to share his burden with her in some small way. Such thoughts were dangerous and skated too close to intimacy for his comfort, but they would not be denied. Adora was a bright, intelligent woman and he valued her insight. That's all these strange feelings were about, wasn't it?

He shook his head in disgust at himself as he walked silently away from her doorway. He was a damned fool. Already half in love with the woman and unable to work up the courage to do anything about it. Too afraid of being hurt again to even try.

"How are you feeling, Lord Darian?"

Adora sat beside the man's bed the next day, as soon as she finished checking on the dragons who had been hurt the day before. Jared had given him a room on the other side of the suite from hers that was similar in design and layout. There were several of these guest chambers in the large suite since Kelzy and Jared were the leaders of this Lair and often entertained guests and visitors.

"Much better today. Thank you, Princess."

"Please, call me Adora. I didn't grow up as a princess and I don't think I'll ever get used to the idea."

His blue eyes twinkled as he smiled at her. "Far be it from me to argue with royalty. I will gladly call you Adora if you will call me Darian, or Dar if you prefer."

She couldn't help but smile. This man was charming, that was certain, and so handsome he was almost hard to look at. Straight white teeth shone in contrast to his tanned skin. He had hair black as a raven's wing and startling, almost ghostly, blue eyes that smiled easily and sincerely at her, though he was still in a bit of pain, she well knew.

She busied herself looking over his leg injury. It was still swollen, but healing nicely now that he was off his feet. "Well then, Darian, how are you feeling?"

"Much better now that you're here."

She laughed. "Much friskier too, I see. Were you born a flirt or did you perfect the art over time?"

"Actually..." His eyes grew serious. "I've been a confirmed bachelor all my life, but I think that's about to change."

"What makes you say that?" She dared not look up to meet his gaze as she changed the dressing on his leg wound.

It had been so long since a handsome man had flirted with her, Adora couldn't be certain she wasn't reading something in to Darian's words that wasn't truly there. Certainly Jared had paid quite a bit of attention to her—and reminded her what

78

pleasure truly felt like—but it felt almost as if it were against his will, or his better judgment at least. By contrast, Darian was very honest about his desire to make her smile. In short, he was a flirt and she almost didn't remember how to deal with a man on that level. Still, it was exciting to try.

Darian's hand covered hers, forcing her gaze up to his. Even the air stilled, waiting as their eyes met.

"You, Adora. You're the reason." There was no easy smile now, no sign of amusement. No, this was a man puzzled by his own reactions but willing to risk...to trust. What she saw in his earnest face nearly stopped her heart for a moment.

"I don't understand it, but I think I'm falling in love with you, Adora. It's like my heart was waiting for you all this time, and now it sees what it's wanted all along." She was at a loss for words but he wouldn't release her hands. His eyes implored hers. "Say something, sweetheart. Let me know if I at least have a chance."

"A chance?" she repeated, stunned witless.

"A chance to win your love. I want you, Adora. My life is a mess right now. I have little to offer, I know, but my heart is pure and it's yours if you want it."

"Darian, I've been alone a long time."

"Don't say no only because you're frightened. I'll do all in my power to alleviate your fears. Just say you'll give me the chance to try to win your heart. Give me hope, Adora. I beg you."

Her eyes grew moist as he held her gaze, tenderly stroking her hands. She realized in that moment, regardless of her growing feelings for Jared, this man was open in a way Jared could probably never be again. This man, brave enough to leave his life behind for the good of her people, was offering his heart on a platter—and it touched her in ways she didn't quite understand. She barely knew him, but she knew his nobility—his courage and his honor—and admired him greatly for it.

Could she know his love as well? She wasn't sure, but a part of her really wanted the chance to try. Another part of her longed for this kind of offer from Jared, but sadly knew it might never come. Should she turn down her chance with Darian because of the attraction she felt for Jared that might never be realized? Or should she take the chance of getting to know this sweet, noble, handsome man who seemed so ready and open to her?

Something about him had fascinated her from the start. He was good-looking, yes, but there was also something in his character that spoke to her on a much deeper level. He had an energy about him that drew her in and she was powerless to pull away.

"I'm not saying no, Darian. I'm saying...maybe, I guess." She smiled crookedly. "I was married young and lost my husband young as well. I raised my daughter alone, on the run. Until recently, I haven't had a man in my life, or in my bed, for a very long time." She blushed a little at her own boldness but she wanted to be frank with the man. She owed him her honesty at least, as he was taking the risk she would refuse him outright. "I honestly don't know if I'm ready for that again. My children are grown and I'm at a crossroads in my life. But I like you, Darian, and I'm willing to call you friend. Perhaps lover, but friend for now. Is that all right?"

He beamed at her as he brought her hands to his lips, kissing them soundly.

"It's wonderful, Adora. For your sake, I'll try to control myself, but you're damn near irresistible. You're a special woman and I'll do everything in my power to remind you of that every day."

She felt her cheeks heat with a blush at his impassioned words while his gentle smile warmed her heart.

That night, after all were abed, Adora went to check on her new patient. Darian was restless, his swollen leg healing well, but still a bit uncomfortable at just about any angle. She caught him trying to reposition it on a little mound of pillows with a frustrated expression on his face.

"Can't sleep?"

She advanced into the room, her voice calm as she moved to his leg and gave just a touch of her healing power to ease the ache.

"You shouldn't spend your energy on me, milady."

She sat on the side of his bed. "It's nothing to me if it will help you rest, Darian. I meant to do a more thorough job of your healing before, but I was too tired that first night because of all the energy it took to deal with the dragons. Let me do what I can for you now, all right?"

Darian lay back, watching her every move as she placed her hands on his leg. The warmth of her power swept through her fingers and into his injury, mending the strained muscles and tendons, coaxing the fluid swelling the area to recede. It would take a while to do so, but she knew he would be out of pain now, and probably good as new by morning.

She smiled as she lifted her hands away. It hadn't taken that much energy after all, and he would be fine now. She was glad of that.

Darian reached up and stroked her cheek with the back of his fingers. "You're a compassionate woman, Adora, and a beautiful soul." His gaze searched hers. "Why did you come here, to me? Couldn't you sleep either?"

This was it. This was her moment of truth.

"No, I couldn't sleep. I kept thinking about what you said about...us." She sought reassurance from his almost ethereal, sky-blue gaze. "You got me thinking, Darian, wanting things I haven't wanted in a very long time."

His hand turned to cup her cheek, then moved down her neck to her shoulder. He sought permission before moving further.

"What do you want, my love?"

"I want—" She sighed as his hand moved lower, parting her robe. She was bare beneath it. Her voice trembled as she forced the words out. "I want you, Darian. I want to be a woman again."

"You've always been that, Adora. You are a desirable, beautiful, brave woman."

He sat up to meet her as she sat on the side of his large bed. With gentle hands, he pushed her robe from her shoulders and moved to meet her lips with his own, taking her in a tender kiss that spoke of desire, passion, and respect. He deepened the kiss and she went with him, following him back down to the bed, her robe hanging open so that she was bare to his roaming, worshiping hands.

Darian kissed her, steadily increasing the pressure on her lips, delving his tongue into her sweet mouth to catch her breathless sighs as his hands caressed her breasts, tweaking the hard nipples, luxuriating in the softness that was Adora. He moved one hand lower, over her back under the satiny robe and down to her shapely, taut backside. She had a muscular body from living off the land and working hard all her life, but she was supple in the places that really counted. Womanly soft and womanly warm, Darian thought, and more welcoming to his lonely soul than any woman had ever been.

She sighed as he rolled her gently on the large bed, pinning her beneath him, the pain in his leg forgotten in her enticing arms. He tugged the robe down over her shoulders, trapping her arms in the thin fabric.

"Say you want me, my love, my beautiful Adora."

"I..." Her breathy voice trailed off as her luminous eyes met his. He watched carefully for any sign of fear, but found only an almost maidenly hesitation that soon disappeared as she made her decision. "I want you, Darian. Make love to me."

He smiled at the soft look in her eyes. She was such a wonder to him, reaching out for what she wanted, what she needed.

"I need you so much." Darian's voice whispered through the dim chamber.

He nibbled on her neck, kissing his way across her body, down to the sweet valley of her thighs. He lingered there, spreading her legs, licking at her tender folds, noting every reaction and cataloging every shiver of delight he brought her. It made him feel so good to see her writhing in passion beneath his hands and mouth. He paused only to pull the long, borrowed sleep shirt over his head and toss it across the chamber, reclaiming his place between her legs with a barely repressed growl of need.

Biting gently, he focused his tender assault on her clit until she came apart under his mouth. She gasped as her body shook through a long, powerful orgasm. This little woman was so needy. He loved the idea that he was one of very few men to bring her such joy—for he could tell this beautiful, shy woman was not too free with her charms—and vowed in his heart this would not be the last night he would pleasure her. He would have her in his bed come morning and every day thereafter, as soon as he could convince her to tie her life to his. She deserved better, it was true, but he was just selfish enough to take her and claim her and spend the rest of his life dedicated to her happiness. He knew he could bring her that at least, if with nothing else but his body, his hands, and his clever tongue.

Darian had never fallen in love before—never felt such immediate, stirring desire for a woman in his life before—but he knew this was the real thing. With a conviction in his heart, he made plans to make her his own. He knew he could no longer be complete without Adora, and only Adora. No other would do ever again.

He moved back up her trembling body, plying her with kisses as he went, bringing her back up to an even higher peak of desire before claiming her mouth and rolling so she was on top of him. He positioned her beautiful, slender but muscular legs onto either side of his hips, encouraging her to cocoon his aching cock in her tender folds. Her eyes met his as she gasped and pulled slightly away.

He dragged the satiny robe down her back, throwing it across the chamber to join his sleep shirt. She was beautiful in the dim light of the chamber, gorgeous to him in all her feminine glory.

"Take me this first time, my sweet Adora." He cradled her head in his hands, stroking her hair as he looked deep into her mesmerizing green eyes. "I know it's been a long time for you. Take me at your own pace."

She smiled down at him, repositioning herself with slow movements that drove him wild. She was so soft and wet for him. He wanted her badly, but didn't want to hurt her with his eagerness, so this was the only solution for this first time. Later he would take her the way he needed to, claiming her and pounding into her without mercy, without restraint.

She moved on his cock so tentatively it was killing him, but this time was for her. She would be tight and tender from so many years of denial. It was like taking her virginity, in a way, and he felt like a king that she would give such a gift to him.

Adora rose up and positioned him with her small, trembling hands, nearly making him come right there, but Darian held on, gritting his teeth as he watched them join for the first time.

Adora sank down on him by slow degrees, taking him a little way, then bouncing back up, only to go a little lower the next time. Within a few agonizing strokes, she was seated fully upon him and Darian was well on his way to heaven.

He placed his hands on her hips, stroking upward to pull at her hard little nipples. She shivered in response, her wet pussy tightening on his cock and driving him higher. He pinched her nipples harder and was rewarded with another little spasm of her inner muscles around him.

"Do you like it a little rough, Adora?" His eyes dared her to tell the truth he could read from her responses.

"I don't know." Her eyes were wide with surprise, and he tugged again, just a little more harshly this time on her nipples, testing.

"I do." His grin widened as he brought one hand down to slap her ass. She jumped, yelping breathlessly as her pussy spasmed and creamed around him. "You've got an adventurous soul, my little love."

She sighed and shivered as she began to move on his hard cock. "I never did before." She gasped as he used his hands to pinch her bottom. "It must be the company."

"Are you saying I'm a bad influence on you?" His hands encouraged her to speed her pace with gentle slaps to the fleshy part of her ass. He knew she liked it from the way she smiled and squirmed in delight on his cock, sending him higher as well. "If so, I'll have to remember to influence you more often." Darian emphasized his statement with a gentle but firm slap right over her straining clit and she took off for the stars, coming around him and gripping his cock so tight with her inner muscles he thought he would go off with her.

But he had bigger plans for his adventurous little love. As she came down from her peak, he rolled her beneath him again, never leaving her body for one moment. He couldn't bear to part from her even for a second.

"Are you back with me, sweetheart?"

"I'm with you, Dar." Her voice was breathy and divine. It fired his senses.

He dipped down to capture her smiling lips with his own. He had plans to tire her out and ride her until she couldn't walk straight tomorrow, but he wouldn't take her any further if she had gone as far as she could go. He measured her response to his kiss, the tightening around his still hard cock and slippery wetness telling him she was ready for more.

"Hang on," he warned, bringing his hips down forcefully into the warm cradle of her thighs. Her eyes jolted open, but her sexy lips curled with delight, reassuring him it wasn't too rough. He would rather die than hurt her.

Darian kept careful track of Adora's responses and pounded more heavily into her tight sheath, reveling in her closeness, her warm body, and her heavenly scent. She was all woman and all his. He loosed the need raging within him and brought himself hard into her again and again, feeling at last her pulsing pleasure as he too was overcome. That final blast of pleasure just went on and on and on.

Darian stiffened above her, tensing in every muscle as his come shot deep within the only woman he would ever love. The idea was startling, but oddly comfortable. She felt so right in his arms, in his heart. He loved her truly and deeply, he knew in that moment. And he would never love another.

When it was over and he could move once more, Darian kissed her thankfully as she began to relax into a boneless, trusting, exhausted sleep beneath him. He rolled off her, tucking her close to his side as he lovingly arranged the blanket over her luscious, bare body.

A movement near the door caught his eye and Darian looked up to find Jared staring back at him. The devastation in Jared's lonely gaze chilled Darian to his core. He opened his mouth to speak, but Jared was gone before he could find the right words.

Darian looked back at the bed and realized Adora was fast asleep. She didn't know Jared had seen them together. She didn't realize how deeply they had hurt him. Perhaps that was for the best. Darian would find the right thing to say to Jared tomorrow. He hoped.

Chapter Five

The next morning Adora was up and out of bed before Darian even woke. He dressed and stepped out of the small chamber, leaning just a bit on the walking stick Adora had left for him, in search of breakfast. He found Jared sipping strong, dark tea, standing over the cooking fire in the small kitchen area.

Jared eyed him hostilely but said nothing. Still, the tension was thick between the two men as Darian poured out a mug of tea for himself and found an apple to munch.

"Jared." Darian tried to find the words to broach the subject that was clearly standing between them. "I'm sorry if I hurt your feelings, but I couldn't help myself. When I first saw Adora I realized very quickly that she's different from any woman I've ever met before."

"You're damn right she's different." Jared was going to be belligerent about this, Darian realized. "She's royalty, Dar."

"She's also a warm, mature woman with a woman's needs. She needs love, Jared." Darian tried to speak gently, not wanting to rile his old friend.

"Love? Is that what you call it? Because all I saw last night was you nailing a willing wench." He shot Darian a look of disgust. "How could you?" Jared's deep voice was hoarse with emotion, accusatory and gruff as he glared at Darian. If looks could kill, he'd surely be dead.

"Look Jared, don't jump all over me for this. If you wanted the woman, you've more than had your chance. She cares for you. Don't you think I saw that right away? But I also saw you, in denial, ignoring her. You were hurting her with your indifference, man. Don't fault me for stepping in and making her happy where you've only made her miserable, longing for things you won't give her. She needs someone to care for her and make her feel wanted, cherished, and loved. She's lost her home, Jared." He shook his head. "That's something I have a little experience with as it happens. She needs someone to hold her and make her feel safe and needed."

Jared rocked back on his heels, deflated. "Damn it all to hell and back." He ran a frustrated hand through his hair and sat hard on the sofa. "You're right, Darian. I'm an ass."

Darian sat down in the nearby chair, watching his old friend closely. Jared sighed hard and shut his eyes tight for a quick moment, the pain of the past hours clear on his face. Darian sensed a break in the wall surrounding his old friend and took the chance to get everything out in the open.

As gently as possible, Darian spoke into the heavy silence. "Ana and James are gone, Jared."

Jared sucked in a sharp breath as every muscle in his body tensed. Darian's heart went out to the man, but this needed to be said. Jared was living in a world of hurt, much different from the carefree, jovial man Darian had once known. He owed Jared his support and help in becoming that man once again. No one should live with the kind of burden Jared kept firmly planted on his shoulders.

"I know that, Dar. I don't need to be reminded. I live with the guilt of their deaths every day of my life."

"Guilt?" Darian was truly puzzled. Jared opened his eyes and ran a hand over his rough face.

"I should have been with them, Dar. I should have protected them. Instead I was off serving my king while they were murdered in their beds by greedy thieves in the night."

Darian was silent a long moment. Could that be what Jared really believed about the attack on his family? How could the man not know the truth of those dreadful days? No wonder he was so changed. Jared blamed himself for something over which he'd had no control or responsibility.

Darian knew he could relieve some of that guilt and perhaps focus the anger of this brave man on something more productive than wallowing in his imagined sins of the past. Darian weighed his words carefully, then finally spoke, albeit a bit hesitantly.

"Those were no simple thieves, Jared." He leaned forward as Jared listened intently. "I found out not long ago that your family was targeted by Lucan. Even back then, he had designs on the throne of Skithdron and worked to throw your country into chaos. You were too close to King Jon and his sons. Too protective. Too smart. Lucan needed you out of the way. He succeeded when he ordered his assassins to kill your family. You left the king's service and his way was clear."

Jared was as near to tears as he'd come since that day he had learned his wife and young son were dead. To learn finally who was responsible was both a terrible shock and, oddly, a relief. Jared felt like the weight of the world had been lifted off his shoulders. It focused him. As did his anger.

Jared's anger was slow to build, slow to burn, but once it got going, it was an unstoppable inferno. He felt the fire rising in his veins, but he needed to have all the facts before he would decide on a course of action. The wisdom of his years had taught him to think before loosing the rage within him. While it was still possible to reason somewhat clearly, he needed to hear everything Darian knew.

"Are you sure? The Lucan I met years ago was a sweet child."

Darian scoffed, "He's a maniac, Jared. I believe he killed his own father. Do you think ordering the deaths of an innocent woman and child would bother such a demon?"

"Sweet Mother of All."

Jared staggered to his feet, emotion overwhelming him. He fought down the sizzling anger, but it bubbled up from within, threatening to break him into a million pieces, never to be reassembled. All the years he'd wasted, blaming himself for something perpetrated by an enemy.

Certainly, he still felt remorse over not being there to defend his family when Lucan's assassins came to call, but knowing their deaths hadn't been random violence somehow made it easier to bear his own guilt. The assassins would have waited until he was gone from home to hit their targets, no matter if he were down the road or in another country. When Skithdronian assassins targeted a person, they didn't miss.

Now that Jared knew where to place the blame for his family's demise, the anger and shock of it boiled through his veins like acid. Lucan had won. He'd succeeded in taking Jared from the work he loved for his king and his land, and nearly succeeded in taking Jared's life too. If not for Kelzy, he would have killed himself in his grief long ago. Only the dragon had saved him, bringing him a new purpose.

But Jared's family wasn't the only one to pay the price for Lucan's political designs. No, the old king and his wife had been murdered too. Not long after Jared left the court because of the tragedy in his life, King Jon and his Queen had been killed, forcing young Roland to assume the throne long before his time.

Like patterns in the sand, the lines of deceit were becoming clear. Jared's mind spun as he realized the depths of Lucan's treachery. His family's destruction was just the beginning of the devastation Lucan had visited upon the people of Draconia. Jared had felt terrible guilt at the deaths of the king and queen, thinking if he'd only stayed at court, he might somehow have prevented their murders.

But Jared had been in too much pain at the time. He'd carried his grief with him every day—for his wife and son—but also for the king he had served and loved as a brother. So much death. So much treachery!

Jared's hands balled into fists, his thoughts boiling up until he thought he might explode. Blindly, he moved toward the door. He didn't know where he was going, but he had to do something. He had to loose the anger, grief, sorrow and overwhelming pain in his soul for all that had been lost. So damn much destroyed! So much pain. So much waste.

Suddenly, Kelzy was there, her warm breath bathing him in comfort as the years of sorrow engulfed him. He reached out to the one living being he'd allowed himself to care for and wrapped his arms around her neck. Jared buried his face against her gleaming hide as the emotion welled up and over, pouring out of him with the tears he'd never allowed himself to shed before. He cried for the family he'd lost. For the king. For the years of desolation and pain.

Darian came up behind him and put a strong arm around his shoulders as Jared wept for the first time in many, many years. Jared barely registered his old friend's presence, but he felt the warm support of Kelzy and Darian, needing it as never before.

Adora found them like that when she walked into the suite a few minutes later. Darian caught her eye and motioned her over, his expression solemn as he supported his old friend with a brotherly arm around his wide shoulders. She looked up into Kelzy's aquamarine eyes and the dragon explained what had happened in her silent way.

Adora felt tears well in her own eyes as she thought of how badly this news had affected the strong man who held a piece of her heart. She reached out, coming up on his other side to offer what comfort she could. Her healing gift reached out to his pain as she put her arm around his waist and snuggled into his side.

A moment later, she was whirled around and grasped tightly in his embrace as he let go of Kelzy, only to cling to her instead. She was shocked, surprised, and so touched she gave freely of her healing energy, wishing only that she could heal his shattered heart. She looked up into Darian's sad eyes as Jared choked out broken, nearly silent sobs, his face hidden in her neck as his strong arms engulfed her. She saw sorrow, love, and approval in the eyes of her new lover as she held the other man. It was confusing, but it felt right.

"It's as it should be." Kelzy's voice was gentle in her mind as her breath puffed over them with comforting heat. *"Do not fear your feelings for either of these men. They are your destiny."*

"Both of them? But how?"

The idea of her daughter having two knights as husbands was still uncomfortable, but she sort of understood the necessity with the way the men were bonded to mated dragons. This, however, was something else altogether. Only Jared was bonded to a dragon and Kelzy was unmated. If Adora was mated to Jared, she would eventually be expected to take the knight of Kelzy's dragon mate as her second husband, if such a thing ever occurred.

Because of the bond dragon and knight shared, when dragons mated, their human partners were inevitably caught up in the sensual frenzy. It was a sacred rule that fighting dragons never mated while their knight partners had no mate. The frenzy as the dragons joined would drive an unmated knight insane and a casual sex partner just would not do. The depth of feeling—the love—had to be there for the mating frenzy to be sated, for it was deeply emotional as well as intensely physical for both the dragons and the humans involved.

"Don't ask how, child," Kelzy counseled her, still sending warm breaths of cinnamon-scented air over them to offer what comfort she could to her heartbroken knight. *"Just accept it will be so. The Mother and we will make it so. We see the way both these men feel about you and how you feel about them. This is the turning point, I think."*

"Who is 'we'?" She had a sneaking suspicion, but the idea was too wild to even contemplate.

"Leave that to us, child. See to Jared now. This storm was a long time in coming and he will feel shame for his actions if you give him half a chance. Best to take him to your bed now and take his mind beyond the grief of the moment. Give him something much more pleasant to focus on."

"You want me to sleep with him?"

"Isn't that what you've wanted for weeks now?" Kelzy's voice was sly with the knowledge only another female could understand.

"Well...yes, I suppose so. But he doesn't want me. Not really."

"Nonsense! The man loves you."

Adora gasped. *"Are you sure?"*

"I know my knight. He's stubborn, but he loves deeply and true. He has a good heart that has been badly hurt and he takes too much responsibility on his solitary shoulders. He needs you, Adora. He needs your strength and your love."

"But what about Darian?"

"Child, the Mother of All knows what She is about. Look at Darian. I think he understands. He knows how much Jared loves you and needs you. He loves Jared like a brother and hates to

see him hurt like this. I think he'll understand. He will help, I think. Take him with you and see where it leads."

"But he's not a knight. He doesn't expect to have to share a woman with another knight."

"He's a man, child. I don't know of too many human males who would turn down a threesome when offered the chance."

Adora smiled just slightly, shyly, as she met Darian's eyes over Jared's broad shoulder.

She saw warmth there—the warmth of care and love, but also the warmth of desire. Darian had shown her just last night that she was not as dead sexually or emotionally as she had thought. He'd given her a boost of confidence along with his tender and commanding loving. She knew he cared for her and was fast falling in love with him as well, but her heart also wanted Jared. Adora had wanted him almost from the first moment she'd seen him.

Jared needed her so badly, she knew it in her heart, and this breakdown only proved it further. He needed love and support. He needed to let people close to him, not just dragons. For the past years, only Kelzy had managed to breach the defenses around his heart. But those walls crumbled and crashed as she and Darian supported him in his soul-deep grief.

Darian moved slowly, coming around her, holding her gaze as long as he could until he was behind her. Sandwiched between two hard male bodies, Adora swept her hands down Jared's back as his weeping began to ease. He was so silent, so needy, but so resolute. Jared straightened by degrees, his warm lips nuzzling into her neck as he moved, perhaps unable to meet her eyes while his own were red from grief too long denied. Or perhaps because he was finally giving in to the attraction between them.

As he moved, so did Darian, reaching to clasp her waist, moving his already hard erection against the soft globes of her ass. So Kelzy had been right. Apparently getting Darian to share wouldn't be such a hard thing after all. Or rather, there was a hard thing involved, but it was a good, hard thing she would see was put to good, hard use. She could barely wait.

Smiling to herself, Adora tugged at Jared's leather shirt, pulling at the laces as he worked at hers. Darian was already stripping down her leggings and baring her legs. Kelzy watched all with apparent approval, puffing her sweet breaths over them to keep them warm as they bared themselves and each other.

Adora couldn't believe she was acting so wanton. Her only lover before last night had been her husband. They had been married young, just teenagers fumbling in the dark until they got the hang of meshing their bodies together, but this was something else entirely. Darian had shown her things the night before that she never would have imagined, and she sensed she was in for another breathtaking lesson here.

Jared seized her mouth with his own, his lips demanding as never before. Her clothing was gone and she pulled at Jared's with his enthusiastic help. Soon he was bare too, but she didn't get the chance to step back and enjoy the view of his masculine body. No, he was too eager. He kept her close, kept his lips fused to hers as his hands roamed, learning and claiming first her breasts, and then the smooth expanse of her abdomen and lower, to cup the wetness between her squirming legs.

Darian was busy too, ridding himself of his clothing and dropping to his knees behind her. His lips left a trail of kisses all the way down her back and up her thighs until he reached his goal, between the soft cheeks of her ass. He gripped her cheeks and squeezed, apparently enjoying the soft flesh, leaning forward to nip and suck, leaving his mark on her and licking the momentary, exciting pain away with his clever tongue.

It was Darian who eased her to the floor, his strong arms taking her weight as Jared refused to let her go. Having two sets of masculine hands caressing her body was an enticing, exciting, amazing experience. The approval she read in both their faces when Jared briefly let her up for air gave her the confidence to reach up and run her hands over Jared's chest and down to his straining cock. He was so hard, so ready, and she knew this first time would be fast.

That was fine with her. She would do anything for him. She realized in that moment that she loved him—truly, deeply and without reservations.

"Come to me now, Jared. Make love to me."

He growled as he bore down on her. Thankfully Darian had made a bed of sorts out of the pile of their discarded clothing. Kelzy helped by scooping a mound of warm sand from her wallow. Darian had covered the sand with clothing until Adora lay on a squishy sort of bed that was much more comfortable than she would have expected.

Jared looked down at the woman waiting for him—her soft thighs spread, her beautiful green eyes wide with acceptance of whatever he might do...and love. He could see the love shining in her eyes and knew he felt the same. He could no longer deny his need for her and her beautiful, open, healing heart.

He settled between her legs, unable to help himself. He kissed her tenderly, then pulled back for one last moment of sanity to look down into her beloved face.

"I don't want to hurt you."

"You won't." Her simple acceptance of him and all he was humbled him.

"I love you, Adora." He held his breath. Leaving his heart out in the open like that was a risk.

She touched his rough cheek, her smile generous. "I love you too, Jared."

Her words touched a place deep in his heart he'd thought was gone forever. But suddenly she was there, in his heart, and he knew she would never be removed. Kissing her sweet lips reverently, the heat between them rose once more to a fever pitch.

"I need you now, Adora. I'm sorry, I can't be gentle."

"I don't want you to be gentle. I want you, Jared." She emphasized her demand with an erotic pulse of her hips that brought his hard cock within the hot warmth of her waiting sheath. And he could wait no more.

With a groan, he buried himself inside her, glorying in her heat, her warmth, her wetness, and her love. He was so far gone in his desire he barely heard her answering sighs of pleasure as he pumped hard and fast into her, straining against the force that pushed him onward, holding out to make this first time last as long as he could, but it was a losing battle. He had waited too long to accept the reality that she was his, and all too soon he felt his balls clench and his entire body tense as he erupted within her, showering her with his tribute, bathing her womb in his essence, making her truly his.

Jared collapsed on top of her, eyes opening slowly to stare down into hers. He kissed her then with a gentleness that had been near impossible only moments ago. Adora sighed into his mouth, her hips quaking in the last rolls of orgasm. Jared felt a sense of relief that he'd somehow managed, even in his blind desire, to bring her pleasure.

He kissed her neck, her shoulders, working his way down to the tips of her breasts, and she sighed. A rustle of leather off to his side registered just barely in his preoccupied mind and Jared looked up.

There was Darian, trying to squeeze a painfully hard erection back into his leggings.

"Where do you think you're going like that?" Jared was sated enough to have regained a bit of his usual good humor.

Darian started, his eyes meeting Jared's with regret. "Look, you two obviously need some time alone—"

"Not alone!" Kelzy insisted in his mind. *"He's part of this, Jared. Make him see."*

"As my dragon partner reminds me, Darian, you're responsible for this. I know you love her too." Jared finally found the strength to lever himself off her luscious body. Caressing her as he got to his knees, Jared removed himself gently from between her slippery legs. How he hated to be apart from her! But things had to be settled between all three of them. He had to make Darian understand the complex feelings he himself couldn't quite figure out, but accepted nonetheless.

"I was jealous as hell when I saw you with her last night, but I know what I saw. There was love there, in every moment. On both sides." He leaned down to kiss her cheek.

"You saw?" She flushed red with embarrassment.

He winked at her. "I saw, all right. Didn't sleep at all for thinking of how he must feel, locked deep inside your beautiful body." Jared kissed her softly. "Now I know." Their eyes held for a moment, her blush fading as her breathing sped up again. "And I also know he's part of this, Adora, in your heart." His gaze shifted to Darian, still standing in indecision, his clothes clutched in his hands.

He saw how Darian watched Adora and how she returned his loving gaze. There was love there, without doubt. Adora would not give herself without it.

Darian shook his head and resumed dressing as Adora sat up on the makeshift bed. "I should go."

"No. You shouldn't." Jared's voice was firm but held more than a hint of frustration. How could he explain something he didn't understand himself? "Look, Dar. It's the way of things for knights to share. If there's love, then there's nothing wrong with us both being with Adora, as long as she wants it." He looked over at the startled but smiling woman. "And I think she wants it." He nudged her knee with his own. "Am I right, darling?"

Adora was confused, but her heart knew what it wanted. Her heart wanted both of them, with her, forever. Her pussy wanted both of them too. It was a scandalous, exciting thought.

"I..." She searched for the right words. "I don't understand it, but...I want you both. You're both in my heart." They stood and Adora went first to Jared and then to Darian, taking each of them by one hand. "I need you both." Blushing uncontrollably, she kissed Jared, then Darian, leaning into Darian a bit longer, convincing him with her mouth, her naked warmth, and her soft sighs that she didn't want him to leave.

When he released her, there was a tentative smile in Darian's sparkling, light-blue eyes.

"Are you certain, Adora?"

She laughed. "I'm shocked by my own behavior, but I know I want and need you both. As crazy as it sounds, I love you both. Please don't make me choose between you. It would shatter my heart." Her eyes grew serious. "Unless the thought of, um...sharing...hurts you. I wouldn't want to cause either of you pain."

Jared smiled broadly at her. "I didn't ever expect to have a woman to love in my life again. You're a miracle to me, and as a leader of knights, I'm used to three-partnered relationships. I see everyday how well they work out. Darian and I have known each other for a very long time. We respect each other as warriors and statesmen, but more so as friends. You'll get no complaint from me."

Darian's head tilted as he seemed to think carefully about his answer. Adora held her breath and waited to see what he would say. He was from another land, after all, where traditions were probably much different. The Mother only knew what he had been raised to expect... Adora realized in that one tense moment she would never be truly happy unless she could have them both. It was that simple and that amazing. She had never thought to have even one man in her life again and now she felt incomplete without two. She was getting greedy in her old age, she thought with an inner chuckle.

"I don't understand this at all, but I need to be with you, Adora. More than I need to breathe." Darian moved a step closer and caressed her cheek with the back of one big hand. "Jared and I have been good friends for a very long time. He's like a brother to me, and if I had to share with anyone, it would be him. I don't pretend to understand how these three-partnered relationships work, but I'm willing to try, if you truly want this."

She took his hand and turned it to press a tender kiss to his palm. Their eyes locked and held as she smiled.

"I truly do. I want to try." Joyous tears slipped down her face as she looked up at him. "Darian, I love you."

"And I love you, Adora." A kiss sealed his words as he pulled her body into his embrace. Adora pushed at his hastily donned leggings until he was naked once more.

"Let's move this into the bedroom," Jared suggested. "I believe we have some unfinished business to attend to."

Tugging on Darian's hand and catching Jared's in her other hand, she led them both toward the largest bed in the big suite. It happened to be in Jared's chamber. Jared winked at her as he caught her up in his arms, strode through the archway and deposited her on his wide bed.

"As my lady wishes, of course."

Darian knew he couldn't go slowly this time. He needed her too badly. Watching Adora make love with Jared, instead of defusing his desire, had only made it rise impossibly higher. A look of understanding passed between the men as Jared stepped back, motioning Darian to take the lead this time. With a nod of thanks, Darian knelt down on the bed beside Adora. She was eager for them both and her responsive little body only made his passion climb higher than it had ever been before.

"How do you want it, sweetheart? Slow, fast, gentle, rough?" Darian whispered as he nipped her tender throat on the way to her sensitive breasts.

"I want what you want," she answered with little guile.

He loved that about her. She was fully a woman, yet so innocent. He would bet her husband, gods rest his departed soul, hadn't taken her beyond basic lovemaking. Darian relished the thought that he could teach her a thing or two about giving and receiving pleasure. There was so much he wanted to experience with her, so much he wanted for her to experience.

"Then hang on for a wild ride, my lovely."

He bit softly at her slight belly, winking up at her as he licked down lower, over her distended clit. A second little nip there as he tested her readiness had him smiling. She was gushing and so responsive to his every move. She was more than ready for him.

Moving with some urgency, yet caressing her skin at every turn, Darian positioned himself under her. He had something in mind and, glancing over at Jared, was pleased to note the fire in the other man's eyes as he watched Adora. It boded well for

Darian's plans. Catching Jared's attention with a patting motion on her beautiful fleshy ass, Darian raised one eyebrow at the knight. Understanding flared as Jared licked his lips, seemingly mesmerized by the sight of Adora's womanly body swaying seductively with her passionate motions.

"How about we all do this together?" Darian made sure his voice was pitched loud enough so that Jared would hear his question to their woman.

"Is that possible?" Adora sat back, looking down at him with questions in her lovely green eyes.

He chuckled. "You're a healer, woman. You should know there's more than one place a man can pleasure himself and his woman."

She blushed so prettily he reached up and kissed her, the muscles in his abdomen rippling and contracting as he sat up under her slight weight. Pulling back, Darian watched her eyes carefully for any sign of fear, but there was none. No, his little adventuress was curious and more than a little excited if he read her right.

He looked over at Jared and caught the other man's eye once more. "What do you say?"

Jared's cock was hard as stone watching Adora climb all over Darian's firm body. The other man was damned near perfect. No huge, ugly scar marred his skin, and Jared remembered how his handsome face and perfect teeth had been sighed over by the ladies of the court. He could understand why Adora might fancy Darian, but he couldn't fathom why in the world the woman would want him as well.

He was scarred badly, his face nothing to write home about. His body was rough, hair flying whichever way no matter what he did to tame it and starting to go gray now just at the temples. He was no longer the handsome lord he'd once pretended to be. He was a rough warrior now, through and through. Yet, the magical light of passion tempered Adora's sultry green gaze when she looked at him.

Apparently love truly did make one blind, for she looked at him the same way she looked at Darian's perfect features. How had he gotten so lucky? Why had the Mother blessed him so well? Jared would never know, but he would spend every moment proving to Adora that her love was not misplaced, demonstrating over and over how much he loved and cherished her in return.

When Darian's raised eyebrow challenged him, Jared was more than up for it. He searched around the sparse room, knowing he would need something to ease his way inside Adora's unused channel. The curiosity in her eyes told him she had never done this before—never taken a man's cock up her pretty ass—but he knew she was game to try. He didn't want to hurt her, so he'd make sure she was well prepared. The only problem was, Jared was totally *un*prepared. He had nothing to use as a lubricant to help ease his way past her tight muscles.

"Look in the top drawer of the table at the side of your bed."

Kelzy's voice came to him seemingly out of the blue. Turning, Jared spied Kelzy's large head watching all from the archway. He should have known Kelzy would be nearby, orchestrating his life as she had since she'd first taken him as her partner.

Jared moved to the nightstand and opened the drawer. Inside was a large tub of a pleasant-smelling herbal concoction tucked neatly into the top that he'd never seen before.

He looked back at Kelzy suspiciously. *"Where did this come from?"*

"I asked Belora to put it there."

"You were awfully sure about this, eh?"

"*I hoped,*" Kelzy clarified. "*I prayed to the Mother of All that you three would come to your senses and see what was right in front of you all the time.*"

Without comment, Jared scooped out a bit of the salve and went back to the lovers entwined on his bed. Adora was impaled on Darian's cock, riding sinuously while Darian held her to a slow pace. The other man knew what was coming and he was coaching her into the experience, thoughtful and tender as Jared looked on approvingly.

Jared caught Darian's eye as he positioned himself. Nodding to each other over Adora's shoulder, Darian reached down and pulled her luscious cheeks apart, helping Jared in his quest to teach her this new pleasure.

He slathered her little hole with the herbal mixture, probing gently at first, then more insistently as she responded with soft sighs and hungry moans to his moves. He sank two fingers into her, stretching gently, urging her to relax as he worked his way inside. A third finger slipped in and after a bit of stroking in and out, he figured she was as ready as he could make her.

As gently as he could, he positioned himself at her opening, pressing steadily inside. She accepted him with surprisingly little fuss, her body shivering just a bit as she was stretched in this new way for the first time.

"Is it all right?" Jared asked, bending to nip the lobe of her ear.

Adora moaned. "It feels so strange! So good. Oh, Jared!"

He smiled and sank completely inside her. Once there, he just waited a moment, both to let her adjust and to savor the feeling. Jared could feel the ridge of Darian's cock through the tissues separating them. Jared knew the other man felt her pussy tighten impossibly around his own straining member, just as he felt the flexing inside her ass. He caught Darian's eye and they began to move in her. This was a true partnership—

the goal of their work to make the woman between them experience the ultimate in pleasure.

They were both dedicated to their work.

While Adora whimpered in mounting pleasure, they each worked their cocks in and out of her, in rhythm. She strained between them, coming to peak after peak as they rode her through the pleasure right into another wave of ecstasy.

"Are you with us, love?" he heard Darian ask her. She moaned in reply as both men chuckled, but the time was drawing near.

Jared sped up, knowing Darian would feel and understand the need for urgency. Together they rode her higher and higher. Jared loved the way her fingers clutched at his hands and arms and her mouth sought purchase on Darian's sweat-slicked skin. She was close to total meltdown and together, they were going to take her there.

"Now, Adora. Now!" Jared called out as he bucked into her, ramming high and tight. He felt Darian do the same as her body convulsed around them in the biggest explosion yet. Adora screamed as she came, over and over, hard and fast, and Jared finally gave himself permission to let go.

He pulsed into her ass, filling her with his come, knowing that at the same time, Darian was filling her womb with his own tribute. It was an amazing feeling and one he never thought he would know. To love and be loved and know that should he falter, there was a partner there, ready and willing to help him, even as he would do the same. Together they would cherish and love this little woman who gave so much of herself to them both, and she would never be in any danger as long as one of them lived.

Pulling from her as gently as he could, Jared took only a moment to clean up before returning to the big bed, claiming one side of her luscious, sated body for himself and falling into a deep dreamless slumber. The crisis was past. There was only the future to look forward to now and it looked bright indeed.

Chapter Six

Before the others rose the next morning, Darian walked through the halls of the Border Lair, needing to exercise his healing leg. The Lair was a truly magnificent feat of architecture and magic, combined to form a place that was hospitable for man and dragon alike. There were few women and children about, but there were some. Most smiled and nodded as he passed, friendly but reserved. It was, after all, quite early in the morning, so everyone kept their voices down to avoid waking those who needed more sleep.

Darian followed most of the early risers in the general direction of the great hall. There, he found quite a few people gathered, eating breakfast. Some knights were clearly just coming off duty, dressed still in their leathers, and some were freshly shaven, in a rush to get out on their patrols.

All of them eyed him suspiciously, though none bothered him as he ate a small bowl of porridge one of the smiling women had spooned up for him. There were those who didn't view him as the enemy, but they appeared to be few and far between. The disgruntled looks shot at him from all around the hall made Darian feel rather conspicuous. Rather than tempt fate—and the angry knights eyeing him hostilely—he finished his meal, then stacked his used bowl and spoon in the area set aside and walked quietly out into the hall.

That should've been the extent of the excitement, but Darian didn't count on the foolishness of youth. A few of the younger knights followed him, walking beside and behind him in the wide hallway as he headed for the landing ledge. It was on the way back to Jared's suite and Darian had wanted to get a bit of fresh air before returning, but the younger knights changed his plans.

They followed on his heels, slowing their pace to match his as they neared the wide landing area. All his instincts went on alert. These knights apparently had some kind of problem with him and they undoubtedly wanted to be heard—or worse.

Normally Darian was light on his feet and good with his fists, but the recently healed injury put a little cramp in his style. Even so, five against one weren't the greatest odds—even for him. And to top it off, Darian didn't really want to fight with these lads. He hadn't the heart for it. The Draconian knights had every reason to despise Skithdron after the unprovoked attacks on the border. Skithdron was in the wrong here and these young hotheads saw him as the enemy, no matter that he'd sacrificed all he owned, and all he was, to come here and warn the Draconian side of worse things yet to come.

To them, he was simply an enemy.

Darian sighed as he stepped out into the open landing area. They would act now, if at all, he knew. They didn't disappoint him.

"We don't want you here, Skithdronian scum."

Darian turned to face the speaker, his back to the wide expanse of the landing ledge. There were seven of them now. Apparently two more had just flown in from patrol and joined with their fellows against the enemy in their midst. Darian had to forcibly hold back a sigh.

"I have no quarrel with you, sir knight." Darian did his best to keep his tone civil but firm.

"What if we have a quarrel with you? Skith bastard." Another of the young fools found the nerve to speak, buoyed by his compatriots.

"Go back where you came from," yet another of them sneered.

Darian didn't want this to turn into a fight. These men were all younger than he was, big and battle-trained. But Darian had skills that—even with his slightly swollen leg—assured him he could at the very least hold his own. Still, he didn't want to harm any of these youngsters. He thought it wouldn't be a good idea to repay Jared's welcome by disabling five or six of his knights on his first full day in the Lair.

"Look," Darian held up his hands, palms outward in a gesture for calm, "I don't want any trouble."

"Then leave," came the quick reply.

Darian was at a loss as to how to defuse this situation. The young knights were attracting attention and others were coming over, some to join and some to simply observe. He became aware of dragons too, pausing to see what their human counterparts were doing, and one dragon in particular, came up behind him, settling at his back.

Almost dreading what he'd find, Darian craned his head around to discover the huge blue-green dragon, shockingly, standing behind him. It was Kelzy, and she clearly showed her support for Darian, eyeing the knights arrayed against him—no, *them*, now—with a baleful glare.

He hadn't dared expect any assistance from the huge dragon, though he thought she was coming to like him a bit better as he got to know her. Still, this sort of show of support was completely unexpected and oddly humbling. Darian didn't know Kelzy well, but knew in his heart she had to be a special dragon indeed to gain the trust of Jared, a man he'd known as wise and honorable to the core.

The young knights didn't back down, but they stopped threatening Darian physically, and before he knew it a full-fledged confrontation was in the works. He cursed himself for going out into the public areas of the Lair alone as other dragons came over to see what Kelzy was doing. Suddenly his morning walk had become an international incident.

"Oh, great," Darian mumbled to himself when a slightly rumpled Adora and Jared elbowed their way through the massive group now gathered around him and Kelzy. He should've realized the dragon would call her partner.

Darian would rather not have forced Jared's hand this way, especially not after the momentous events of the day, and night, before. He had no idea if Jared would be welcoming or wounded this morning. The chances were good either way after the emotional upheavals of the night.

"What's going on here?" Jared demanded of his knights while Adora stood back, watching with wide, nervous eyes.

One of the ringleaders stood forward from the sizable throng that faced him now.

"We want him gone, Jared. He's Skithdronian scum and probably a spy."

Jared stared at his knights in deep disappointment. He thought he knew these men. He thought he knew their hearts, but apparently he'd been wrong. They didn't know him well enough to trust his judgment and really, when had he ever opened up to them? It was his own fault.

Sadly, he shook his head. There was nothing he could say. Leaders led by example, not by making speeches. Jared took the time to look each and every one of his knights in the eye. He noted the ones who stood against him directly in defiance of his leadership and those who merely watched from the sidelines. Gareth and Lars were nowhere to be seen, though he would have hoped those two, at least, would have stood with him and trusted his judgment.

Saying not a word, Jared turned his back on the doubters and strode forcefully to Darian's side. Clapping him on the back, Jared demonstrated his support of the Skithdronian lord who had become more than a brother to him, more than just a friend. This man was part of his family now. No matter what complications might arise from it, he would be there for Darian.

Kelzy moved away, surprising Jared, but it didn't change his mind. He would stand with Darian against all comers. Alone if need be.

But they weren't alone.

A moment later, another dragon loomed behind them. It wasn't Kelzy and for just a second Jared feared some new form of attack, but when he looked up, his mind spun as his thoughts sped. The looming presence could only mean one thing. He just hoped his old friend was ready for what was to come. Oh, the Mother of All was having a grand joke on all of them today. Her influence was clear in this new development. Jared just hoped Darian would understand what Fate had in store.

The huge copper dragon loomed over Darian's shoulder, a solid presence, somehow even more comforting than Kelzy had been. Sandor's voice boomed through Darian's head as it had only once before. But this time, he felt a thickening of the connection, an opening of the pathway that led from the dragon's mind to his own.

"I claim you as my knight partner, Sir Darian, former Lord of Skithdron. You have proven yourself worthy and if you will have me, I will be your companion and partner for the rest of your days."

"Merciful gods! What are you talking about?"

"You heard him?" Jared asked loudly. Darian was puzzled. Why would Jared ask such a thing? It was plain they'd all heard the dragon speak.

"Of course I heard him."

"Lord Darian has always had the ability to hear me. It was just untapped. I have spoken to him before."

"Is this true?" Jared wanted public confirmation for some reason.

Darian nodded. "He spoke to me once before."

"Then it's his right to choose you as knight partner. Our law says any male who has the ability to communicate with dragonkind may be claimed if he is deemed worthy by the dragon who wishes to partner with him."

"What are you talking about?" Darian looked from the astonished knights, to the huge copper dragon, to Jared and back again. Something cold and nervous settled in the pit of his stomach, while at the same time, something eager and joyous wanted to shout from his heart. Could this huge dragon really want him? Could this ancient and wise creature really see anything of value within a man who'd turned traitor to his own country?

"I do claim you, Darian. If you will have me, I'll be your dragon partner for the rest of your days and you will be my knight."

"Me? A knight of Draconia?" Darian could hardly believe it, though something deep in his soul wanted desperately for it to be true.

"You have already proven yourself willing to put your life on the line to warn the humans and dragons of this land of grave and serious danger. You are a brave and honorable man. There are few knights here who are your equal, Lord Darian. Accept me as your partner and we will continue to do good work for the humans and dragons of this land."

113

Darian considered the copper dragon's words for a long silent moment. The boy who never aged within his heart was jumping up and down in excitement. Sandor was such a noble being and it was such a rare and splendid thing to even hear a dragon speak, much less want to be your partner for life. Darian knew he'd be a fool to pass up this magical opportunity. If he didn't accept the dragon now, he'd live with regret for the rest of his life.

Still, agreeing to be a dragon's knight partner wasn't something to be undertaken lightly. Darian ran through the various possibilities in his mind, but there was really only one answer for the dragon's request.

"All right." Darian breathed deeply, his chest expanding with excitement and joy. "I accept. And I'll do all in my power to live up to your high opinion of me, Sir Sandor. I only hope you know what you're doing."

The dragon chuckled smokily. *"Trust me, my friend. Let it be your first act of faith in our new partnership. To make this official, you must accept me like this, Darian, mind to mind. Follow the path I have forged between us."*

With the bright wonder in his heart spilling over into joy, Darian followed the path in his mind used only once before. It was wider now, more direct and easier to access. It felt as if the connection had always been a part of him and it gave him just a bit of insight into the soul of the incredible, magical creature who had just managed to alter the course of his life forever.

"I accept, Sir Sandor. I will be your knight partner for the rest of my days."

Sandor turned and trumpeted his joy skyward, a noble acknowledgment of the newly made knight. All the other dragons followed suit, welcoming the new knight with a huge crescendo of sound that shook the very mountain itself.

Adora wept openly as she watched it all. First Jared had made her proud, his noble heart beating true as he stood up for his friend against the younger knights. She knew Jared's honor demanded he stand for what was right rather than bend to pressure and she loved him deeply for his nobility and honor.

Then Sandor arrived, making such a public display of claiming Darian for his knight partner it took her breath away. Adora suddenly realized exactly who Kelzy's co-conspirator had been all along. All they needed now was for Kelzy and Sandor to declare themselves mated and it would all be tied up with a nice, neat bow.

Adora was about to confront Kelzy with her surmise when Gareth and Lars strode in, having learned from their dragons what had just transpired. Without a word, they went to stand firmly at Darian's and Jared's sides. Even their dragon partners, Kelvan and Rohtina, lumbered over to stand with Sandor. Kelzy moved to stand beside her son, Kelvan, and Adora finally saw the resemblance that had escaped her before.

"Kelzy, is Sandor Kelvan's father?" She sent the question privately, amusement lacing her tone.

"It took you long enough to figure it out. And here I thought you were such a bright child."

"Sandor is your mate, then? That's what you were talking about when you said the Mother of All knew what She was doing, wasn't it?"

"Sandor came to the Lair to meet Kelvan's new family, but when he first saw Darian, he knew he had found his next knight partner." Kelzy bowed her great head in acknowledgment and Adora suddenly knew what she had to do. Moving to stand before the two men she loved, Adora reached up and kissed them both, deeply, in front of the entire Lair.

"Do you trust me?" she asked both of them as quietly as she could.

Both men nodded.

"Do you love me?"

Again, they nodded and their eyes were filled with the flames of their love as they looked at her. Adora offered up a silent prayer to the Mother of All, then turned to face the doubters who still stood against them.

"I am Princess Adora of the House of Kent." There were a few surprised looks from those who hadn't ever heard public acknowledgment of her royal status. "I claim these two brave men, these knights, as my mates and Prince-Consorts. They deserve your respect, and if you don't like it, you may take it up with my cousin, the king."

So saying, Adora linked her arms through both of her men's and walked regally through the throng, which parted as if by magic in front of them. The dragons followed behind as they promenaded out of the area, leaving stunned silence behind.

When they reached their suite, both men turned on her.

"What did you just do, Adora?" Darian eyed her with suspicion, then turned his gaze up to the copper dragon who stood next to Kelzy trying to look innocent. "And you! What was that all about, Sandor? I'm no knight. I'm not even Draconian."

"I beg to differ. Every action you have taken since I've known you has been more than worthy of a knight. You are an honorable man and one who puts the good of others above his own. Those youngsters could learn a few things from you, Sir Darian."

"I agree with Sandor," Adora said with some conviction as she moved to stand with the copper dragon. "He is, after all, Kelvan's father." She looked accusingly up at the dragon, but her smile softened the teasing. "And Kelzy's mate."

"Sweet Mother of All!" Jared sat heavily on the sofa. "You two were planning this all along."

"Planning what?" Darian wanted to know.

"Last night, and now Sandor claiming you...it's all so they can be together."

At this the dragons appeared to take offense, rearing their great heads.

"So you three can be together, you ungrateful swine," Kelzy berated her knight. *"We saw right away that you three belonged together. You need each other. You were made for each other. Sandor and I have been mates for many years, it's true, but we will outlive you all many times over. How could we sit by and watch you waste even one more of your precious years when love was looking you in the face and you were turning away? Ungrateful—"*

"Now, Kelzy, he's just young. He'll learn." Sandor's deep voice sounded amused to all three humans.

"Young?" Jared was clearly upset. "I've already lost a wife and son." His voice broke on the words as his emotions threatened to overtake him. "Or did you forget?"

"No, we can never forget them. Nor will you." Kelzy had calmed in the face of Jared's sorrow.

Adora went to him and took him in her arms. "Nor *should* you, Jared," she said. He held her fiercely.

"I don't deserve you, Adora."

"Now that's the first sensible thing you've said since we got here." Kelzy's tone was teasing in all of their minds.

Jared kissed Adora deeply then, as if he needed to feel her in his arms, grounding him in the changing situation.

"We have little choice, I'm afraid. We've been outmaneuvered by generals greater than ourselves." Jared smiled briefly up at the dragons.

Darian gave Jared and Adora a lopsided grin, his eyes somewhat uncomfortable. "I can hear them in my head."

Adora chuckled and reached out, pulling Darian into the embrace as Jared shifted her around in his arms.

"And so you should, *Sir* Darian." She kissed him soundly. "Sandor couldn't have chosen a knight who couldn't hear him speak, now could he?"

Darian shook his head, smiling faintly. "I guess not. I still don't quite believe it. Or understand it."

"All you need to know for now, Darian, is that by choosing you, I've fulfilled the Mother's design for us all. It was fated that you three join and that by doing so, reunite me and my mate." Sandor's deep voice was wise and gentle. *"The rest will come to you in the fullness of time, my friend. I believe you still have a role to play in protecting our world from King Lucan. He threatens to upset the balance of Nature with his evil plans and the Mother of All must have some purpose for you left to fulfill. Believe in that, believe in yourself, and believe in me. You will never be alone again, Darian, as long as any of we five here now live. We are a family."*

There was a mating feast, of sorts, held that night in the great hall of the Lair. Many were still injured from the battle and many others were on patrol. The merriment was low-key, but the congratulations were heart-felt from most of the revelers. Some still eyed Darian with suspicion, but most of the younger dragons had been trained by Sandor or Kelzy, or both, and trusted in their judgment. With encouragement from the dragons, most of the younger knights were willing to give Darian the benefit of the doubt.

Surprisingly, Darian was familiar with the traditional mating feast dances from his years spent as ambassador to Draconia and was able to dance easily with Adora and Jared. It was Adora who had a tough time keeping up with her newly claimed men. Certainly, she had seen her daughter learn the steps to the odd three-partnered dances favored between the mated sets of knights and their ladies, but she had never performed the steps herself.

At the beginning of the dancing, when the patterns called for her knowledge and input, she stumbled, but either Jared or Darian was always there to catch her. As the night wore on though, the dancing got hotter and the men did most of the work. By the time they got around to the traditional mating dance, she had little to do—and little to wear—as the men tossed her around between them, holding her close, kissing her deeply, and fondling her nearly naked body.

She was all too ready to leave for their suite when the dragons took to the sky in their first mating flight in years. She knew Kelzy and Sandor were eager to renew their relationship and her men were even hotter than they'd been the first time the three of them had joined in passion. That first time had been a catharsis for Jared and even for Adora in a way. They'd worked through all their old pains and offered them up on the altar of passion, wiping away past hurts and forging new ties that were stronger and deeper than anything any of them had known before.

This time the joining would be joyous. This would be a mating, a claiming, a joining of pure hearts and souls. There would also be the frenzy of the dragons, influencing the men and probably Adora as well, as closely bonded as she was with Kelzy, not to mention the unpredictable influence of her own royal blood.

The closer they danced, the higher their passions rose, and when Kelzy and Sandor trumpeted as they took to the sky, Jared picked Adora up bodily and made straight for their bedchamber, Darian following close behind. Other mated pairs and threesomes headed out of the main area as well and Adora had only a glimpse of her daughter and her two mates leaving before she was out of the great hall.

Jared was kissing her even before he placed her in the center of the large bed in their suite. Darian undressed her and himself in between biting kisses to her backside and her hips. For her part, Adora pulled at what remained of Jared's clothing, removing the loincloth with eager hands as she began to feel the echoes of the dragons' passion through the bond she'd formed at a young age with Kelzy and the bonds that were even now strengthening between herself and her chosen mates.

Darian was nearly beside himself and she knew he would find this night the hardest to deal with of the three of them. He had only bonded to Sandor hours before and hadn't had any time to get used to the dragon who now shared a connection to his soul. Jared had been partnered with Kelzy for years now but had never felt the intense mating heat two grown dragons could create. He would have a little more chance of tempering it, but Adora knew she was in for a wild ride that night.

She wouldn't have it any other way.

Darian looked at his new lover and realized she was his home. Adora was comfortable in a way he had never before experienced. The moment she touched him, he'd known that she was the last woman he would ever desire and the only woman he would ever love. It was that sudden, that harsh, and that true.

"It's like that for knights," Sandor had told him earlier that day when his thoughts turned once again to Adora. *"Lest you doubt you are truly a knight, you should know most knights recognize their mate the moment they lay eyes on her. It's part of being a knight and joining with my kind. We too know our mate the moment we see her and for us, there is usually only one mate for all our many years."*

Sandor's words came back to Darian as he looked at Adora now. She was it for him. He was certain of that as he had never been certain of anything in his life before. This was love—plain and oh, so simple. There would never be another woman for him. Only Adora.

He couldn't get enough of her. He couldn't get close enough and couldn't seem to control himself when he touched her. He felt her fire, her steam, her desire as if it was his own, but then perhaps it was the dragons' fire he was feeling. Darian shook his head to try to regain some sense of normalcy, but it would not come.

He was linked to the soaring dragons as they circled and dived, climbing higher in their joy before joining and taking that dangerous plummet to earth as they pleasured each other, only to separate at the last possible moment of freefall. To do it all over again.

Adora was on the bed now. All three of them were naked and wanting. Darian tried to cool his ardor to give his beloved Adora a chance to catch her breath. Struggling for control, he sat back, but she would have none of it. Adora rocketed up, grabbing him by the ears so that he had no choice but to follow where she led.

"Come into me now, Dar. I need you and Jared both."

"I don't want to hurt you. I'm just barely in control here." The admission was ripped from his soul, but her smile made everything all right.

"I don't need your control tonight, Darian. I need you. I need your passion, your lust, your cock. And your love."

Freed by her harsh gasp of excitement, Darian watched as Jared pulled her back onto the bed, mounting her swiftly. He moved in time with the dragons Darian could feel in the back of his mind.

Bianca D'Arc

Jared's hard cock slid home as he rolled beneath her, pulling her ass cheeks apart, making room for his partner in this strange marriage. Darian prepared her, entering slowly but steadily, using the special ointment Adora had placed on the nightstand before they even left for the feast. She'd apparently known what to expect from this night and she was getting it in spades, he realized as he slid home within her.

When they were both seated fully, Darian met Jared's eyes over Adora's shoulder, pressing deep within her. With a nod, they began to move, slow at first, then getting longer and stronger as the frenzy grew within them all. Dimly, he heard Adora's panting cries of ecstasy as she came to peak after peak between them. Darian felt the powerful contractions of her orgasms around his hard cock, but he couldn't come until the dragons did.

Higher they flew, the dragons and the humans locked in coital bliss. As the dragons began their freefall, so too did their human counterparts, both knights spurting their come deep into the woman they both loved, adored and cherished with all their hearts. She was claimed—filled and marked for all time by the hard, merciless loving. As she smiled lazily at them, Darian knew she loved every minute of it.

The dragons rose again, only an hour later, searching for the stars as their bodies joined, beating wings into the night. First though, the men treated Adora to a long soak in the heated tub where they teased her mercilessly. They lifted her out, stepping free of the huge tub and drying her inch by precious, tantalizing inch, licking her flame higher.

Darian caught Jared's eye as they brought Adora back to the bed. Both men could feel the dragons taking off for the stars and they knew their time of rest was almost at an end.

"Are you up for something a little different, my love?" Darian whispered in her ear as he ushered her toward the bed,

122

his legs right behind hers. He rubbed his chest against her back, his arms caging her breasts as she giggled like a young girl.

She turned in his arms to place a teasing kiss on his lips. "Anything you wish, Master."

Darian growled. "Mmm, I like it when you call me that." He nodded to Jared as the other man finally noticed the cords Darian had left out before joining them in the bath. "Have you ever been tied, Adora? Will you trust us to see to your pleasure completely? Will you let yourself be helpless in our arms?"

She looked uncertain at first as her gaze moved between the two men, but then she smiled and the twinkle in her eyes brightened his soul.

"I trust you."

Darian kissed her deeply, backing her onto the wide bed as Jared prepared the soft ropes Darian had scrounged earlier from elsewhere in the large suite. While Darian held her arms up, Jared tied them tightly together above her head, using one rope to secure her to one corner of the large bed.

Darian lifted his head to survey the work and nodded with a broad grin. Jared had done this before, he could tell. It amazed him that they were alike in this way, but he didn't question his good fortune. He had work to do before the dragons took him beyond reason and into their own brand of wild lust.

Adora lay diagonally across the wide bed, hands bound together, then secured to one corner. They could maneuver her easily into just about any position either of them could dream up.

Darian flipped her over onto her knees and elbows, positioning her just so as he surveyed the enticing sight her spread, wet pussy made against the bedclothes. Jared slid beneath her upper body, seating himself within easy reach of

123

her mouth. Darian realized Jared was letting him have her pussy for this round and thanked the other man with a sly grin as he slid his fingers into her slick well.

The dragons rose now, their passions echoing through the knights as both his and Jared's rods stiffened beyond bearing. The level of arousal he felt was inhuman. It was but an echo of the immense desire filling the dragons and influencing their bonded knights to be more than men in those moments. It was humbling and invigorating at the same time. Darian saw the incredible need he felt reflected in Jared's expression and knew they were both caught up in their dragon partners' lust.

"Suck him, Adora. Take Jared in your mouth and swallow him down."

That she complied so eagerly pleased him. He liked directing her actions in this way and would heartily enjoy it when Jared and he reversed their roles, he knew.

He lay down on the bed and pulled her down slightly so that her pussy rested over his mouth. He used his tongue to sink deep within her tight hole, licking upward, spreading their combined moisture and making little circles around her sensitive clit. He felt her tremble against his mouth and he knew she was close.

So was he for that matter. The dragons neared their zenith and he just had to be inside his mate before the passion overtook him completely and drove him mad. With a growl, he lifted her hips, rose up, turned and sank home within her in one smooth but forceful motion. If she could have screamed with her mouth stuffed fully with Jared's cock, he knew she would have in that moment. As it was, she made a sound deep in her throat that both knights enjoyed.

Darian knew from Jared's gasp and the way he clenched his fist in Adora's auburn tresses that her vocalization had reverberated through his shaft. For his part, Darian just enjoyed hearing the proof of her enjoyment as they both possessed her.

He began shafting in and out, his rod harder and stiffer than it had ever been before. Darian began to realize just how fully the dragons affected both he and Jared in ways he never would have imagined, allowing them both to bring Adora to peak after peak before coming themselves.

But this wasn't one of those times. This time was hard and fast, harsh and earthy. Darian plowed into her, slapping her ass just once as she tightened on him, coming for him nicely before he totally lost control as the dragons did. After that, he lost all rational thought, driving home within his new mate the only goal.

"Adora!" he shouted as all of them neared the stars with the dragons.

Darian's eyes shut hard and every muscle in his body tensed as he joined with Sandor in a hard, long release inside the warm welcoming depths of his mate. He felt what the dragon felt in that moment, sharing in the glory that was the physical expression of love no matter the species. He felt the pleasure multiplied through him and Sandor and through Sandor to Kelzy and to Jared, magnified and sent back to him. It was a true sharing, a completion and a new start for them all.

Darian realized in the aftermath that he was linked with Jared through the dragons, but Adora had a direct link to him as well, somehow. It was a phenomenon he vowed to explore further now that he'd decided to make his home in this land and among these people.

This was his home now. Wherever Adora, Jared, Kelzy and Sandor were. Without all four of them, he would no longer be content or complete. They were his family.

As he came down from the fast, hard high, he realized the dragons were plummeting to earth in the freefall of their spent passion, their wings outstretched at the last moment to prolong the pleasure and allow them to glide on the wings of love for a long, satisfying moment. They were basking, as he was too, in the glory that was his mate and his new family.

Chapter Seven

As leaders of the Lair during a time of war, there was no long honeymoon for Darian, Jared, and Adora—or the dragons. They were back to work the next day, yawning a little, but with wide, satisfied grins as they went about their business.

As a previously mated pair, Kelzy and Sandor were better able to manage their frequent urges to couple, though they did catch their human partners off-guard a time or two over the next few days. Each time, though, the men raced to their suite, throwing off clothing as they ran, only to find Adora waiting for them already naked on the bed. She welcomed them both with open arms...and legs. They varied their positions, but the love between them never varied, never altered, never changed, except to grow deeper and surer with each passing day.

Darian was a novice when it came to fighting from atop a dragon but proved himself an able student and an innovative strategist as he trained with Sandor. His added insights into the workings of the Skithdronian army were invaluable as they prepared their defenses. Darian had spent most of his younger days as a warrior before becoming an ambassador, so fighting and training was nothing new to him. Nothing, that is, except flying on the back of a huge dragon. Now *that* was new and absolutely thrilling.

Sandor was a great teacher and Darian learned as much and more from just watching the way Jared and Kelzy worked together. The four of them were a fighting team now, since the dragons were mates, and would fight side by side. They trained together, lived in the same suite, and shared the same wife. It wasn't as Darian had always expected his life to work out. It was much better than that, actually. Though he still believed in the gods of his culture, he had to admit this "Mother of All" his new family believed in certainly did know what She was doing when She brought them all together.

Still, Darian felt his years when he returned to the suite late at night after a full day of riding patrol and drilling with Sandor, Kelzy and Jared. Jared just laughed at him and shook his head, but Adora was more sympathetic. She went to him while he soaked in a hot tub of water in the bathing chamber. She had an herbal mixture for his bath and later gave him a rubdown with a warm, fragrant massage oil she'd prepared to relax his overstressed muscles.

After such delicious treatment, he was ready for the dragons to take off for the moon and drive him and his mate to a frenzy of pleasure. Darian positioned himself under Adora this time, where he wouldn't have to put any extra stress on his already abused muscles, but when she took Jared and him both into her beautiful body, he forgot all about his aches and pains. The only ache he felt was one at the center of his heart for this lovely, giving woman who had become the center of his universe.

The skirmishes continued over the next few days, but the reconnaissance reports indicated the Skithdronian army was massing just over the border. They were waiting to start the second wave of attack, Darian surmised, for something...or someone.

The answer came the next day when their patrols reported movement on the border. Skiths slithered across the already destroyed fields and farms, heading for the few villages that remained populated after the first round of attacks. Jared was a sight to behold as he decisively took charge of the Lair's fighting forces, marshalling the knights and dragons to mount an effective defense against the renewed attack.

When the first dragon fell, all trumpeted in horror and sadness. It was a youngster named Jizra with an equally young knight named Bennu who fell first to the new, deadly weapons Skithdron had unleashed. Diamond-tipped bolts took him down, and the deadly, horrifyingly organized skiths did the rest. Both knight and rider were lost in a matter of moments.

Jared called a retreat to reorganize and Kelzy sent out the message through the dragons. They fell back to a rocky outcropping, Darian silent as he thought through what he'd seen of the Skithdronian lines carefully before voicing his observations.

"I think they were waiting for the weapons to arrive before they launched the second wave. We have to assume there are more of those catapults and diamond bladed bolts. I also have a suspicion about who now leads this army."

"Who?" Jared's voice was grim as he looked over the stunned knights who were finding places to rest a moment until the order came to regroup.

"Venerai. An old enemy of mine. His symbol is a white skith on a field of blood red. I think I caught a glimpse of his banner toward the back ranks. He's one of Lucan's *pets*." He practically sneered the word. "Jared, if he's here, we also have to look at the skiths. I don't think these are wild skiths. These are the trained ones. Did you see the way they went after poor Bennu and Jizra? They're organized, working together."

"So we'll have to expect some kind of coordinated attack from them as well, I gather."

Darian nodded grimly. "I want Venerai. If we take him out, there's a good chance the skiths will lose their cohesion. From what I was able to learn before leaving the palace, the trained creatures only respond to certain favorites of Lucan's." Darian felt the anger burn through him for the evil Lucan had loosed. "I want to try for Venerai."

Jared nodded. "Then I'm with you."

"Kelzy, tell Kelvan and Rohtina to take point with the majority of our forces," Jared ordered.

Darian knew that meant Gareth and Lars would lead the attack with their dragon partners. They were all excellent warriors who worked so well as a team they were nearly unstoppable.

"I'm with you, Dar. If you say we can end this by getting this Venerai, I believe you."

Darian didn't know he'd been holding his breath until that moment. He was touched and gratified to know this man, this friend, this new brother, trusted him enough to place his very life—and those of his people—on the line.

"Thanks, Jared." Darian nodded around the knot in his throat that threatened to choke him.

With a silent signal, Sandor and Kelzy took Darian and Jared into the sky. Using the other dragons for cover, they worked their way higher and higher until few on the ground could see even the dragons' large bulk against the bright sun. Coming out of the sun, they used it to their advantage to drop down steeply behind the enemy army. Darian guided Sandor to the disguised command tent he knew would house the opposing general.

With a rending tear, Sandor burst through the thick canvas of the huge canopy followed closely by Kelzy, both spewing flame as they went. Darian jumped to the ground, clutching his sword, still better suited to fighting afoot than on dragonback. Besides, he was looking for someone.

While the dragons created a ring of fire around them, Darian sought and found his target. He bounded over to stop Venerai from slithering away.

"Stand and face me, Venerai!"

The bold shout brought the man's head whipping around and Darian couldn't suppress the gasp of surprise that sounded from his throat.

"Darian? You dare come here?" The words hissed through the altered face, no longer quite human. Darian could see the slitted eyes that looked like a wild skith's, the dark mottling of the man's once golden skin. He almost looked...scaled.

"I've come to kill you, Venerai, as I should have long ago." Darian felt a presence at his side and knew without looking that it was Jared, ready to back him up if need be.

"And who's this? Is that the old troublemaker Jared of Armand?" Darian was surprised Venerai would recognize Jared. He didn't think Venerai had ever been dispatched to Draconia, but then Venerai had worked behind the scenes for Lucan for years.

Venerai sneered at Jared as he drew his sword. "I thought I'd done away with you when I killed your wife and that pathetic whelp of yours."

Darian had to hold Jared back, so great was the anger coming off his fighting partner.

"Don't let him rile you. This man is evil straight through," Kelzy cautioned them both. *"Sandor and I will hold the ring around you as long as we can. None will be able to see or interfere with what transpires within."*

"I suggest you kill him quick, though," Sandor put in. *"They're bringing up reinforcements and we won't be able to hold them off forever."*

"Fight me like a man, Venerai. Or maybe you're no longer a man, are you? You look like a fucking skith." Darian grimaced as he stalked Venerai, sword drawn and ready. "What in the hells happened to you? Or is it your true nature finally coming out after all these years?"

131

Darian circled the other man, noting Jared coming up behind to block and guard. They already fought well together, like brothers. He knew he could trust Jared to kill Venerai, should he fail, and take care of Adora. It was a secure feeling, though he vowed to himself not to fail. He had waited too long for this.

"No, Darian, this is how Lucan rewards loyalty." He raised his arm, allowing the wide sleeve of his shirt to fall back and reveal deep acid burns in his skin, partially healed over with reptilian-looking scales. It was disgusting and downright scary. "I am one with the skith and they are one with me."

He lowered his arm and suddenly there were skiths attacking the dragons from all sides. Sandor bellowed in pain as some of their venom singed one wing, but he flamed even higher, crisping the skiths that dared to answer their new master's call. Kelzy fought on the other side of the ring, and though they drew in toward each other, lessening the space they must keep aflame, they held off the skiths and roasted every last one.

"Your pets can't seem to overcome our partners, Venerai. Or were they your cousins? No matter, they're dead now."

Venerai's eyes narrowed as he charged with his deadly sharp blade, his animal rage momentarily overcoming his human intelligence. Good, Darian thought, that was just the reaction he wanted, but Venerai had the strength of ten men and the sinuous motion of a skith. It was difficult to anticipate his moves and Darian paid the price a few times in shallow cuts to his exposed body. The areas where Adora had incorporated dragon scale into his leathers were holding firm, protecting him, but there were too few precious dragon scales and too much of his large body left vulnerable to this almost inhuman attack.

Jared jumped between Darian and Venerai and took some of the blows, allowing Darian just a moment to regroup. Jared had a fire in his eyes that Darian well knew was the light of revenge. His new fighting partner finally faced the man who claimed to have killed his family and he wanted justice. Darian vowed he would get it this day, no matter the cost.

With renewed effort, Darian rejoined the fight. Whatever had been done to Venerai, it made him stronger than either Darian or Jared and it took both men to fight this one deranged, half-skith-looking monstrosity. They managed to push him back, but only just barely, each knight suffering shallow wounds that hurt fiercely and bled enough to be downright annoying.

"You must end this now, boys," Sandor advised them, *"before they get those giant crossbows into position. They're setting up the machines too far away for us to flame before we take to the sky."*

"We hear and obey," Darian sent with just a touch of wry humor to his new dragon partner, *"but this son of a skith has changed since I knew him and not for the better. I should have killed him years ago."*

"The Mother of All knows that's true." Sandor continued to flame all who dared come near the wall of fire he and his mate kept going around them. *"Get your asses in gear, knights! We must end this with haste."*

Jared saw his opportunity a moment later. The grotesque creature before them was starting to weaken as his eyes showed pain. He didn't understand where the pain came from since neither of the knights had managed to score any major hits on the bastard, but Jared knew that look could not be manufactured. He was trying too hard to hide it.

With a flourish, Jared moved in and struck at the joint where Venerai's arm met his body, double striking to the knee with the same complex, arcing sweep. Venerai went down hard on one knee. Darian came up behind and ran his sword through the vulnerable part of Venerai's plate armor, near the waist, putting the enemy general in the perfect position for Jared's next powerful swing.

"This is for Ana and James," he whispered, recalling the happy young boy and laughing woman who had shared his life and died by this enemy's hand. With one final motion, he separated Venerai's head from his body, killing the bastard who had killed his family. Justice had finally been served.

Both knights panted, their breathing harsh, as Darian searched the enemy general's pockets for any bit of intelligence that might be helpful to their side. Jared slung the evil bastard's head into a sack. He would take it and burn it to be certain no sort of evil magic could ever bring this bastard back to life. Jared never would have believed such a thing before, but then he had never seen the kind of magic that would turn a normal human man into the grotesque monster they had just faced. Lucan had access to powerful, demented magics, and Jared wasn't taking any chances.

Darian scanned the area, taking anything that might be of some kind of use to the Draconian cause, then ran for Sandor's side. He saw Jared do the same, tying something to the pack around Kelzy's neck that they used sometimes during battle. Within moments they launched skyward, the dragon wings beating with all their might for the high ground that would mean their safety from those dragon-killing weapons below.

They were almost out of range when a simple arrow screamed out of the sky from below, jamming itself through Jared's chest. The shock of it sent him scrambling for a hold, but he tumbled off Kelzy's back and went plummeting toward the ground at an alarming speed.

"Jared!" Kelzy's distress trumpeted over the field of battle.

Without pause, Darian and Sandor, both of one mind, turned and dove, positioning themselves beneath the tumbling warrior. Darian reached upward, his own position increasingly precarious as he caught Jared and settled him onto Sandor's broad back, holding him tight.

"We've got him! Kelzy, we've got him!" Darian's thoughts were stronger each day he worked and trained with both dragons and he knew Jared's partner would hear him.

Flying as fast as he could, Sandor raced for the Lair, his mate at his side. *"We'll save him, my love. He's a strong human, in the prime of his life. Adora will not let him die."*

Adora was beside herself when Sandor landed at the Lair. Jared had lost a lot of blood and she feared the arrow might have pierced his heart.

"Praise the Mother!" she cried as she realized the arrow had not hit either his heart or his lung. It had gone through the muscle near the shoulder joint and it looked a lot worse than it really was. She sobbed as Darian helped her break off the arrow and pull it through cleanly, then got herself together enough to continue his treatment.

Jared stopped her with a hand over hers when she would have healed him as fully as she could, draining herself in the process.

"Don't you dare, my love. I need you beside me, talking to me, caring for me. Not unconscious from exhaustion that could put you in danger."

She smiled at him and it was a watery smile. "Let me just do a little, Jared. Just start the process. We can do it a little at a time over several days. That way I won't be drained and you won't lose any of your ability to use your shoulder fully."

"You drive a hard bargain, my love, but I agree as long as it puts you in no jeopardy."

She kissed his cheek, his lips, and his brow. "None at all. I promise. Jared, it hurts me to see you injured. Let me do this for you."

He pulled her head down with his good hand, kissing her soundly. "All right," he whispered as he released her. "Do your worst."

She laughed as she knew he had intended and let the healing energy flow through her fingers and into his shoulder. She concentrated on knitting the tears and rejoining the muscle and blood vessels that had been disrupted by the arrow. Once this part of the healing was accomplished, she knew he would rest easier and there would be little lasting injury from the wound. Adora sighed as she felt the first ebb of her power. It was enough for now. She'd promised him not to tire herself too much and she knew he'd be watching closely for any sign of fatigue, chastising her lovingly if he suspected she was the least bit tired.

Adora pulled back and Jared sat up, gingerly at first. Then a broad smile crossed his face and he tumbled her into his embrace, kissing her soundly. After a long, joyous moment, he moved back, keeping her on his lap while he searched around them.

"Darian! Thank you, brother, for the good catch, and you, Sandor. I can never repay either of you for saving my life."

"Think nothing of it." Darian winked at his fighting partner. "I expect you'll do the same for me someday."

Jared laughed shortly, then his eyes sharpened. "How goes the battle?"

Darian's broad smile was answer enough, but he stepped back to let Gareth and Lars move closer. Both younger men were flushed with excitement, fresh from the battle and high with their victory. Gareth stepped forward, the usual spokesman for the duo.

"Whatever you two did, it did the trick. Just before Sandor and Kelzy burst into the sky, the ranks of skiths lost focus and started to scramble. They turned on the Skithdronian army and started fighting them as they fled across the border for their home rocks. Their forces, both skith and human, are in retreat, running for the border as fast as they can."

A cheer went up from the knights surrounding them now and all were smiling. Adora put her hand over Jared's shoulder when he tried to stand, she and Darian supporting him as he faced his warriors.

"You've done well this day, my lads!" Again they cheered as he buoyed their spirits. "Send out patrols to watch the retreat and make certain no stragglers remain on our side of the border. Gareth and Lars, you're in charge of the patrols for now. I have some recuperating to do with my family."

Many of the knights stepped forward to pat him on his good shoulder as he passed. Adora noted that just as many offered congratulations and a respectful hand on the shoulder to Darian. All of them talked about the brave and magnificent save Darian and Sandor had performed by plucking Jared out of freefall and flying hell bent for leather back to the Lair. They'd saved Jared's life and unwittingly earned the respect of many a knight that day.

When they reached their private suite, Darian and Adora helped Jared to bed. Adora undressed him, surprised to find his cock hard and wanting as she uncovered it.

"What's this?" she teased, dipping her head to kiss the tip of his erection.

"It's what always happens when you touch me, my love." He reached for her hand, pulling her onto the bed. "Dar, she's wearing too many clothes. Can't you do something about that?"

Jared's deep blue eyes twinkled up at her as the knights amused themselves with a lighthearted seduction.

"Are you sure you're up to it, Jared? You just almost died."

He dragged her down for a deep kiss. "No better time to reaffirm life than when you've almost lost it, Adora. The question is, are *you* up to it? You expended a lot of energy healing me. Do you need to rest, or can I make love to you first?"

"As long as I can sleep sometime tonight, I'll be just fine." She tugged his head down to hers. "Make love to me, Jared. I'm so grateful you're alive." She kissed him deeply, cooperating with Darian as he moved around them to remove her clothing. When she was bare, Darian turned to leave. Adora stopped him with an outstretched hand.

"Where do you think you're going?" Jared asked, his voice rough with desire and strong with the vitality of returning health.

"You should celebrate together."

"Not without you," Adora said softly.

"I thought we'd settled this already." Jared sighed loudly, clearly exasperated. "She's right, Dar. You're part of this family. This is for the three of us to share together."

The other man looked truly touched as he stood silent for a moment, clearly caught off guard. Adora tugged him closer so that he stood between her legs as she sat on the edge of the bed. With slow, deliberate hands, she undressed him, easing his leather leggings off and sucking him deep when she uncovered his hard cock. Darian's head dropped back, his beautiful eyes closing as her lips closed around him.

Jared knew the ecstasy Darian felt. He didn't envy his new brother the love of their mate—instead he reveled in it. Adora was theirs to pleasure, theirs to protect, and she in turn would pleasure them and give them all the love they needed. It was a rare gift and one he would never deny again.

"Enough, wench!" Darian called out with a laugh when she would have sucked him to release. Stepping back, he dove for the other side of the bed, careful not to jostle Jared's injured shoulder, but eager now for more loveplay.

Jared caught Adora gently by the neck and turned her to face him. "Give me some of what you just gave him, little one."

Her eyes flamed brightly as he pushed her head down near his straining erection. Without hesitation she took him deep and wide, her eyes holding his as she positioned herself to take all of him—all the way to the back of her throat. Adora was truly talented that way, Jared knew, thinking again what a lucky son of a bitch he was.

"She really likes sucking cock," Darian observed from beside him, leaning negligently against the headboard as he fingered his long, stiff rod. "She's got a talent for it, I think."

Jared couldn't answer around the rumble of pleasure rising from his throat as she swallowed around the tip of him. With a groan, he brought her off his dick and urged her face up to his.

"Ride me, little love. Ride me hard and fast."

She did just that as Darian moved to the side, watching her ass jiggle up and down on Jared's thick cock. When she slowed, Darian slapped her butt cheeks, making her yelp and clench around Jared. When Darian inserted his wet finger into the tight spot between her cheeks, she nearly shot off the bed.

"Do you want him in you too?" Jared asked as she writhed on him. "Do you want him up your ass while I'm in your pussy?"

"Yes!" The scream was torn from her throat as she came hard over him.

Jared nodded and jerked his chin over at Darian. The other man wasted no time positioning his quickly lubed cock at her rear entrance. He eased in, not wanting to hurt her, but they both knew by now she liked the little edge of pain this position put her in. They wanted to bring her as high as they could, to show her how much they both loved her. They were of one mind in that moment, with their willing mate writhing between them. No words needed to be spoken, they simply were connected, hearts and souls.

When Adora came again, she brought both her mates with her in a glorious fireball of ecstasy that had all three of them gasping and collapsing into a dreamless sated sleep, side by side by side in the huge bed.

Chapter Eight

The next morning the dragons woke them. Kelzy nudged the huge bed with her chin, her long tongue reaching out to playfully tease her humans awake while Sandor watched and laughed in his dragonish way, smoking up the vented dome above their sandpit.

"Go away, Kelz, can't you see I'm injured here?" Jared groused as a ticklish dragon tongue prodded their feet.

"The children are coming to visit. They have news you will be happy to learn and can't hide it any longer. Do you want them to find you lounging in bed, naked as the day you were born?"

"What children?" Darian asked sleepily as Adora slid over him, pausing only to kiss him good morning on her way to the bathing chamber.

"I think she means my daughter, Belora, and her mates."

"And our son, Kelvan, and his mate, Rohtina," Sandor added with just a hint of fatherly pride.

"They're all coming here?" Jared finally sat up and scratched at his chest. "What for? Is there a problem?"

"Not a problem, worrywart," Kelzy laughed at her knight. *"Get dressed and you'll find out shortly."*

Darian decided to stop trying to fight the inevitable. He stood and joined Adora in the bathing chamber, cleansing himself before dressing for the day, stopping a few times to tickle and fondle her because he just couldn't help himself. She was so sweet, so womanly, so much of everything he had always wanted in his life. He only wished he had found her sooner, but Fate apparently had other ideas.

He realized by joining with Adora, he had also inherited an extended family in her daughter, Belora's mates, and their dragon partners. He'd gone from being all alone in the world to having a large, loving family almost overnight. The gods must be smiling down on him, indeed. Darian didn't know what he'd done right, but it must have been something big for them to grant him such happiness.

After they were all dressed and Adora had the morning tea going, the promised guests arrived with a spring in their steps and sparkles in all of their eyes. Belora rushed over to hug her mother, her face sporting a wide grin.

"What is it, baby?" Adora asked her youngest child.

"Make that babies, plural," Gareth joked, reaching out to clasp hands with Jared, then Darian as Lars did the same.

Adora's eyes drew together in suspicious delight. "Are you?"

"Mama, I'm pregnant!"

Adora shrieked and hugged her baby girl close. "Are you sure?"

"Yes, the prince told me."

"Nico?" Jared asked quickly, a grin splitting his face as well. "Was he here again?"

"No, he told me days ago, but things were too hectic, and then I didn't want my news to overshadow your wedding. I had morning sickness and the prince calmed my stomach with his healing gift. Then he told me..." Her eyes grew wide with tears of joy as Lars pulled her back against his broad frame in comfort. "He told me I was going to have twin boys. One from each of my mates. And they were both going to be black dragons."

Jared sat heavily, his knees seeming to crumble at the startling news, but Darian and Adora were both puzzled.

"Black dragons, praise the Mother!" Jared spoke softly from his chair.

"What?" Adora pounced on him for answers, her eyes bright with suspicion, her mood happy but uncertain. Darian felt the same uncertainty reflected in her beautiful eyes. He sought Jared's gaze for answers, reassured by the happy expression he found there.

"Dar, since you're part of the family now, I guess you're allowed in on the secret." Jared looked over at the dragons for confirmation and both Kelzy and Sandor's heads went up and down in oversized nods of agreement. "The royal lines of Draconia are descended from Draneth the Wise."

"What's ancient history got to do with my grandbabies?" Adora wanted to know. Jared took her hand and pulled her onto his lap with a smile.

"Patience, my love." He kissed her cheek before continuing. "Draneth the Wise was the last of the wizards. He made a deal with the dragons who allowed he and his heirs to live peacefully with the dragons forever after, by becoming one of them."

"One of what?" Darian cocked his head, trying to follow.

"Draneth became part dragon. As are all his heirs. You, my dear," he squeezed Adora, "and your lovely daughter, are descended of Draneth. Your sons will have his gifts and your daughters will most likely have the gift of healing dragons."

"What were Draneth's gifts?" Darian was intrigued now.

Jared smiled broadly. "Draneth was the first black dragon. Only the males of royal blood have the ability to change form from human to dragon and back again. Only they are black of all the dragons in our world."

"My grandbabies will be dragons?" Adora's eyes shot to her daughter excitedly.

Belora came over and grasped her mother's hand. "Dragons and human, just like us, only they'll be able to change back and

143

forth, like Prince Nico. He said he showed you, Mama, like he showed me. Isn't it great?"

"It's amazing." Adora's voice trembled, her expression stunned.

"By the gods!" Learning the secret of the royals of Draconia suddenly made it all clear to him what Lucan was trying to do. He looked over at his new fighting partner. "Jared, this is what Lucan is driving at."

"You mean like what we saw in that tent with Venerai? You think that was the result of him trying to emulate Draneth the Wise?"

Darian nodded grimly. "In his twisted mind he probably figures he can be just as great as Draneth, can conquer the entire world, if only he has the power of the skiths on his side."

"That's insane!" Gareth stepped forward, taking Belora protectively in his arms. Lars stood beside them, a united front.

Darian nodded at the younger warriors. "Lucan is insane. Last year he brought in a witch from the north and closeted himself with her for over a month. We all thought he was just screwing her brains out, but when she emerged, she was no worse for wear and he's notoriously hard on his bed partners. Then he started canceling audiences and has since gone into semi-seclusion within the palace. Only his favorites are allowed in to see him and they ferry messages and orders back and forth. He appears in public only rarely, and only when he can wear ceremonial robes that hide most of his body, come to think of it."

"You think he's like Venerai?" Jared asked shrewdly.

"Probably worse. Venerai was normal the last time I saw him at the palace, only two months ago. What we saw had to have been done to him in the last weeks. Lucan was with the witch over eight months ago. I hate to think what he might look like now."

"Who is Venerai?" Gareth wanted to know.

Jared shook his head. "He was the leader of the enemy army. We killed him when we went behind their lines. His skin was...changed somehow. Like scales. And his eyes weren't human. They were slitted like a skith's."

"Lady Kelzy, did you destroy the head yet?" Darian turned to ask the dragon.

"It is over there." She pointed with one wing to the bloody sack in a far corner.

"Keep the ladies here." Darian nodded and went over to the corner, taking Lars with him. He handed the grisly burden to the other knight with grave eyes. "We need to show this to the king. I want you to keep it safe for now. Devise a case out of treated leather for it that will keep it from harming anyone. Don't touch the blood. It's probably as venomous as skith blood. When you've got it in a case, have your dragon partner burn this sack and anything else that could be contaminated. I don't want a single trace of this left anywhere in this Lair, do you understand?"

Lars nodded solemnly as he took the gruesome burden and walked briskly out of the suite, followed by his dragon partner, Rohtina. Darian shook off his fears for the future as he made his way back to the small gathering.

"I'm sorry to ruin your announcement, Belora. Your news is amazing. I can't say I ever thought I'd have littles in the family to spoil and play with."

Belora shocked him by hugging him tightly. "They're your grandchildren, Darian. I expect you and Jared to spoil them rotten."

"Grandchildren?" Darian shook his head, pleasantly stunned. The women of his new family had a way of doing that to him, no matter what their age, he realized.

Belora laughed up at him. "And Mama's not too old to have more children of her own, you know. She had my sisters and me when she was just a child herself."

Now he was completely speechless as he looked over at his blushing bride. The thought of her growing round with his child completely floored him, but that was in the hands of the gods. He would never pressure her to have a baby if it weren't what she wished also.

"Belora, have some pity on the poor man!" Gareth chided his mate as he drew her back into his arms. Gareth looked over at him with a smile. "She's a whirlwind at times, Darian. You just have to learn how to put up with it."

All of them laughed then as Belora squirmed happily in her mate's arms, showing a bit of her feisty spirit.

They left shortly after and Adora put Jared back in bed, despite his protests. She used her healing gift to treat his shoulder once more, tiring herself a bit more than she wanted, so she lay down on the sofa outside in the main chamber. Darian joined her, stroking her hair as they shared a quiet moment.

"Did your daughter say you had other children besides her?"

Adora yawned daintily and pillowed her head on his thigh. Her eyes stared straight ahead at the huge wallow where Sandor and Kelzy rested after returning from their hunting trip.

"I had twin girls who were stolen from me when they were ten winters old. After that, Belora and I hid in the forest. I had three girls, Dar. Only one was mine to raise past her tenth birthday."

"I'm so sorry, my love." He stroked her soft hair, lulling her to calmness as she recalled the sad memories. "I want you to know that I would never pressure you to have more children."

She sat up then on the wide couch and faced him. "What if I wanted more children?"

He frowned. "Do you?"

"Honestly, I don't know." She settled into his arms, snuggling close. "As a healer I know how to prevent pregnancy, of course, but since I had no bed partners until you and Jared, I haven't been doing anything to prevent it. I could be pregnant, I suppose, but it's harder to conceive for older women." She craned her head up to look into his eyes. "Would you want a child, Darian?"

He hugged her close. "What kind of question is that? I would welcome any child of yours into my heart, Adora. I would love it and teach it, be a good father to it, regardless of whether it was my seed or Jared's that did the job." He squeezed her once in reassurance. "I love you, Adora. I love everything about you. I would love your child as well. Simply because it's a part of you."

Kelzy lifted her big head and stretched lazily over to them. *"You're wrong about one thing, child."*

Adora lifted her head from Darian's chest to regard the dragon. "Oh, yeah? What's that?"

"You are not too old to conceive easily. By bonding with our kind, your knights will reap the benefit of a long, extended life. You're a descendant of Draneth the Wise, as well as having mother-bonded with me when you were just a toddler. You will live three or perhaps four normal human lifetimes, as will your mates. You could have many children in that time, if you choose to do so."

"Sweet Mother of All! Mama Kelzy, I had no idea."

The dragon quaked with smoky laughter. *"I thought as much."*

Sandor raised his head and moved over to face them in his gentle way. *"Princess, this land once teemed with black dragons.*

147

It's been many years since even one black dragon was born and my kind was beginning to despair. Now, with Belora's news, we have new hope for your race as well as our own. Any child of yours would be a blessing to our world, Adora. I hope you'll consider having at least one set of babies for your new mates. I think it would make them both happy as well."

"Sets of babies?" Darian's voice rose in question.

Kelzy swiveled her head to look at him. *"Royal blood often inspires twin births, as does mating with two knights. The Mother has a hand in all, Darian. She often blesses knights with twin sets—one from each knight. Perhaps it's Her way of equalizing things so that one mate or the other doesn't feel left out."*

"I had twins before Belora." Again sadness nearly overwhelmed her. "Arikia and Alania, we named them."

"Princess," Sandor intoned, *"the search for them is already underway. Every knight and fighting dragon in the land has been told to watch for them. We'll find them. I know we will. Have faith that the Mother will bring your children back to you."*

"You're a kind being, Sir Sandor. Thank you for trying to comfort me. I'll keep your words close to my heart."

Jared walked out to the sofa, scratching around his healing wound, careful not to get too close to the sore skin around the arrow hole. He sensed the tension in the air as he drew closer to Darian and their mate. He still couldn't believe Adora was his...well, theirs. All in all, he didn't mind sharing her love with Darian. He felt good knowing Darian would be there for her if the Mother of All should decide it was time for him to leave this world.

He had come awfully close when that arrow hit him. A few inches to the side and it would have pierced his heart. Regardless, if Darian and Sandor hadn't caught him, the fall would have killed him with certainty. He had been spared that day, and he could only guess as to the reason. Apparently the Mother still had work for him to do here.

The first order of business was to cheer up his partner and their mate.

"Why so solemn?" He sat down on the couch, pulling Adora's lithe, muscular legs across his lap.

"I was just telling Darian about my twin daughters." She wiped at the wetness that leaked from her eye with a flustered smile.

"And learning that we'll have three or four lifetimes to enjoy each other."

Jared laughed. "I guess that came as a bit of a shock to you, Dar. I forgot you wouldn't necessarily know about that aspect of partnering with a dragon." He nodded over at Sandor. "Hundreds of years to drive each other crazy. Can't wait." He chuckled dryly as his shoulder itched.

"And time to have more children," Adora said quietly, shocking his eyes back to her. "If you want them."

"Sweet Mother!"

"Now who's caught off guard?" Darian teased him. "Or didn't you think about the fact that Adora could bear our children. She could already be pregnant."

Jared felt the blood drain from his face. He'd lost his son and it had nearly killed him. He didn't think he could face such devastation again.

Darian clapped a hand on his shoulder. "There are two of us now to protect her, Jared. Two fierce dragons and two warriors, not to mention her daughter's mates and dragon partners. Nothing will happen to Adora or any children we might be blessed to have."

Jared took Darian's words to heart. Relief worked its way through his system, a huge weight lifting off his shoulders that he had not even been aware was there. Adora crawled across the couch into his arms and held him as tightly as his wound would allow.

"Nothing will happen to me, Jared. I'm afraid you're stuck with me." She chuckled and he leaned down to kiss her luscious lips.

Jared sensed Darian moving around them, making a place for them all on the wide couch. They were out in the open, in the middle of the public area of their suite, but he figured it was relatively private as long as uninvited guests didn't come barging in unannounced.

He pulled back from her mouth, helping Darian undress her. Adora's leggings were already gone as Jared pulled off her top. She had her hands in his leggings and before he knew it, his cock was hard in her mouth.

"Suck me, baby." Jared's eyes closed as his head tilted back to rest on the padded back of the couch. "Oh, yes."

Adora went down on him with relish as Darian feasted on her dripping pussy. Jared opened his eyes wide enough to watch Darian's tongue delve between her legs and Jared reached out with one hand to squeeze her swinging breast. She whimpered around his cock as he pinched her nipple. Her eyes shot up to his with a devilish sparkle as she sucked harder, using her tongue in a way that threatened to unman him right then and there.

She was shoved forward a bit as Darian rose over her bent bottom, sheathing his hard cock inside her with a deep groan of pleasure. The pistoning motions in and out of her sweet pussy moved her mouth on Jared's most sensitive flesh, making him even hotter.

Darian sped up as they neared completion, driving all of them forward. With a grin for his fighting partner, he slapped Adora's ass playfully. Both of them enjoyed it when she yelped and clenched on them, so he did it again with Jared's nodding encouragement. They were close to the edge now and with a final whack to her taut ass, she climaxed hard around them both, Jared coming in her hungry mouth while Darian spurted deep inside her womb.

All three were speechless for long moments, but finally Darian drew himself out of her tight depths as she licked Jared's cock completely clean. Adora rested her head in Jared's lap as Darian lowered her hips to the couch, taking only a moment to seat himself under her lean, gorgeously naked body.

Both men closed their eyes as they caught their breath, leaning their heads on the back of the padded couch.

"I've been thinking," Darian said after a long while.

"You can still think after that? You're a better man than I." Jared chuckled as he stroked Adora's silky hair while she dozed lightly in his lap.

"Lucan keeps a woman chained to his bed, but she isn't his fuck toy." He kept his voice low so as not to wake the sated woman in their laps. "It's rumored she's a healer."

Jared's eyes popped open and he looked over at his fighting partner. "A healer?"

"I've seen the girl, Jared. Just once. She was skinny and dirty, but she had the most luminous green eyes I'd ever seen...until I met Adora." He looked pointedly at the woman sleeping softly over them both.

"Sweet Mother! Do you think—?"

Darian nodded grimly. "That poor creature could be one of our lady's lost twins."

Master at Arms

Bianca D'Arc

Dedication

To my family and fans, in equal measure. Both are my main source of inspiration, support and happiness.

Prologue

"Faedric! Get out of there!" Rath shouted into his new partner's mind. Faedric was fighting with too little skill against an enemy that vastly outnumbered the knight, even with his dragon backing him up.

"The king!" Faedric shouted, too caught up in the heat of battle to project his thoughts to his dragon partner, but Rath heard him anyway. Rath's heart plummeted. The king was down there in the melee that had suddenly erupted on a narrow city street.

Rath folded his wings against his sides and charged downward like an arrow—an arrow with big, sharp teeth and the ability to breathe fire. He aimed his trajectory for his knight who—to his credit—was fighting his way to the king's side.

Old King Jon was a good and just king who had done much for his land, but he had enemies. Draconia was rich in natural resources and its neighbors were not nearly as peaceful as the inhabitants of this fertile land. The king and his large family had come under fire many times, but this time...this time was different.

He'd been ambushed in the heart of Castleton—the city beneath his towering castle. Caught unprepared on the ground by a superior force, with only three knights and no dragons at his side.

Worse, the king would not shapeshift into the dragon that shared his soul because his mate was there, on the street, with him. Rath knew King Jon would never leave his wife unprotected, and the attackers were too numerous, and too close, to allow him to defend her in dragon form.

But Rath could help. If he could just get down there in one piece.

Of all the dragons beginning to swarm above, only Rath dared the narrow city street and the hazards between the tightly packed buildings. He was an excellent flyer and more agile than the others who were racing to answer the king's call. He hit the ground with his sharp claws, slipping a little on the cobblestones, but he would not let the hard conditions deter him.

He'd had to land down the street from the knot of fighters. The enemy had chosen their spot well. Only a few places in the old city of Castleton remained where a dragon could not easily land or maneuver.

The king and queen had gone to a merchant's shop on one of the older streets. The king had commissioned a surprise for his wife on the occasion of their wedding anniversary and had decided to take her into the city as part of the special celebration. It had been a spur-of-the-moment trip and he'd taken minimal protection with him—only the knights who had been stationed outside the royal chambers as honor guard.

The dragons who partnered with those three knights had been relegated to flying above or perching on rooftops as the small, royal party made their way over ground. As a result, Rath had been too far away to help when the trap had been sprung around the king and queen.

Swords clashed and clanged as Rath used his foreclaws to tear attackers out of his path. He couldn't flame down here among the buildings unless he wanted to start an inferno that would kill hundreds of innocent citizens. That left his teeth and claws. And the swords of the knights who had been with the royal couple.

Faedric was young. Ill trained. He was not a swordsman. Not yet. Rath worried as he tossed assailants—too many of them—out of his path.

Other dragons were arriving, following his perilous path downward toward the street with mixed results. A few of the smaller ones had made it down safely and were following his example, following right behind Rath or approaching from the other side of the bottleneck.

Several other dragons screamed in pain as they failed to find a safe path down to the street and fell hard, breaking bones and crushing parts of buildings and street lamps. Rath worried anew as he worked his way closer to the king.

There were two older knights who were acquitting themselves well with their swords as they fought back to back to back with the king and poor Faedric, keeping the queen at the center of their small group. The king fought valiantly alongside his knights and they all had to know—as Rath did— that Faedric was the weakest point in their defense.

Even as Rath watched in horror from too far away, Faedric fell.

Everything happened in slow motion as Rath watched, feeling Faedric's pain as if it was his own. Then the queen screamed as blood pulsed red around the knife sticking out of her chest. She had been stuck through the heart.

The king, seeing his beloved wife fall, turned and was run through the neck by one of the assassins. The two knights tried to help, killing those who had struck the king and queen, but they could not last long against such overwhelming odds. They too were struck down.

As Rath made his way to the pile of the fallen, he slashed out, killing all in his path. His talons were stained with the blood of the enemy, but it was not enough. It would never be enough to bring back Faedric. Or the king and queen.

Dear Mother of All. The king and queen!

Rath howled his pain to the heavens as he realized they were both dead.

All dead. The royal couple. The two older knights. Faedric.

Rath's pain knew no bounds. He crouched protectively over the pile of bodies as the other dragons took out their anger, sorrow and pain on the remaining assassins. The street ran red with blood. Blood of the enemy. Blood of friends.

Not one of the attackers lived to tell the tale and the air was filled with the roars and cries of dragons. The sound of despair. The feel of anger and mourning.

Rath felt the pain of loss and the guilt he would bear for the rest of his long life for choosing a man who had not been ready to defend the king and queen...or even himself.

Chapter One

Golgorath was an old dragon. Not past his prime, but old enough to have taken more than one knight as his partner. The last had died before his time, in a battle he had been ill-prepared to fight. Rath blamed himself for picking Faedric for the goodness of his heart alone, thinking that the young man would have time to learn the warrior's skills he'd need. The guilt Rath had felt over his misjudgment sent him into seclusion for decades.

When he came out of self-imposed exile, Rath had decided to wait for the right man to be his next knight. That man, he decided, had to have both the pure and true heart worthy of being a knight *and* the skills of an expert warrior. Rath didn't want to go through the kind of loss he'd experienced with Faedric again.

Nor did he want to put his mate, Sharlis, through it. She was an excellent female and together they had raised five wonderful dragon children and been second-parents to over twenty human offspring. Theirs had been a long and fruitful union and he looked forward to the day that he found the right man to partner him, so he could reclaim his mate.

Sharlis had already chosen a knight. Thorn was a newly appointed Weaponsmaster of the Border Lair. He was good enough to teach the other knights about archery and spear. No one in the new Border Lair could match his skill with long-range weapons, which were a knight's first line of defense when on dragon back. In fact, few in the kingdom could best him with either longbow or crossbow.

Sharlis and Thorn had been fighting partners now for almost ten years. Golgorath was impatient to find his own knight so those two men could begin the search for their mate. Only after the men had found a woman to share their lives and passions would the dragons be free to consummate their lifelong bond once again. For if a dragon bonded with a knight, the bond was so close that the dragon's passion spilled over into his or her knight.

Only the deep abiding love and acceptance of a mate could sate the passion the dragons inspired in their knights. No other woman would do. A casual sex partner would not satisfy the need and could drive the knights insane from the emotional overload.

Long ago, it had been decreed that fighting dragons who bonded with knights must abstain to protect their human fighting partners until the knights had a mate of their own. Only then could the whole family—dragon and human—all be happy and safe.

To be near his mate and some of their offspring, Rath had come to the Border Lair and agreed to teach the younger dragons flying techniques he had perfected over his centuries. Rath had a certain aerodynamic shape to his wings and superior tail control that made him one of the best flyers in the kingdom. He shared those skills that could be learned, freely with the other dragons, and always had. He was not one of those to lord it over anyone because he'd been born with a better wingspan than most.

But he did admit to a certain amount of parental pride in the fact that all of his offspring took after him. They were fierce flyers who had mastered the art of keeping their knights safely on their backs through almost any maneuver. He had schooled them himself and imparted his knowledge on the subject to many fighting pairs over the years.

Sharlis was just as gifted, and between them, they had been named Flightmasters of the Border Lair. It was an honor he wore with suitable humility. Any time he started to feel full of himself, he remembered that one horrible mistake he'd made in choosing Faedric as his knight. Faedric had been good in the air but abysmal on the ground. He couldn't heft a sword to save his life—and that's what it had come down to. His life.

Caught on the ground, Rath could not protect him completely. If they'd been in the air, Faedric would have lived to fight—or at least lived to *learn* to fight—another day. But caught on the ground, Faedric had been the next best thing to helpless. And for that, Rath would always bear guilt.

He should have chosen better. Faedric had a knight's heart, but not the skill.

Rath swore this time he would choose a knight fully trained and worthy of the name from day one.

Rath was one of the first in the air when the call to arms went out. By chance, he had been leading an entire battle wing in an exercise designed to teach the young pairs of dragons and knights to fight together more closely as a cohesive group. They were positioned closest to the area of attack, and though these were all young pairings, they were good fighters who had seen some action in the recent skirmishes.

The Skithdronian army had been mounting surprise attacks along the border for the past several months. The escalation in border violence was the main reason the king had decided to create a new Lair in this region. It didn't hurt that there seemed to be a larger than usual number of young dragons choosing knights lately. The surplus of young fighting pairs along with the increase in hostility in this area didn't bode well for the future. The king and his council had decided to take the rather drastic action of creating a new Lair from scratch, which was quite an undertaking. In fact, it was something that hadn't been done in generations.

Unlike the paired dragons, Rath didn't have to wait for a knight to remount, so he was one of the first on the scene of the latest border crossing. The entire young fighting wing was behind him and would soon be along to help him defeat this latest incursion. For now though, he and two other unpartnered dragons were the first to arrive.

It was a familiar battleground. The keep was old, and dearly held by one noble family who had already lost their patriarch to the constant incursions onto their land. The Fadoral family was unlucky enough to live on the border with Skithdron. Though many noble families held lands along the border, the Fadoral lands offered one of the easiest border crossings and were therefore, constantly tested.

Elsewhere along the border, steep cliffs and a wide river caused the invaders much more difficulty. House Fadoral's holding had many farms with acres of cleared, relatively flat land that offered little natural resistance to the invaders and the Goddess-cursed skiths they drove before them.

Skiths were evil creatures of magical origin. Much as dragonkind had been nurtured by ancient wizards to protect and guard, the skiths had been created by one rogue wizard—the thrice-cursed Wizard Skir. He and his allies had been defeated in the last great war among wizardkind, but his pets lived on and thrived in the land that was named for them.

They were massive, snake-like creatures with sharp teeth and voracious appetites. They would eat anything that moved and could cleave a human in two with one fast chomp. They had one other weapon that was good at some distance too—a venomous spray they could spit from their fangs for several yards. The liquid was so acidic, it could even burn through dragon scale.

For dragons were the skith's only real opponent. Dragon fire could burn a skith to cinders, but it took time and cunning.

Rath had polished his skith-hunting skills all too often over the months since they'd been tasked with setting up the new Border Lair. He'd fried dozens of skiths since moving to the border and had no doubt he'd kill many more before this conflict was ended once and for all.

The only good skith was a dead skith as far as he was concerned, for they had no conscience. No real intelligence either. Not like dragons, who had as complicated a society as their human partners and felt the same emotions. Love, pride, joy and yes, hatred, disgust and anger were all part of the common ground between dragonkind and humanity.

Skiths, by contrast, had little emotion other than mindless hunger. The all-consuming appetite drove them to hunt and kill at all times. There was no compassion in a skith. No heart. No love. And not much intelligence.

Rath took stock of the battlefield. It had once been a thriving farm with both an orchard and a shady copse of trees where goats and sheep would graze. That wooded area provided cover for the enemy now, to the disadvantage of the defenders. Some were on horseback, but many of the men at arms were on foot, wearing dusty and damaged armor that had been patched together more than once.

This small group of defenders had been attacked repeatedly and only recently had the dragons and knights been close enough to come to their aid in any numbers. The battle was already engaged, with more than a dozen skiths sent out before the enemy fighters as a first wave, driven ahead of the men to attack all in their path.

They were making inroads in the tattered defense, but Rath and his fellow dragons would put an end to that shortly. Flaming carefully as he went, Rath made a first pass to distract the skiths from their human prey. He wanted the creatures to focus on the new threat from above, allowing the men on the ground time to retreat to safety before the dragons could engage the skiths directly.

In a maneuver he had personally taught to many of the younger dragons, he flamed downward at an angle as he flew past with dangerous accuracy, toasting skiths but not the human fighters who were fleeing to safety. Rath made the first few passes with two other unpartnered dragons but was soon joined in the sky by many bearing knights. The rest of the fighting wing had arrived in good time.

"Naru and Venri," he called mentally to the two unpartnered dragons. *"Will you come to ground with me and engage directly while the dragons with knights flame from above?"*

"Lead on Flightmaster, I'm with you." Naru answered readily while Venri positioned himself for another pass.

Venri was one of Rath's older sons. Venri had recently come out of mourning for the loss of his first knight partner—a pairing that had lasted more than a century. The first loss was so very hard, Rath remembered from his own experience. Not that losing a fighting partner—a family member—was ever easy, but the first was a deeper learning experience that somehow hurt more because you were unprepared for the intense pain of the loss. At least that was how Rath felt.

He'd talked long with his son on the subject in the past weeks since Venri had come out of his solitude in the mountains and rejoined the ranks of working dragons. It had been Venri who had volunteered to join his sire at the Border Lair and that had been a proud moment. That his son would want to work alongside him meant a great deal to Rath.

"I am with you too, Father," Venri answered as he finished the pass over the top of the spitting skiths. Flame mostly protected him from the acid, which vaporized when it came in contact with fire.

"Good. Ven, take the north flank. Naru, take the south. I'll come down the middle and we three will hold the line while our brothers in the air flame from above." Quickly communicating his plan to the leaders of the fighting wing now forming ranks in the sky above, Rath led the attack, landing in the center of the cleared space between the human defenders and the vicious, spitting skiths.

Fighting on the ground was not his favorite thing to do, but in this case, it was the most effective use of resources. Rath knew the young pairs that made up the newly formed fighting wing were unused to fighting together as a unit. Normally an unpartnered dragon like Rath would not dare to lead a mixed group of knights and dragons, but of those present, as Flightmaster, Rath was the highest ranked and most experienced.

It was his decision to allow the knights to remain aloft, where they would be safest. By having only unpartnered dragons on the ground facing the skiths, those above could freely flame. Their fire would not harm other dragons, but it would fry the skiths. Flame from above as well as below would take the creatures down fastest and with the least amount of danger to human and dragon alike.

As they put Rath's plan into motion, a few of the skiths made a break for it. They tried to go backward toward the copse of trees, but whatever the enemy used to herd them was enough of a deterrent to keep them from going back. The line of creatures became ragged as some tried to bolt forward.

They only had three unpartnered dragons. Rath's strategy relied on the dragons on the ground being free to bathe in their brethren's flame without endangering a knight. Three dragons against more than a dozen skiths wasn't very good odds, but it was all they had to work with.

Venri and Naru were being pushed farther outward as the line bowed. Rath had one rough moment when a skith got past him, but he was too preoccupied with the remaining creatures to worry about that single rogue at the moment. He flamed constantly, pushing the creatures back with his fire, but he felt the telltale burn of acid on the sensitive spot where wing met body and realized that one rogue skith had gotten behind him.

Rath peeked backward, craning his long neck to the side so he could take stock of what was going on back there. The sight that met his eye shocked him so deeply, he froze in place for several seconds, astounded.

A single man in battered armor was climbing onto the skith's back in a maneuver that was completely unheard of. All the while, the skith flipped and tried to roll, a maneuver designed to crush the man beneath the skith's giant body. The man was either insane or had some kind of death wish.

But as Rath watched in those few seconds that seemed like a lifetime, the warrior wrapped his legs around the skith's bucking neck and, using both hands in an upraised strike, he plunged the point of his sword downward into the skith's brain. Acidic black blood oozed out from around the hilt of the sword, which was buried in the top of the skith's head.

The creature wavered for one long moment, then collapsed to the ground. Dead.

The man slid off the creature's neck and looked around himself, seeking a new enemy. Rath was amazed at his audacity and completely impressed with his skill and bravery. This man was a warrior worthy of the name...and then some. Never had Rath heard of a single man bringing down a full-grown skith without magic or some sort of aid and walking away unharmed.

"Flightmaster! We flame!" came the warning cry from one of the dragons above.

"To me, soldier!" Rath trumpeted both mentally and with a roar as he turned his head to flame the skiths in front of him once more.

Rath spread his wing to cover the warrior on the ground a split second before fire rained down from the sky above them. Either the man had heard Rath's silent warning or he'd realized he was about to be toasted and sought the only protection available. Whichever the case, Rath was glad the brave man was protected from his brethren's fire as the area around them was bathed in a nearly continuous stream of dragon fire.

One after another, the knights and dragons aloft made one long pass that took out the remainder of the skiths beneath them. Rath and his two companions on the ground flamed constantly, creating an impenetrable wall in front, while the main attack force in the air reduced the rest of the skiths to smoldering cinders.

After several minutes of this concentrated attack, the skiths were no more.

And the courageous man who had in all likelihood saved Rath's skin, remained crouched beneath his wing, protected as best Rath could manage, from the rain of fire all around. He was probably hot, but hopefully not burnt.

Chapter Two

"It is safe to come out now, warrior." Rath spoke mentally, hoping the man sheltering beneath his wing would understand as he retracted his protection. *"The skiths are no more."*

The man stood from the crouching position he'd taken and looked around. Rath noted the dual sword sheaths on his back and realized this two-handed fighter was still armed. He had lost one of his curved blades to the skith's skull, but he still had another, already gripped in his hand.

The warrior paused to take stock of the situation before turning to look up at Rath. All was quiet for the moment, but they both seemed to realize that would not last. The enemy soldiers were even now regrouping. They might attack, even with the dragons present, or they might retreat. The defenders had to remain vigilant.

"Thank you for protecting my back, warrior. Never before, in all my years, have I witnessed a lone man kill a full-grown skith. I have never seen the like." Rath wondered if the remarkable man could hear him. It was a rare gift to be able to speak with dragons.

"I have never seen the like of the fire storm you and your fellows just unleashed, Sir Dragon." The warrior smiled broadly, the exhilaration of battle clear in his every move. "Thank you for shielding me." The warrior bowed low, a sparkle of adventure in his gray eyes as he moved quickly. "But for now, I have to muster the troops in case the enemy is fool enough to press forward. I bid you good day."

The man moved nimbly away, already calling battle commands to the soldiers who awaited his orders. This, then, was the keep's new Master at Arms so many of the knights had been gossiping about. They had said he was a warrior the likes of which they had never seen and judging by what Rath had just witnessed, they were right to talk of him. His courage was either completely foolhardy...or the stuff of which legends were born.

He was not a young man, so perhaps it was the latter. He would not have lived so long if he were truly a fool with more courage than brains.

But had he heard Rath when he spoke into his mind? Rath couldn't be certain but was intrigued enough to want to know much more about this strange warrior. Rath tried to follow the man, but the stinging burn along his shoulders made him hiss in pain.

Damn. He'd forgotten the venom.

Rath craned his neck around to inspect his shoulder joint. It was angry and red. Already the acid had eaten through the top layer of scale, which was thinnest at the joint. He needed to do something about this before it got any worse.

Water. He needed water—and lots of it—to dilute the acid. Looking around, Rath spotted the old well that was pretty much all that was left of a once-beautiful farm. He began walking slowly and painfully over to the well.

More dragons were arriving. More experienced fighters from another battle wing that had been dispatched from the Border Lair. Rath spotted two knights circling, coming in for a landing near the well.

"Gareth and Lars will help you while we guard, Flightmaster," a young dragon named Kelvan said in Rath's mind. He knew both of the knights the youngster named and had been glad when they found their mate, a lovely woman

named Belora, who was a lost daughter of the Royal House of Kent. Such a happy mating among the younger generation of dragons and knights boded well for their new Lair.

"I would be glad of any help you can give. I got sprayed from behind." Rath deliberately included both Gareth and Lars in his communication, along with the lovely young female dragon Rohtina, who was Kelvan's mate.

"We saw," Rohtina answered. She was somewhat soft-spoken for a dragoness, but that was probably because she tempered her words around Rath. Oddly enough, she seemed in awe of her own grandsire. Rath could only imagine the tales his daughter Rohna had told her daughter about him while Rath had been in the seclusion of mourning for Faedric. *"That man killed the skith,"* she went on haltingly. *"All by himself."*

Her tone captured perfectly the amazement they all felt at such a feat. The dragons landed and Gareth and Lars jumped down from their backs, but there was someone at the well already. A small figure in battered armor was already pulling buckets of water up from the deep well and positioning them at the ready, Rath saw as he stumbled the last few feet. One of the locals must have realized he needed help, thank the Mother of All. The sooner they diluted the acid, the better.

The two knights thanked the busily working local fighter and grabbed the buckets, running to Rath's side and delivering the blessedly cool water just where he needed it most. Both knights had seen such burns before. They had learned dragon anatomy from their partners and knew how best to apply the small buckets of water to the greatest effect. They ran back and forth many times, while the small figure at the well kept them supplied with bucket after bucket of much-needed water.

When it became clear the enemy was in full retreat, others came over to help. The Master at Arms sent them to Rath's side and the knights and the figure at the well organized them into a line that passed the buckets even faster between the dragon and the well. It didn't take long after that for the burning pain to ease. The venom was diluted enough to be harmless on the ground and on the dragon's scaled back.

"I don't think you can fly on this for a few days, Flightmaster," Lars said aloud, inspecting the wound. Rath had suspected as much, judging by the pain he still felt when he tried to move the joint. The acid had burned deep.

"We will care for him," a feminine voice called from in front of him.

Rath moved his head to regard the slight figure that had labored so tirelessly at the well. It was not a small man or boy, as he had thought. As she walked toward him, she took off her helm and a tumble of golden-red curls fell around her shoulders. It was a woman. A *swordswoman* who had fought alongside the men, then come to his aid when she had seen Rath walking painfully toward the well.

He looked at her anew. This was a woman not only of courage and strength, but of intelligence as well.

"Lady Cara," Gareth said with some surprise, moving forward to meet her, his hand extended in welcome. "I did not realize you led the keep's forces now."

"Lead?" She laughed as she took his hand in a friendly clasp usually reserved for warriors. "I do not presume to lead. I leave that to our new Master at Arms. But we have so few able-bodied fighters left, it is important for all who can heft a sword with any skill to answer the call when Skithdron renews its attack. I thank you on behalf of my brother for coming to our aid this day. Especially you, Sir," she addressed Rath directly. That was something most humans who did not often mingle with dragons seldom did, especially females.

Gareth escorted her closer to Rath. "Flightmaster Golgorath, this is Lady Cara Fadoral, sister to the new Lord of House Fadoral, daughter of old Lord Harald, who fell in the first waves of fighting along this border." Gareth's tone was suitably solemn as he made the introductions.

"In fact, he fell defending this very farm," Cara added with a heartfelt glimmer of tears in her pretty blue eyes. "My brother Envard and I used to play in this orchard when we were little. It used to be a place of great joy but has been turned by our enemies into a land of sorrow."

Rath bowed his head to the young lady. *"I am sorry for your loss, Lady Cara."* He spoke the words, though it was doubtful any but the nearby knights and dragons would hear.

She returned his bow, greeting him as if they were not on a battlefield, but in a receiving room. She had grace, this lady did, and a courage he had seldom seen in the few human females he had known.

"Thank you for helping us, Flightmaster. My brother lies abed under the healer's care for grievous wounds suffered in battle, but I extend the hospitality of our keep to you. For without you, there surely would not be a keep left by now. Never before have such numbers of skiths been shepherded to our doorstep. I can't imagine what we would have done without your timely intervention."

"He won't be able to fly without danger of making the wound much worse until the burns have a chance to heal a bit," Lars said, walking forward and greeting the lady. "We can arrange for medicine and a healer to come to him, but he will need a place to rest for a few days while he recovers. If you won't mind having him in the keep courtyard, we can rig up a shelter for him."

"I would invite him into the main hall!" Lady Cara said with a smile. "But I fear he would not fit through the door. The place was not built with dragons in mind and for that, I am sorry. Whatever I can do to make your stay with us more comfortable, I will do with gladness. Can you get him there on your own or should I arrange for a cart or something?" She looked at Rath with a measuring eye and a bit of humor that appealed to him. "Though I don't think we have anything big enough to carry him, much less enough horses to pull it."

Rath appreciated her humor in the face of the horrors of the day. She had come perilously close to facing skiths one on one. He liked the way she bounced back from such a grave threat. He chuckled along with her, sending smoky ringlets into the sky with his laughter. She caught his eye and winked at him, clearly realizing they shared their amusement. It was a rare moment of bonding with a human he had only just met. So few non-Lair people were comfortable around dragons. Certainly few newcomers dared to tease them. He enjoyed the moment even more for its novelty.

"I can walk," he grumbled, already beginning to move. *"I'm not the most elegant on land, but I can still get where I'm going."*

With that, he turned and began to make his way toward the keep he could see in the distance. It might take a while, but he'd get there eventually. Hopefully with his dignity intact.

"Flightmaster, I will go ahead to make a place ready for your arrival," the lady said, jogging up beside him. A servant approached with a lovely little mare that was well trained and did not shy away from him.

He watched with some surprise as she vaulted into the saddle and rode off at great speed, stopping only a few times to consult with some of the fighters that had remained to guard and clear the area of debris or anything that could be used against them the next time the skirmishes started. Rath noted the Master at Arms organizing his troops and the way his eyes followed the lovely lady as she rode across the fields toward her home.

If Rath wasn't much mistaken, the Master at Arms had more than the normal admiration for his employer's sister. Rath liked the man even more. He had appreciation for a fine woman who was not quite the norm. That showed good judgment, in Rath's opinion.

He was looking forward to staying at the keep for a few days. He needed to know more about these people. They were by far some of the most interesting humans he had come across in all his years.

Rohtina walked at Golgorath's side, her knight off talking with some of the soldiers from the keep. She was hesitant to talk to her grandsire, but she wanted to get to know him better and this seemed like a good opportunity.

"Flightmaster, are you in much pain?" She made the first foray into conversation.

"Sweetheart, I am your grandsire. Can you not call me such?" His head swiveled to look at her even as he continued to move slowly forward.

She ducked her head. *"I did not want to presume."*

"We are family, Rohtina." The great Flightmaster sighed, sending a small stream of smoke toward the heavens. *"I regret that my mourning period coincided with your fledging. I would have liked to have known you as a youngster. But it could not be helped. I had no idea Rohna had mated, much less had a daughter, until I returned to duty."*

"That's all right, grandsire. Mama told me all about you. So much so that I felt as if I always knew you."

"Then why are you so shy around me now, child? I will not bite you. I promise," he teased her. She liked the warm tone of his voice, something she had not heard from the fearsome Flightmaster before.

"You are the Flightmaster," she replied, hoping he would understand.

"And my Rohna probably filled you with all kinds of stories about my legendary flying ability." He seemed to understand what she was getting at. *"I suppose being your teacher doesn't help either. Being a figure of authority before being your grandsire has caused an awkwardness between us. I begin to see your dilemma."* He moved quickly to twine his neck partially with hers. *"But you are family, little girl. My granddaughter. Do not let the title of Flightmaster scare you away from me. One day, if you continue as you are, you could very well be Flightmaster in your own right, Rohtina. You have the wings for it. Now all you need is time and practice to perfect your aerial skills."*

"Really? You truly think so?" She hadn't dared hope he thought so highly of her, even if he was her grandsire.

"I know so. Your mother and father are excellent fliers and you already have all the basics down pat. As the years progress you and Kelvan—who has very good wings as well—will turn into a great team. You're good now, but in time, you will be great. Mark my words."

His words gave her such hope, she felt a little bounce in her step as she walked with him. *"Do you mind if I walk with you to the keep, grandsire?"* she asked shyly. *"And while you're here, can I come visit you?"*

"I would be most disappointed if you did not, young lady."

She liked the teasing tone and twinkle in his sparkling eyes. He was much less scary now that she'd taken the initiative and talked to him, as Kelvan had suggested. She was glad now that she'd taken the chance.

Chapter Three

Cara raced ahead to the keep, astounded at the day's turn of events. Not only had the most magnificent dragons arrived in the nick of time to save the day, but one would be staying with them for a few days at the keep. Cara had always wanted to spend time among dragons but had never had the opportunity. Her father had kept her close to home and never included her in his few travels to the capital and court. Until today, she'd only ever seen dragons at rare times when Sir Gareth or Sir Lars and their dragon partners paused briefly at the keep to impart messages or exchange greetings.

Sir Thorn had dined with them on several memorable occasions, but his dragoness, Sharlis, usually spent the evening hunting among the flock kept for dragon consumption and Cara didn't get to see much of her. Thorn had never even bothered to formally introduce them, which counted against him in her books, though she was undeniably attracted to the handsome knight.

Her brother, Envard, didn't like the attention Thorn had paid to her. No, Lord Envard wanted her safely married off to a faraway nobleman and out of his hair. Younger by five years and born of her father's second wife, Envard had always had a chip on his shoulder where Cara was concerned. He'd tried to get rid of her as soon as father had died, but then his own injury had prevented him from putting his plans into motion. Instead, she'd been left to run the keep without his interference, which was good for the time being. What would happen when he recovered was anyone's guess, but for now, she was able to do as she pleased.

And right now, preparing for a dragon guest was on her agenda. She was intrigued beyond measure by the dragons that kept their country safe. This would be her first real interaction with one and she hoped she could make a good impression for both herself and the keep that had come to depend so greatly on the protection of the new Lair.

Sir Golgorath would be their guest for a few days and she would be able to look at him and help him, if he was receptive to her offer of assistance. She didn't want to overstep the bounds of hospitality. Dragons were said to be sticklers for manners and she intended to be on her best behavior while the fierce dragon was in residence.

Now she just had to figure out a way to do all this without Envard butting his big nose in. Since their father died, her brother had become a real stick in the mud. He'd been fun before, but lately...

It wasn't worth worrying about, Cara decided as her favorite mare brought her through the gates of the keep at a fast gallop. She only slowed when they neared the stables, which was close enough to where she wanted to go that she vaulted from the saddle, calling for help from the nearest stable hands. They set about a multitude of tasks at her direction so the dragon would be comfortable here while he healed.

By the time Sir Golgorath limped in some minutes later, the dragoness Rohtina at his side, things were as organized as she could get them on such short notice. She ran over to the walking dragons, stopping several yards before them and making her bow.

"Sir and lady, if you will follow me, I think we have an area set up that you will like."

Without comment, the weary dragon followed her. Lady Rohtina accompanied him, craning her long neck to look all around the keep. Cara had no doubt the dragoness's sharp, jewel-like eyes took in the damage the keep had suffered in recent battles. Cara hoped she would not hold battle damage against them. The keep had been lovely once upon a time, but recent events had been hard on both the place and its inhabitants.

She pushed aside the dark thoughts as she led the way to the enclosure she had rigged for the dragon. It was well away from the stable and the all-too-flammable hayloft. It was a corner nook formed by the stone wall of the keep and another stone wall that stood at a right angle. Behind that inner wall were the bakery ovens. That wall radiated warmth from the ovens, in which fires were kept banked at all times and whipped up to full blast before dawn. In the summer, the stone helped dissipate the heat, but in winter, the area was enclosed to form a warm place for guardsmen to shelter on breaks from the cold duty of standing watch on the walls.

Lady Cara had organized the stable lads to remove the rough furniture the Guardsmen used and to sweep the packed dirt floor clear of any debris. She had then sent a few of them to cut fragrant young pine boughs to cover the floor. He would probably enjoy their clean scent and could possibly build a nest for himself of the soft green boughs that would not burn easily. She left the canvas roof in place. It was high enough that the dragon would not have to stoop to enter and low enough to help keep in some of the warmth.

The front of the enclosure was usually left open except in the worst of winter weather, but Cara had asked the lads to rig up the heavy fabric that could be used to give the dragon some privacy. She had even devised a knotted rope looped through a pulley that the dragon could operate himself to open and close the heavy curtain.

She'd also had a bathtub brought in and filled with clear water from the well so the dragon would not have to go far if he wanted a drink. A crate of apples had been put next to the water, in case he wanted a sweet snack.

Cara reached the enclosure first and pulled back the heavy curtain. "I wasn't sure what you might like, but I hope this meets at least some of your needs, Flightmaster Golgorath," she said as the dragon's neck craned past her to inspect the area.

Just then, the blue-green dragon she'd seen earlier caused a stir by landing inside the keep's walls. Both Golgorath and Rohtina paused to look, as did every being inside the keep's protective walls. The newly arrived dragon landed lightly, touching down with one back foot first while he backwinged to a neat, gentle landing. A moment later, two men jumped down from his back.

It was Sir Gareth and Sir Lars. They walked right up to the curtain and into the enclosure, taking a look around.

"This is good. Really good, Lady Cara," Sir Gareth said, taking in her preparations with an approving glance. "You seem to have thought of everything and it's nice and warm in here." He cocked a questioning eyebrow in her direction.

"The baking ovens are on the other side of this wall." She patted the stone nearest her. "I thought perhaps Flightmaster Golgorath would enjoy the heat."

"Dragons produce quite a bit of their own heat, but they enjoy warmth from the outside," Lars confirmed in a quiet voice. He wasn't as gregarious as his fighting partner, but he was efficient and friendly enough.

"Lars will stay to help get him settled while I go back to the Lair and get our mate. She is a healer and may be able to help speed Flightmaster Rath's recovery."

"What about his knight?" Cara asked quietly, following as Gareth pulled her to one side while Lars helped settle the injured dragon into the enclosure.

"Sir Rath isn't partnered at the moment," Gareth explained as they walked toward the blue-green dragon who was waiting nearby.

"Oh." Cara was surprised. She hadn't realized unpartnered dragons also lived in Lairs, but she probably should have thought about it. Where else would they live? "If he needs anything, I will be nearby. All the resources of the keep—such as they are—are at his disposal."

"I'll tell him. Thank you, Lady Cara. Your preparations are much more than any of us expected. You seem to have thought of everything he'll need for the moment. Now it will just take time—and perhaps the attentions of my wife, Belora, who will be able to help him as few others can."

"Then may I invite you and your lady to stay to dinner with us in the hall after she sees to Flightmaster Golgorath? It won't be grand, mind you, but we'll do the best we can to honor those who have helped us so greatly this day."

"I am honored, Lady Cara, but my wife might be too tired after the healing session. We will have to wait and see."

That was interesting. The lady must be a true healer if she gave of her own energy in healing. Cara had heard of such, and had seen it only one time in her life. It was a rare thing. A magical thing.

"I understand," Cara replied as Sir Gareth climbed aboard the dragon's back. "Fair winds to you both. We will await your return and keep the fires lit on the walls, should you arrive back here after dark."

"My thanks many times over, Lady Cara. We will return soon."

She stood back as the dragon moved a few yards away to a clear spot. He leapt into the air and winged away, a majestic sight against the afternoon sky. Cara glanced toward the enclosure, but the curtain was down, Lady Rohtina sitting in front of it as if on guard duty. Cara decided to leave the dragons be for the moment. She had preparations to make inside the keep, just in case the knights and their lady decided to join them for dinner.

She also had to get out of her armor and hide it before Envard got a look at her. With any luck, nobody would tell him what she'd been up to for the past few hours.

Tristan watched Lady Cara disappear up the back stairs into the keep. The new Master at Arms couldn't help following her with his gaze, even though he knew he should not. She was a fine lady, for all that she took up arms in her people's defense. While some might foolishly think such behavior was unladylike, Tristan silently applauded her willingness to defend her home with every skill she could bring to bear.

She was a fair swordswoman. Tristan would not have let her anywhere near the front lines if she weren't. He probably should have kept her farther from the action than he had, but Tristan couldn't seem to deny her anything. All Lady Cara had to do was look at him with those clear blue eyes of hers, and he would give her the moon if she asked.

He was smitten. Well and truly under her spell. They'd shared one amazing, never-to-be-repeated, tempestuous night together when he had first arrived at the keep...before he knew who she was.

When he'd found out she was the daughter of the lord he had contracted to serve, he'd nearly had a fit. Remorse and guilt ate at him. He'd been hired to safeguard the lord, his family and his keep. And on his first night behind the security of the keep's stone walls, he'd seduced the daughter of the house—though he hadn't realized until later.

It was his dishonor. A shame he would have to live with, even as he remembered the most amazing night of his life. Tristan had bedded many women in his past, but none could compare with the lovely Cara. She was the light in his darkness, the sun in his sky. And he feared he would be in love with her for the rest of his life.

He had hurt her that night, when she'd finally revealed her true identity. That was another regret in a long line of them that night. He had not meant to be so brutal with his words, but he'd been shocked by her deception.

Tristan had wrongly thought the daughter of the house must be a child. When he'd met with old Lord Harald, he'd described her as a young maiden, but the woman who'd come so willingly to his bed that night was mature and utterly lovely. So sure of herself. So strong willed and fiery.

He had met her in the soldiers' practice yard, going through sword drills with some of the younger men at arms. Tristan had admired her skill and willingness to teach what she knew to those who needed to learn it. Tristan had joined the small, impromptu class, helping the swordswoman learn a few things as well, and when she'd suggested sharing an evening meal, he'd agreed readily.

The private meal had surprised him, but he was new not only to this keep but this land as well, and he'd enjoyed the quiet moment with the lovely swordswoman. She had seemed surprised when he'd made advances, but after only a slight hesitation, she'd joined with him wholeheartedly.

He would always remember the way she had touched him. She'd seemed hesitant about some things but willing to learn what he liked as he learned the secrets of her body. She'd been adventurous and playful, trying things he had not expected.

When she'd taken his hard cock in her mouth, he'd nearly jumped out of his skin. Her mouth haunted him to this day. The memory of the pleasure she'd brought him would be with him all his life. Never had anything felt so right.

And when he'd slipped into her welcoming sheath, she surrounded him with her warmth and the tight clenching of her inner muscles that drove him wild. He'd been out of control, but thankfully she'd met him move for move. Her sleek, muscular body had been a temptation and delight beyond measuring as her strong limbs clutched him to her beautiful body.

He'd ridden her hard, bringing them both pleasure before collapsing at her side. Moments later, she'd teased him back to hardness and switched places. She climbed over him and took his cock into her body, allowing him a vision he would never forget. He watched her take him, then ride him to ecstasy, groaning as he came in her sweet, welcoming warmth.

They'd slept, limbs tangled and bodies entwined until she woke before dawn and he caught her trying to slip away from his bed. He'd wrapped one arm around her waist and tried to cajole her into staying. That's when she'd revealed just why she could not be found lying abed with the Master at Arms. She was the daughter of the house and was expected to be found chastely sleeping in her own bed.

Tristan had been stunned. Then outraged. Then cuttingly sarcastic. He'd seen the hurt he inflicted on her lovely face, but was powerless to stop himself from being so hateful. He knew in that moment that their night of passion could never be repeated. Never.

He had driven her away and she had gone, a cold distance between them ever after. He regretted many things about that night and its results, but he would never regret the sweetest pleasure he'd ever known.

Lady Cara had been distant with him ever since and, after that initial encounter, seemed to not care one way or the other about what had happened. She probably would laugh if she ever realized just how deeply in love with her he was.

She was a lady. A noblewoman. Tristan wasn't fit to shine her boots and they both knew it. Their stations in life were too different. She would never be permitted to become involved with someone like him.

But he could watch her from afar and dream of what could have been.

Over the next months, Tristan had been tempted to comfort the woman who had invaded his dreams, both waking and sleeping, several times. He'd given in to his instincts when old Lord Harald fell in one of the early battles. She had been distraught and when he'd found her crying softly against her horse's mane in the dark stable one night, he'd put aside his pride and taken her in his arms. She'd wept all over him for a time, but gradually, she found her courage and inner strength.

He'd been touched by the way she grieved for her beloved father privately but was strong in public for her people in the days to come. Tristan hadn't liked the way Lord Envard had treated her after their father died. He'd been petty and short with her in public and more than once, Tristan had found her pacing in the stable, a look of mixed fear and worry on her lovely face.

He knew the new lord had plans for his sister that were not to her liking. Exactly what they were, he didn't know. Not yet. He was certain that as the day for action drew nearer, Lord Envard would have to consult with the Master at Arms if he was sending Lady Cara away. At the very least, she would need a group of Guards to travel with her. If he was inviting visitors to the keep, likewise, the lord would have to arrange for the Master at Arms to provide security. Either way, Tristan hoped to learn what caused the lady such upset. He'd wanted to comfort her, but until the threat became real, he refrained—

even though it was one of the hardest things he'd ever had to do.

But then things changed drastically. Envard had been grievously wounded in battle, and Lady Cara was suddenly free to be who she really was. She'd organized the healers and servants to see to Envard's care and recovery, then taken over, seeing to all the little decisions that needed to be made to keep the place running.

The very next time the alarm bell sounded, Cara had jumped on her horse and galloped right beside Tristan all the way to the battlefield, though he'd tried to dissuade her.

That first time, he had stayed glued to her side, watching as she defeated several opponents, as he did the same. Once he realized she could handle herself in real battle, he felt better about having her there. Between them, they felled many of the enemy soldiers and lived to tell the tale. Neither of them had been unhorsed and they rode back to the keep together in the dusk before night fell in earnest.

They had dismounted together in the dark stable and when she stumbled, he'd caught her against his chest. Her lithe form had felt so right against him and he'd longed for her for months now. She had looked up, seeming to be as stunned as he was, and in the dark of the stable, with the grim euphoria of victory clear in her dazed eyes, she had crept up on tiptoe to match her soft lips to his.

Heaven had opened up and let him steal another small glimpse of paradise in that moment. Tristan became convinced that Cara had ruined him for all time. She had ruined him for all other women. She had stolen his heart that one, fateful night they'd spent together. He didn't know later if he would have allowed the moment to stretch into the next morning, but when her horse shifted, it jostled them apart and he saw the confusion in her gaze as he pulled back.

He couldn't take that look. It reminded him of their stations and how their relationship could never be. Tristan had set her away from him, steadying her on her feet before turning on his heel and walking away. He would care for his mount later. At the moment, he couldn't get away from her fast enough.

Tristan had been careful to never be alone with her again after that night. He'd let her find her own way in the skirmishes they'd fought, though he always kept her in his sights. He would not allow her to come to harm if he had anything to say about it.

They had an uneasy wall between them now. A wall of silence on all but the most mundane of topics.

But deep in the night, as he tried to sleep in his lonely bed, Tristan's thoughts often turned to what it had felt like to hold Cara in his arms. He remembered the magic of her kiss, and he both hoped and feared he would remember it always...

Chapter Four

Lars and Rohtina stayed to help Rath get comfortable. That was nice of them, he thought, but really, Lady Cara had seen well to his comfort. The enclosure she had devised was toasty warm and smelled of the fresh-cut pine she had thoughtfully provided. It wasn't the usual sandy pit that Lair dragons favored, but it was both clean and comfortable.

"This will do nicely." Rath spoke to both Lars and Rohtina, who stood guard outside the curtain. Lars was inspecting the mechanism and smiled when he turned back to Rath.

"The lady has rigged it so you will be able to open and close the curtain yourself." Lars proceeded to demonstrate, pulling the rope a few times, much to Rohtina's enjoyment. She chuckled, sending spirals of smoke up into the darkening sky.

"Lady Cara is very thoughtful. Did you notice the crate of apples? Give some to my granddaughter. They are tasty." Rath crunched another apple as he said the words.

Lars opened the curtain and left it that way, bending to pick up an apple. He threw it toward Rohtina's mouth and she caught it with a single chomp.

"Oh, these are good," she agreed. *"Thank you, grandsire."*

"You are very welcome, sweetling. Now, both of you have been here before," Rath said, turning the conversation. *"What do you think of the Master at Arms?"*

"He is a gifted fighter," Lars said, answering in his serious manner. "He favors matched, curved blades. You probably saw the sheaths on his back. A foreign style. It is said he comes from a land far from here."

"Truly? Which land? Do you know?" Rath asked, intrigued.

"I'm sorry, Flightmaster. I know not," Lars admitted.

"His skill was already the stuff of discussion and gossip before he killed that skith single-handedly today, grandsire." Rohtina added. *"If I had not seen the carcass with my own eyes, I would doubt the truth of it. I have never seen the like."*

"Nor I, my dear. It makes me wonder..." Rath trailed off, thinking.

"What do you wonder, Flightmaster?" It was Lars who would not let the subject drop.

"For one thing..." Rath turned his head to look at Lars. *"I wonder if he can hear me. I spoke to him today and I cannot be certain, but I think perhaps he heard and understood."*

"Really?" Lars sat on the edge of the bathtub full of drinking water and folded his arms. "And if he did, would you consider choosing him as your knight?"

"Now there's a question." Rath nodded his head, unsure of his own thoughts. *"I will have to observe and examine him more closely while I am here. If he has honor and a pure heart, then I will have to think carefully about doing so. We could use his skills in the Lair. He would be an asset in teaching the less-skilled swordsmen. The Border Lair does not have an expert swordsman of his caliber and I have noticed the lack."*

"That's because you're obsessed with preparing us all to fight," Lars said in a calm voice.

"My obsession—as you call it—is born of bitter experience, as you should know, young Sir." Rath knew his mental voice took on a chiding tone. He was the grandfather here, imparting his wisdom to the younger generation, even if they didn't want to hear it, or thought he was *obsessed*.

"What happened to Faedric wasn't your fault, you know. It was just bad luck and bad timing. Everyone agrees," Lars added quietly.

"I see the gossip mill still runs strong, even in a newly made Lair," was all Rath would reply. *"Leave me be for a bit, children. I want to close my eyes for a few minutes before the princess arrives."*

Dismissed, Lars mercifully closed the curtain and went outside to join his partner. The lad had hit a nerve, talking about poor Faedric so openly. The wound of losing him had not fully healed, even now. Rath knew it never would. He closed his eyes and let the weariness of the day take him.

A short while later it seemed, Rath woke to a feeling of magical warmth being applied to his wing joints. A light touch told him Princess Belora had come and was already treating him.

"Don't let me disturb you, Sir Golgorath," she said softly as she moved around near his back. "You know as well as I that rest is what you need most right now. I'll do what I can, but burns take time to heal."

"I know, Princess. Thank you for your help. It feels much better already."

"Good. I will leave a supply of burn jelly salve for someone from the keep to apply overnight, but I will stay here if you want me to," she was quick to add.

"No, Princess. You need not inconvenience yourself on my account. I have been stung by skith venom before. I know what to expect. As long as one of the people here will help with the salve, I'll be fine."

"And from what Lars and Rohtina tell me, you have reconnaissance of your own to carry out," she added slyly. "Shall I ask the Master at Arms to check on you?"

Rath had to laugh, sending smoke toward the ceiling. *"I see I shouldn't have confided in my granddaughter or her quiet knight."*

"Is it so wrong for your family to want to help you? We've all been concerned for you, grandfather. We want to help you be happy."

Rath was touched by the princess's heartfelt words. He craned his neck around to look into her eyes. *"That means a great deal to me, Princess. More than I can adequately express. But you of all should know that the Mother of All will let things unfold in Her time."*

"I will pray that She brings you a new knight worthy of your partnership," she answered solemnly.

Princess Belora left him after a few more minutes of her healing magic. She and her mates went into the keep to share a meal with the lady and her retainers while raw meat was provided for the dragons who waited in the courtyard. Both Rohtina and Kelvan seated themselves in front of the open curtain of Rath's enclosure and the three dragons shared a lovely feast of fresh meat provided by the keep's butcher.

It was much later that night, after dinner was over and the children had left to fly back to the Border Lair, that Rath had his first visitor. Much to his surprise, it was indeed the Master at Arms, come to check on his comfort. Rath was glad he'd left the curtain up, indicating he was receptive to visitors and desirous of the night air.

The Master at Arms walked very silently for a human, approaching without making much sound at all. Rath saw him before he heard him, turning his head to regard the naturally stealthy human as he approached.

"Greetings, Flightmaster," said the Master at Arms. "I'm sorry. I do not know your name, Sir. I am called Tristan Dalen and I have served as Master at Arms for this keep for only a few months now."

"I am aware of your newness to the position," Rath thought hard at the man, hoping he could hear. *"My name is Golgorath, but my friends call me Rath."*

"Pleased to meet you, Sir Golgorath."

There it was. Confirmation. The man could hear him. Rath felt a thrill of excitement race down his spine. Perhaps the Mother of All was about to answer Belora's prayers much sooner than she could have expected.

"Pardon my shock, but it is a rare thing that humans can hear my kind when we speak. It marks you as a very special being."

"Really?" Tristan asked conversationally, seeming unimpressed. "It is a skill somewhat common in my family. In my homeland, there are small creatures we call *virkin* that are able to communicate simple thoughts in this manner. They are not as intelligent or articulate as your kind, but their speech method is similar."

"I have never heard of this creature, but I would be interested to know more about it and your land. Where do you hail from, Master Tristan?"

"Please, just call me Tristan, if you don't mind the informality. I am only recently become the Master at Arms. I am not one to stand on titles. But to answer your question, I was born in Elderland, far to the east. The curved blades I carry into battle are more common there, though I admit few have the patience to learn my chosen style of fighting."

"I will call you Tristan and you must call me Rath. I too get tired of formality at times. I have heard tales of your land, but have never met anyone from there in all my years," Rath admitted. *"Will you tell me of it...and what brought you to Draconia?"*

Tristan leaned against the edge of the filled bathtub, much as Lars had done, his shoulders drooping with fatigue. Tired as he appeared, the fact that he had come to check on Rath before seeking his own bed meant that he put other beings' welfare before his own. That was a good sign.

"It was a woman that sent me out to find my fortune in other lands. My sister, to be precise. She is an oracle of sorts. The family situation being what it is, it was pretty clear for a long time that if I stayed in my homeland, I would cause..." he seemed to grope for the right words, "...inconvenience to the rest of my family. You see, I am a twin. My brother holds a hereditary position of power. I was for the army.

"It caused some confusion because we are identical in looks, but not in temperament. If the army rallied to me, as they were beginning to do, I could easily cause a coup, which I did not want. I love my brother. He is a deep thinker and the wiser of we two, even though he is hard to get to know. Being the heir was always a heavy burden on his shoulders as we grew. I was allowed to follow more dangerous and fun pursuits while he was protected and schooled in all he would need to know to run the empire."

The empire? Rath thought carefully to himself. Was this man brother to the Emperor of Elderland? It was just possible that fatigue had loosened his tongue even more than the subtle magic Rath was using on him. Rath had done this a few times in his life—when choosing a new knight he had to be careful to choose wisely. Only then was it permitted for a dragon to use his magic in such a way.

As if he had only just realized what he'd said, Tristan straightened from his slouch. His eyes grew wide, then narrowed in suspicion as he gazed at Rath.

"I have heard dragons are both crafty and intensely magical. Are you subjecting me to your magic, Sir Rath?"

Rath ducked his head. *"I admit I am curious to know what drives you, young Tristan. You are a mystery to me and a stranger to my land. Yet you have proven yourself in battle and saved me even graver injury, perhaps death. I owe you a debt of gratitude and I would like to call you friend, if possible."*

"Well spoken, Sir," Tristan continued to eye him with both suspicion and humor. "But I beg you keep what I have said private between we two. My birth means nothing here or in any other land. My brother reigns. I am but an inconvenient spare. I am a warrior only. A newly made Master at Arms. I am nothing."

"I beg to differ on that last point. Just from what I have observed in this single day, you are a warrior of skill the likes of which I have never seen. And let me tell you, I have seen many warriors over my centuries." A small chuckle sent smoke wafting toward the ceiling. *"The circumstances of your birth aside, you have already proven you have the courage of a lion. You took on a full-grown skith all on your own and won. That is a rare thing in any land."*

Tristan's head bowed and Rath could see high color on his sharp cheekbones. Was he embarrassed to be praised? Curiouser and curiouser.

"How old are you, exactly?" Tristan changed the subject. Yes, he was definitely embarrassed and avoiding the topic.

"Exactly? I'd have to get back to you on that. Suffice to say, I have buried three knight partners over my years. The first two lived long, full lives, but the most recent, poor Faedric, died much too young."

"I am sorry for your loss," Tristan said solemnly. "I have lost comrades in my time. It is not an easy thing."

"Thank you, but you should know—a dragon's knight is more than just a comrade in arms. My knights and I bonded on a

soul-deep level. They were part of my family, as I was part of theirs."

"I do not pretend to understand. We have nothing like it in my homeland. My experience with dragons is limited to only the past few months."

"How long have you been in Draconia?"

"Almost half a year. I came by sea, landing at Tipolir. I spent a few weeks there, getting my bearings before traveling north toward the border. I heard this was where the action is, so I decided to try to help."

"Sounds like a foolhardy pursuit. You came seeking danger? Or was it adventure that called you?"

Tristan grew silent for a small time before answering. "I came first because my sister told me to seek out the *battle among giants*. If that doesn't describe the conflict between dragonkind and the skiths, I don't know what does. Second, I came here to be of service. I'd heard in Tipolir about the vulnerable points along the border—especially this keep—that needed protection. Even in Elderland, we have heard about skiths and their gruesome penchant for human heads. And when I got here and I met the people of this keep, I had my third—and perhaps most important—reason for being here."

"The Lady Cara," Rath said, not unkindly.

Tristan let out a huge sigh. In it was all his fatigue and frustration. All his pent-up desire for something he probably believed could never be.

"The Lady Cara," he finally agreed. "She is everything to me. Everything and nothing, for it can never be."

"I'm not so sure about that," Rath replied, raising his head as soft footsteps came closer over the cobbled path in the courtyard. The lady herself was about to make an appearance, if he wasn't much mistaken.

"I should go." Tristan stood, making as if to leave, but Rath lifted one clawed hand, barring his exit.

"Stay," he ordered in a gentle voice. *"I would like to test a theory."*

Tristan didn't look happy but nodded and subsided back to his resting position on the rim of the bathtub.

"Sir Golgorath?" came Lady Cara's tentative voice from just outside the entrance.

"Come in, Lady Cara. You are very welcome here," Rath said to her, testing his so-called theory. Things were lining up and he'd be a fool not to recognize the Mother of All's hand in these affairs.

She entered the small enclosure and Rath's heart sped up. She'd heard him! Hadn't she?

"Thank you, Sir Golgorath."

"Just Rath, please. My given name is a tongue-tripper for humans, I have found, milady."

"Sir Rath, then." She confirmed his suspicions nicely. "And you must call me Cara." She hesitated when she caught sight of Tristan, but to her credit, she recovered quickly. "I'm sorry. I didn't know you already had company."

"The more the merrier, as they say." Rath tried to sound casual, though his heart was racing. Things were coming together and his future looked brighter than it had in many years.

"I don't mean to intrude. I just wanted to check on you and ask if there was anything you needed. Princess Belora left the salve for your burns with me and gave instructions on how and when to apply it. She said you would need some applied before you settled down to sleep."

As she came closer, he could see Cara was holding a large crock in the crook of her arm. Tristan stood to take the heavy item from her and Rath noted the way she blushed when their fingers touched. The attraction wasn't one-sided, Rath was glad to note. This was getting better and better. Now all they needed was one more element...

And he could hear wingbeats on the night wind. Any minute now, the last part of this little tableau would arrive.

Chapter Five

"Yes, some salve would be welcome," Rath answered. *"Perhaps Tristan could assist? It is not easy for one as petite as you to reach the area that needs to be treated, milady. He could help you up and hold the heavy crock."* Rath seemed to be laying it on a bit thick, but it wasn't Cara's place to question a dragon, even if it would put her in uncomfortable proximity to the Master at Arms.

Cara had loved the way Tristan had made her feel. But his rejection when he realized who she was still didn't sit well. She didn't give her favors easily. Usually, not at all. But there was something about the foreign warrior that called to her. Something that made her act out of character and climb into his bed when they had only just met.

Things between them had been strained ever since and she almost regretted the night they spent together. Almost. But she couldn't quite bring herself to regret such magnificent pleasure. Or the deep and abiding love she still held in her heart for the troubling man.

Following the dragon's instructions without any show of reluctance, Tristan helped her up behind Rath's wing. The dragon didn't make it easy for her to climb aboard, and she thought maybe it hurt for him to move. But Tristan put down the crock to slide his hands around her waist and boost her up. She balanced awkwardly over the dragon's back while Tristan bent to retrieve the crock of salve. He was only gone a moment.

Tristan was very close. Closer than he'd been in too long a time. As she worked on Rath's injuries, she could feel Tristan pressing against her legs and backside with his chest as he held her in place. He supported her with one hand, hoisting the crock upward with the other so it was within her reach. It was very intimate and reminded her of other, more sensuous touches. Her breathing hitched in her chest and she realized she needed to get herself under better control. She had to concentrate on the dragon. Sir Rath needed her help now.

"Sorry to interrupt." A familiar male voice sounded from the entrance, making Cara jump.

She lost her balance and fell backward into Tristan's arms. He grunted but managed to catch her. She heard the thump of the heavy crock of salve as it fell to the ground. Luckily, it hit a spot covered by soft pine boughs and didn't break. She saw it as they nearly overbalanced and she tipped a little too far forward and to the right.

Then more arms came out of the darkness to support her and she felt the warmth of the newly arrived man in front, with Tristan still holding her from behind.

Oh, boy.

Everybody froze for a moment as balance was restored. Equilibrium was another thing. Surrounded by two well-muscled warriors—both of whom she admired more than any other men she had ever met—Cara was more than a little breathless.

"My apologies, Lady Cara, I didn't mean to startle you." The deep voice came from the newcomer standing so close, facing her, his big hands bracing her arms.

His words seemed incredibly intimate, spoken in such a low, almost breathless tone. His grip went from bracingly supportive to gentle as she steadied, and his gaze held hers in a new and exciting way.

"Sir Thorn," she whispered. If Tristan had competition for her heart, this was the man. The only man besides the Master at Arms that she reacted to so strongly.

Tristan's arms relaxed, letting her slide a short distance down so that her backside rubbed along him until her feet settled on the floor. Only then did she realize how tall both men were compared to her. She looked upward to find that they were eyeing each other warily over her head.

But neither of them moved. They both seemed engaged in some kind of dominance game with her as the prize. One part of her thrilled at the idea, while another part of her wanted to laugh at their posturing. Although...maybe she wasn't giving either one of them enough credit. Maybe they were both trying to protect her from the other? That was very possible, given that both men were warriors who were in the business of protecting those more vulnerable than themselves.

And she was definitely vulnerable. If either one of these men ever crooked a finger in her direction, she'd follow wherever they led and damn the consequences. She would have worried about her morality, but in her entire life, only these two men had ever inspired such a heathenish response. She'd only had one other lover, and that a long time ago, when she was just a youngster experimenting with her blossoming body. She would cut any other man down who tried anything she didn't welcome—and had in the past.

But she knew the truth of her own responses, and if either Sir Thorn or Master Tristan invited her to their bedchamber, she'd probably jump the man and never look back. Quite a realization for a woman who prided herself on her independence.

"Sir Thorn." Tristan greeted the knight.

Thorn nodded. "Master Tristan."

Both men lowered their arms from around her, leaving her to sway slightly on her own feet. She steadied and then the men moved exactly one step away from her at the same time as if by some unspoken agreement. She noticed they didn't look at her, but kept their gazes locked on each other, a measuring look on each chiseled face.

Thorn had luscious light brown—almost golden—eyes that usually looked at her with warm amusement. They were speculative now, with a hard glint of anger. She could only guess at the challenge in Tristan's sky blue eyes. She'd seen him wither the keep's men at arms with a single glance and she had no doubt he was causing Thorn's strange reaction now. That had to be why they were eyeing each other over her shoulder. Simple male posturing. Right?

Then why did it feel like something altogether more thrilling? Cara had never been one to get excited by the idea of men fighting over her, and she wasn't about to start now, but there was something about this situation that made her little, female heart skip a beat.

"I'm sorry my arrival took you by surprise. I hope I'm not interrupting." Thorn looked down at her, speculation lighting his warm golden gaze.

"Master Tristan was helping me put the burn jelly salve on Sir Rath's wounds." She bent to retrieve the heavy crock which had landed slightly tilted in the pine boughs but thankfully had not broken or spilled any of its slippery contents.

Thorn looked from the crock to the dragon, then shot another undecipherable look at Tristan before turning back to her. She had no idea how to interpret his gaze. Was he upset? Was he amused? Angry? She really couldn't figure him out.

"We came to check on Rath and keep him company. My dragon partner, Lady Sharlis, wanted to see for herself how he was faring." Thorn stepped back and only then did Cara notice the female dragon who stood just outside the entrance.

Where Rath's scales were a pale, glimmering silver in color, the dragoness was a gleaming red, like the deepest embers of a flame. They made a striking pair together, though Rath was slightly larger. In fact, come to think of it, he seemed slightly larger than most of the dragons Cara had seen.

The dragoness craned her long neck through the curtain opening to twine slightly with Rath's. It was clear to Cara that the dragons were sharing a moment of greeting that went beyond mere friendship. They were in love. She could feel it in the air all around them and see it in the caring motions of the dragon's necks, smooth scales sliding against each other in a gentle caress.

"Let's give them a minute," Cara suggested, moving toward the entrance. She turned and fled, hoping the men would follow.

Sure enough, when she looked behind her, the two warriors were following a few paces behind. Neither of them made any noise. They were almost cat-like in their unconscious stealth, which impressed her. She'd tried to learn the art of moving silently when she learned swordwork and self-defense, but she wasn't a master of stealth by any means.

She walked to the nearby well and set the heavy crock down on top of a barrel that served as a tabletop. There were a few barrels of varying size ranged around the well, set in a semi-circle. She sat on top of one that was just the right height for sitting and waited for the men to catch up.

Tristan went straight to the well and began pulling up a bucket of water. He offered the cool refreshment to Cara and Thorn using the metal cup he'd found among the spare utensils and implements that sat in another bucket. The men didn't speak, which unnerved Cara a bit. What were they thinking? Were they still sizing each other up, thinking one or the other might be a threat to her in some way?

"I thought mated dragons had to have knights before they could be together," Cara asked Sir Thorn. She'd said the first thing she could think of to break the silence.

He sat atop a barrel near her and seemed to ponder her question before answering.

"Both dragons need knights and those knights need a wife before the dragons can consummate their bond. But both Sharlis and Rath are older dragons. They have been mates for centuries and have several offspring and grown grandchildren," he explained. "They have not been able to actually mate in several decades, but that doesn't mean they don't still love each other and long for the day they can be together again."

"But why? If they love each other..." Cara trailed off. She was probably being too outspoken—something her brother constantly chided her for.

"Because a knight's bond with his dragon partner is soul-deep. What one experiences, the other feels to a lesser extent. When the dragons mate, their knights feel it too." He shifted on his seat as if uncomfortable. "If the knights do not have a true mate with which to express the same kind of soul-deep love, it can drive them to insanity. That is why it is forbidden for the dragons to mate until the family unit is complete."

"Two knights and one woman? That is the normal family unit in your Lairs?" Tristan asked, seeming somewhat intrigued by the idea.

Thorn nodded slowly. "Two knights usually marry one woman, yes, but the family unit includes the dragons. Two sets of mates—one dragonish and one human. Five people living and working together, raising their offspring together. The dragons are second parents to the human children as the knights and their lady are to the dragonets. It is a beautiful arrangement that has worked well for fighting dragons and knights—and their ladies—for millennia here in Draconia. Since the time of Draneth the Wise."

"But why only one woman for two men? Are there ever times when each knight has a wife of their own?" Tristan wanted to know.

"It is rare for a woman to be able to live among dragonkind," Thorn explained. "Rarer still for a woman to have the gift of speech with our dragon partners. Some knights never find their mate and their dragons cannot consummate their bonds for centuries. It is sad, but an unfortunate reality for some of our number."

Silence reigned for a moment as they all seemed to ponder Sir Thorn's quiet words. Cara felt bad for those men who would never know the joy of sharing love with a partner. And the dragons that would have to wait so long before circumstances allowed them to join together in a mating flight.

"Lady Cara can hear Sir Rath when he speaks," Tristan said quietly. Shockingly.

Cara recalled what Sir Thorn had said about it being rare to be able to speak with dragons. She'd never been so close to a dragon before today. She hadn't really thought about what her being able to hear him might mean. What it *could* mean for her future.

Possibilities were opening up in her mind that gave her hope for the future for the first time since her father had fallen. Perhaps there was some way she could serve in one of the Lairs. Even if she didn't find a husband—or two!—among the knights, she still had skills that could prove useful to a Lair. If Envard continued to trouble her, she could always run away to the Border Lair and offer her services.

Sir Thorn's reaction to Tristan's hushed words was remarkable. He grew perfectly still except for his eyes. His gaze went from her to Tristan and back again with renewed suspicion but much less hostility. Instead, there was a sort of hopeful eagerness to the set of his broad shoulders that confused her. Maybe she wasn't reading him right. She didn't know him that well, after all.

"How do you know Lady Cara can hear Rath?" Thorn asked Tristan in a carefully modulated tone.

"He said so," Tristan answered as if it were obvious.

"And you heard him speak as well?" Thorn's gaze narrowed on Tristan as a strangely eager smile began to form at the corner of his mouth.

Tristan seemed to catch on to the knight's change in mood.

"It really is an oddity, then? Sir Rath said as much, but it is something most of my family is able to do."

"Talk to dragons?" Thorn seemed surprised.

"Not dragons, but small creatures in Elderland that seem to speak in the same way."

"Leave off for now, Thorn," came Rath's deep voice in all their minds. *"I have already settled the matter. Both Lady Cara and her Master at Arms can communicate with dragonkind."* He paused as all three humans turned to look at the dragons across the open space of the yard. The two dragons sat side by side now, both squeezed into the small enclosure that was just big enough for them. *"Raises some interesting possibilities, does it not?"*

"Indeed." Thorn rose from his seated position and offered a hand to Cara. She took it and allowed him to escort her back to the dragons. "Lady Cara, this is my dragon partner, Lady Sharlis."

He made the introduction as Cara bowed to the seated dragoness, holding her gaze in respect, as was only polite. "It is an honor to meet you, Lady Sharlis."

"The honor is mine, Lady Cara," the dragoness answered in her mind. Her voice was slightly different than Rath's. More feminine in some way, or maybe Cara was letting her

imagination run wild. *"Thank you for helping Golgorath and for constructing this fine shelter for him."* The dragoness cocked her large head so she could look from the curtained entryway to the heavy canvas ceiling. *"This arrangement shows you put great thought into his comfort and for that I thank you."*

"It was my pleasure," Cara answered softly, feeling the true joy of having the dragoness's approval. It meant more than she could say. "If there is anything else I can do to make his stay more comfortable, please do not hesitate to ask. The resources of the keep—such as they are—are at his disposal."

"I could use more salve on my wing joint," Rath's voice reminded her. A smoky chuckle accompanied his words. *"It was just starting to penetrate when you left off."*

"Oh! I'm sorry!" Cara looked around for the crock she had placed on the barrel by the well, but Tristan had it in one of his big hands. He'd apparently had the presence of mind to bring it with them when they walked back to the dragon enclosure.

Cara tried to take the crock from him, but he gestured instead for her to precede him back into the enclosure. It was a much tighter squeeze now with two dragons taking up the space she'd intended for one, but she managed to get back in position behind Rath's wing.

She heard a bit of jostling behind her and realized both men were trying to fit into the limited space to assist her. Both of them were large—too large to fit in here with her and two full-grown dragons. Cara rolled her eyes, wondering why they would nearly come to blows over something so mundane, but the dragons stepped in and put an end to it.

"Thorn, be gracious. Let the outlander help her. Otherwise my poor Rath will suffer all night with no salve on his wounds." Lady Sharlis's voice in Cara's mind sounded wryly amused.

Sir Thorn gave in, but not entirely graciously. He leaned back against the tall pole that held up the canvas roof at the corner of the enclosure and watched as Tristan wrapped his hands around her waist and hoisted her halfway up the dragon's back once more. She thought maybe she only imagined that Tristan's hands stayed on her backside a bit longer this time.

Chapter Six

Thorn came straight out and asked his dragon partner the question burning a hole in his mind. *"Shar, is Rath thinking of making this outlander a knight by any chance?"*

He was careful to do it in the privacy of only his and the female dragon's minds. Nobody else was able to eavesdrop on the incredibly tight bond between their two souls.

"Even you have to admit, it would be the perfect solution," she replied, one jewel-like eye blinking lazily as she watched the two humans see to her mate's wounds. *"Do you like the girl? She seems nice. And has some backbone despite the fact she was raised as a keep lady. Rath says she rides to battle with her soldiers and fights alongside them from horseback with spear and sword. She has some skill, he told me. And is smart enough to realize she is not and should not be a leader of men. She defers to the Master at Arms, allowing him to lead the battle charge and defensive strategy. He commands on the field of battle, not she, despite her higher social rank. She does not seem to stand on ceremony, and unlike many silly girls raised in these cloistered keeps, she does not seem to have an overinflated opinion of her own worth."*

"That's a lot of observation, Shar, but to answer your question, I do like her. A great deal, as a matter of fact." Thorn could not keep his eyes from the small human woman tending to the huge dragon. *"You probably noticed that I volunteered to come to this keep more than any other. It's not just because I have some suspicions about the young lord. I admit, it was to see Lady Cara, even if nothing could ever come of it."*

"*But it appears now that something could definitely come of your attraction to the girl. She can hear us when we speak to her, Thorn. You know how rare that is.*" Sharlis blinked, casting her gaze on Thorn and then back to Lady Cara. "*If you do not see the hand of the Mother of All in this, then you are being deliberately dense. You are attracted to her. And she is attracted to you too, if the way she was stammering and blushing is any indication. Plus, there is this startling outlander...*" Shar's voice trailed off as she moved her gaze to the man standing so close—too close—behind Lady Cara.

"*Is he truly worthy of being Rath's knight?*" That was the crux of the matter. If Tristan was not pure of heart and strong of character, this arrangement would never work.

"*Rath is beginning to believe so, though he will probably observe the man further before making the decision. You must remember what happened last time. My mate is perhaps overly cautious, but I do not blame him. The pain of losing one's knight is not something I can explain in words. I have felt it myself, and I do not wish that agony on my beloved again too soon.*"

Only rarely did the dragoness speak to him of the knights that had come before him. Sharlis had lived for many centuries already. She was a seasoned veteran and one of the wisest beings Thorn knew. She was the sister to his soul—an older, wiser sister who shared both her laughter and her experience with him in the here and now. She did not dwell on the past, though of course everyone in the Lair knew the story of poor Faedric and Rath's grief over his loss.

"*How can Rath think to put such faith in a warrior who was not born in this land? From everything I have heard, this Tristan is new here. He has no loyalty to us—dragon or human. How can that work? How can he be a knight to dedicate his life to defending Draconia?*"

"*Sometimes it is enough to dedicate one's life to defending the innocent and the true—those who are firmly on the side of light and life, and goodness, and what is right. These are the qualities my mate is beginning to see in this warrior. Although he may have been born in a strange land, he's a good man."* Shar blinked and settled her gaze on Tristan again. *"Rath was telling me a little bit about why Tristan left his homeland. I will not betray confidences, but I will say that he is much more than he seems. More than he even believes of himself."*

Thorn was impressed. *"Rath got that much from a single battle and a few words spoken between them this day?"*

"When something is meant to be, youngster, you will find that things can fall together into place quickly and with little fuss. Not everything in life has to be a struggle. Sometimes the best things in life come to us easily. It is for us to accept the goodness that comes when we least expect it and recognize the opportunities when they present themselves—for they seldom come again. Much of the quality of our lives is all about timing."

Thorn thought about the dragoness's words for a long moment as he watched Lady Cara finish with the worst of the wounds on one wing joint, then move on to the less serious venom burns. Tristan's hands and body held her in place and he did not imagine the tingle of attraction in the air between them. She was drawn to the outlander and he to her. Thorn didn't know whether to be jealous or content.

"They say he is quite a warrior," Thorn offered, hoping to rekindle the conversation and willing to listen to his fighting partner's sage advice. *"I've heard more than one man say that Tristan is the best Master at Arms this keep has seen in many a year. They seem to universally respect him, which is rare when an outsider comes in to take over an established group."*

"True," the dragoness agreed. *"But even the dragons are talking about his actions on the field of battle today. Rath may just owe the Master at Arms his life. The creature that bestowed those terrible burns could easily have done much more damage had not Master Tristan intervened."*

"Did he really kill a skith all by himself? Did you get the story from Rath?"

"Oh, he did it all right. In a most unconventional manner. Rath told me that Tristan climbed on top of the skith and sank one of his swords right into the creature's puny brain."

"That must have been a sight to see." Thorn kept the whistle of admiration to himself.

"Of that I have no doubt. The fact is, we all owe him a debt of gratitude for his actions today."

"Making him a knight goes far beyond gratitude, Shar." The skepticism in his tone could not be hidden from his fighting partner.

Smoky circles of her amusement drifted toward the heavy canvas ceiling far above. Tristan and Lady Cara didn't seem to notice. They were too wrapped up in each other. Or perhaps that was Thorn's jaded opinion. Perhaps the lady was concentrating on helping her over-large patient, but there was no doubt in Thorn's mind that Tristan's thoughts were firmly on the softly rounded backside presented so appealingly, right in front of his face.

"Time will tell what, if anything, Master Tristan is destined to become. If I were a betting dragon, my money would be on him, though. This situation smacks of the Goddess's involvement. I have seen it many times before in my centuries. The Mother of All has a great deal to do with affairs of the heart and family bonds in the Lairs of Draconia."

Thorn kept his thoughts about Cara's noble family carefully to himself. He had an inkling that not everything was as it should be between her and her brother. He hadn't liked the way Envard treated her, even in the presence of visitors. Something was seriously wrong there and Thorn had been quietly trying to discover exactly what it was for some time, to no avail.

Now that Envard was injured, though, he might have more luck. For one thing, Envard wasn't able to deny Thorn access to the keep's archives now that he was stuck in bed. Thorn decided to have a look at what he might be able to find in the records at his earliest convenience.

Thorn was good at ferreting out secrets and he'd solved more than one mystery by careful study of old, forgotten records. He'd wanted to see what he could dig up at Fadoral Keep for a long time and finally had an opportunity to search without impediment. He would make the most of his time here while the young lord was incapacitated.

Lady Cara finished her task and Master Tristan helped her down, his hands lingering on her trim waist perhaps a fraction too long, but Thorn couldn't fault him. If it had been Thorn with his hands around the lovely lady, he would probably have pressed his advantage much further by now. All in all, Thorn had to admit Tristan treated Lady Cara as fine as any noble gentlemen—or any knight of the realm, for that matter.

Cara was well on her way to being overwhelmed by the two men. They were both huge and muscular, taking up far too much space in the increasingly small enclosure. Tristan was at her back, walking close behind her as she left the narrow space between the two dragons.

She could feel not only the heat generated by the dragons, but also the warmth of Tristan that seemed to surround her from behind. He smelled good too. Like leather and the pleasantly fragrant oil he used on his blades. It was something he'd brought with him from his homeland and the scent intrigued her almost as much as he did.

Sir Thorn waited in front of her. There was no way out except by passing very close to him. He didn't seem inclined to move either, which made her excitedly wary. Why wouldn't he shift to let her pass? What was he up to?

The moment of truth was at hand. She'd walked as far as she could without brushing past Sir Thorn and he hadn't moved. She stopped, looking up into his golden eyes, surprised to find a teasing sort of arousal in his gaze. Was she reading him right? Was he truly interested in her? And why now—with Tristan halted only inches from her back?

Thorn stood from his leaning position and faced her. They were very close now and when Thorn moved, Tristan had followed suit. She was sandwiched between the two big men, confused by their actions. Were they competing over her in some way? She didn't think it likely. Even though she and Tristan had spent one amazing night together, he'd been studious in avoiding her presence except in extraordinary circumstances. In fact, he'd made her feel as if he regretted the incident, which broke her heart a little.

Sir Thorn, on the other hand, had been nothing but friendly to her. Although she often got the impression he liked her, he had never taken it any farther. He'd never kissed her. Not even on the cheek. He'd never sought her out to be alone with her on the many visits he'd made to the keep. He'd been pleasant, but he hadn't once given her any indication that he might be interested in something more than friendship.

Until tonight.

"Thank you for taking such good care of Rath," Thorn said in a low, intimate tone she had never heard from him before.

"It's my pleasure to be of service to him," she replied, somewhat formally. Thorn was standing much too close and Tristan was mirroring him behind her.

Thorn moved even closer and she backed up—right into Tristan. His hands went to her hips to steady her and...stayed there. She liked the warm feel of his big hands on her hips, but she couldn't concentrate with Thorn moving in even closer.

"What are you doing?" she asked, breathless.

"Yes," Tristan added over her shoulder. "What *are* you doing, Sir Thorn? Cara is a lady and I will defend her honor even against a knight of the realm."

She heard the anger and confusion in Tristan's voice, near her ear. He sounded firm and challenging, though clearly puzzled by the strange turn of events. Goddess help her, the closeness of the two men was working on her senses. If either one wanted to have her at this very moment, she would be powerless to resist. In fact, she wouldn't even want to resist.

"Are you drunk?" Tristan added, almost as an afterthought.

"Not drunk, Master Tristan. Merely...curious," Thorn said, adding to her confusion. The heat of his body in front and Tristan from behind was making her giddy.

"What are you curious about that you would accost Lady Cara in this way?" Tristan demanded, a bit more anger showing.

"I am curious about something Sharlis told me earlier. You can both hear the dragons when they speak. And it's clear to me that we are both attracted to the lovely Cara. Are we not, Master Tristan?" He paused, raising one brow as he posed the rhetorical question. Tristan didn't answer, but she heard a slight gulp as he swallowed hard behind her. "I think perhaps the lady is drawn to both of us as well." One of his eyebrows rose in speculation, but he didn't push her for an answer, thank goodness. "It is just possible that all of us can have what we want."

"I do not understand," Tristan said after a moment.

In that moment of silence, Cara thought she understood what Sir Thorn was driving at and the very idea made her mouth go dry. The thoughts raised by his words both tantalized and confused her. She couldn't have spoken, even if she'd wanted to. As it was, she was dumbfounded by the idea that the dragoness had been discussing such intimate matters with her knight.

Cara had to take a couple of deep breaths to help her gather her wits. But every time she breathed in, she was engulfed in the delicious essences of the two men, blending together into something so intriguing and sublime that she was hard pressed to think clearly.

She had to dig deep to find her courage. The same courage she'd had to encourage within herself to go out to battle with the soldiers of her brother's keep. That very same courage would help her now. If she was going to deal with these two men at all in the future, she had to assert herself now or they'd run roughshod over her forever. Just as Envard did. And that she would not allow.

"Sir Thorn," she began in as strong a voice as she could muster. She was proud of herself when it didn't quaver. His eyes narrowed as he gazed at her, seeming intrigued by what she might say. That was a good start. "I do not think my brother would consent to such a union."

"Is that your only objection?" His voice dropped to low, husky tones as he smiled at her.

"What union? What are you two talking about?" Tristan groused from behind.

But Thorn wasn't listening. He wasn't even waiting for Cara's answer. His head dipped lower and then his lips met hers in their first kiss. It was delicious and mysterious, hinting at more than she had ever dreamed of. Her blood heated with his nearness and the rough feel of his beard stubble against her skin.

It took her out of time. Out of place. He made her feel as if all was suddenly right in her world.

But it couldn't last.

Tristan's hands tightened on her waist and pulled her sharply backward, away from Thorn.

It was the wrong move. Her defensive training kicked in and she delivered a sharp elbow jab to the midsection of the man *attacking* her from behind. At least, that's how her cloudy mind perceived the action.

Tristan gave voice to a huge *oof* of mixed surprise and pain. He backed up, doubling over as Cara realized what she'd done.

Thorn was laughing at Tristan's predicament, which made her feel ridiculous. Anger swept in to replace embarrassment as she pushed her way past Thorn, out into the dark night.

Chapter Seven

"Very smooth, gentlemen," Rath commented dryly, sending rings of smoky amusement wafting toward the ceiling.

"Why did you molest her in that fashion? I fail to understand this land or its people." Tristan shook his head, his breath returning after the wallop Cara had delivered, which had knocked the wind from him.

He remained slightly bent at the waist, one hand rubbing his abused midsection as he looked up at the knight and dragon. He'd been alarmed at Thorn's actions—and even more alarmed when watching the other man kiss her brought a wave of sexual excitement the likes of which he'd never known before. Something was happening here. Something he didn't understand. It was as if he was operating with only half the information he needed, something any good battle commander would not—and should not—tolerate.

Thorn gave a long sigh before answering. "That could have gone better," he seemed to remark to himself. Tristan didn't like the long, lingering look the other man gave Cara's retreating back. "I'm sorry, my friend. You took the brunt of my bungling attempt to find out if she was receptive." Thorn clapped Tristan on the shoulder, surprising him.

"Receptive to what? A bad attempt at romance? You should have waited until you were alone. Or not done it at all. Can't you see you've upset her?" Tristan was getting angrier by the moment. "Why would you do that in front of me?"

Thorn turned and gave him a speculative look Tristan didn't quite understand. "To see if you were open to it as well."

"I repeat—open to what?" Anger was coming much closer to the surface. The knight had better start explaining his cryptic words soon or Tristan was going to beat some sense into the man—knight of the realm or not.

"To sharing," Rath said abruptly, bringing Tristan's focus to the dragon.

"Sharing? Sharing what?" It took him only a moment to draw some startling conclusions. "You don't mean..." Tristan was scandalized, but if he was being honest, he was also aroused by what had just happened and what these two Draconians were hinting at.

"Sharing her life with you and Thorn. And with us. So we can all be a family," Rath said, twining his neck with the dragoness's in a clear display of affection.

"You've made your decision, then?" Thorn addressed the dragon directly, bypassing Tristan, who still didn't understand exactly what was going on here. He had thought he'd figured out the strange way Draconians used language, but apparently he still had a lot to learn. These people were talking in circles!

"Truth be told, the decision was made when he climbed up that skith's back and showed more bravery and skill than any warrior I have ever beheld." Rath's voice sounded warm as the dragon referred to Tristan's actions that very afternoon. But other than that, he was still having a hard time following the conversation. The dragon turned his large head, untwining his neck from that of his mate and bending low to meet Tristan's gaze directly. *"I have been searching for a warrior of great skill, with a pure heart and the willingness to sacrifice of himself for others. Your actions today and the magic that rises when a dragon seeks a knight show me that you are that man. If you can forever put aside your homeland and make your life here in Draconia, swearing allegiance to our king and people, I will*

217

choose you as my knight partner, to share my life and that of my family for the rest of your days."

Tristan couldn't believe what he was hearing. Or feeling. The dragon's warm magic rose up and surrounded him for a moment, giving him a glimpse of what his life here, with these people, could be like. So different from the lonely path he had envisioned for himself—and very like the promises his prophetess sister had made of the life he could find when he left Elderland. Could it be true? Could he have such a rich and fulfilling life? Tristan hadn't dared believe it could be so.

"I have already given up all claims to the throne of my homeland and severed all ties with my family in a formal ceremony before I left. It is as if I was never born to that family or Clan. I am alone... I thought I would remain alone for all my days, wandering without a home." Tears formed in Tristan's eyes as he spoke the words straight from his heart, somehow drawn to the surface by the dragon's magic. Tristan knew only the dragon's jeweled gaze and the connection he could already feel tentatively forming between their souls. "What you offer seems like a dream, Sir Rath." His voice dropped to a whisper.

The dragon nodded. *"A dream of the best kind. One that can come true, if you agree."*

"I admit, my grasp of your use of language is poorer than I thought. If I agree to be your knight, what must I do in return? It seems as if I gain much more than you do from this arrangement." Tristan's early training in diplomacy prodded him to ask the particulars before consenting to anything.

"You agree to serve Draconia for the rest of your days as my knight. In due course, Sharlis and I would like to resume our relationship. That means you and Thorn will have to convince a woman—Lady Cara, if my senses do not deceive me—to marry you both and share your lives." Rath nodded his big head toward where Cara had disappeared into the front door of the keep. *"Your life will be filled with joy and hardship. Happiness*

and sorrow. Just as all other people's lives. The only difference is that you will be part of a Lair family, living among warriors, fighting alongside other knights and dragons, and sharing your mate with Thorn. We will raise any young—human child or dragonet—together. You will live out your life with us as part of a much larger family and Draconia will be your home for the rest of your days."

Tristan was nearly bowled over at the idea. Shocked and hopeful. Could he really have what the dragon described? Did he dare accept?

"May I have time to think about all you have said?" Tristan asked, stalling. He could not make such a leap without thinking it through—and at least talking to Lady Cara.

He did not want to leave the keep if she did not come with him. From the moment he'd first seen her, he'd vowed to protect her. The new lord was not kind to his sister and Tristan would not leave her without a champion if she decided to stay.

"As you wish. I will be here, healing for a few days. Thorn and Sharlis will stay as long as they can. Perhaps Thorn can give you a better idea of what being a knight is all about from the human perspective." Rath bowed his head and broke the connection that held Tristan in place. He seemed disappointed, which made Tristan feel bad, but there was little he could do about it at the moment.

"Come, Master Tristan," Thorn said, grasping Tristan's shoulder and guiding him toward the keep. "Let's find a cask of wine and a quiet corner to discuss this. If we are to be fighting partners, we should get to know each other better."

Feeling somewhat bewildered by all that had just happened, Tristan allowed the knight to usher him out of the dragons' enclosure. He had a great deal to think about and Thorn's suggestion of wine and conversation would be welcome to help Tristan sort out his thoughts and questions about the dragon's offer.

Cara ran back into the keep and up to her room without looking back. The men had confused her and yes, she would admit to a bit of fear. Not fear of *them*, per se, but more a fear of what her future might hold. Did she dare dream of a different future than the one Envard had planned for her? Could she really escape the bonds of being a keep-bred noblewoman and grab the life she wanted with both hands? Or would it be denied her? Again.

She had already stretched the bounds of the precisely prescribed borders of her life. Her father had indulged her—over her brother's objections. She'd been allowed to learn to fight and ride alongside the men. Envard hadn't liked it and took every opportunity to try to cut her down to size. He didn't realize his constant teasing and testing had only made her want to be better and try harder.

She was a better warrior than Envard, at any rate. He'd fallen in his first battle after their father died. It was for the lord of the keep to lead the charge and he'd done so to disastrous effect. His first battle as lord and he'd been knocked off his horse, unable to rise. His only bit of good fortune was that he hadn't died. He had a very serious leg wound that kept him abed, but that wouldn't last forever.

Cara's short days of respite would come to an end when her brother rose from his sickbed. She wouldn't be allowed to ride with the soldiers anymore and Envard would probably send her packing as soon as he could sign a marriage contract on her behalf. He wouldn't let her choose the man he sold her to. For that's what it was. He would sell her off to some old man in exchange for lands or goods or whatever he could gain from the match.

He'd have to send a dowry, but Fadoral Keep had riches to spare. What they needed was land and people to work it. Land away from the border would be preferable and there were quite a few lords on adjacent holdings looking for suitable brides. Envard wouldn't care if she liked her husband or not. He'd sell her to whoever offered him the best deal.

Cara couldn't stand the thought of it.

But could she become a knight's lady? Could she handle all that implied? Frankly, she wasn't sure.

She loved the dragons, but the idea of having not one, but two husbands, filled her with trepidation. She wasn't naïve. She knew what went on between a man and woman. She'd enjoyed her one night with Tristan and longed for more. But being with two men at once was beyond her.

The idea did fire her imagination though. She was attracted to both Thorn and Tristan. She'd fantasized about both of them—the one she'd been with and the one who was forever out of reach. But those fantasies had never starred both men at the same time.

Troubled dreams of the two men followed her into sleep and didn't let up until morning. She woke tired, with a headache that didn't bode well for the rest of her day. Things only got worse when she went to check on Envard, to find him sitting up, eating a huge breakfast. He was clear of the fever that had plagued him, on the mend and apparently eager to start running her life again.

"Where have you been?" His tone was accusatory and he didn't wait for her to reply. "I want an accounting of the battles since I was injured. Why hasn't the Master at Arms been delivering reports to me?"

"You were gravely ill, Brother," she reminded him. He was always more unreasonable when he was sick.

"That means nothing. He should have been giving me daily reports at the very least. I have sent for him and will sack him if his words are not to my liking." Now he sounded petulant. Oh dear. It was going to be one of those mornings.

"If you sack him, the keep will be overrun in less than a fortnight," she muttered, taking the dishes he'd already discarded and stacking them on a table by the door.

"Don't think I didn't hear that!" he yelled at her back. "And don't you dare to question my decisions. I am lord here."

His tirade was preempted by the entry of a grim-faced Tristan into the room. She was glad of the reprieve, but she didn't want there to be a confrontation as a result of her back talk to the brother that despised her. She didn't want Tristan to suffer because of her.

"My apologies, Brother. You are right, of course."

He pushed his tray away, not caring that the costly dishes clanked and could have broken at the violent treatment. She rushed to take the tray before he did real damage to her mother's prized tableware.

"Damn right, I'm right. And you best remember it...for the short time you have left here." He sneered at her and she felt pain in her heart at the obvious hatred in his gaze.

Had he ever loved her as a sister? She thought not and regretted it bitterly. She would have liked to have been able to lean on a sibling. Instead, she'd been shunned by him at every turn since their father's death.

"My lord," Tristan interrupted, stepping between her and Envard's glare.

"Where in the hells have you been? You should have been reporting to me all along." It seemed Envard's wrath had a new target.

"I have attempted to speak to you every day since your injury, milord. You have been out of your mind with fever and speaking incoherently for the most part. The healers advised me to leave you be until your fever broke. I am glad to see that it has." Tristan's delivery was rapid fire and matter of fact. He didn't give Envard a moment to get a word in and Cara had to admire the way he managed him. As if he'd been dealing with difficult people in positions of power for a long time. "Now," Tristan went on, unrolling a large, deerskin map of the border. "We need to discuss the attacks since you were injured. There appears to be a pattern. I have conferred with Sir Thorn on this matter in your absence and he agrees. The news is troubling indeed."

That was the first she'd heard of a pattern and she wanted desperately to stay and listen, but another glare from Envard made it clear she was to leave. Cara gathered the discarded dishes and made her way to the door, not sparing a glance for Tristan. If Envard caught her looking at the Master at Arms, he might see something she'd rather he not be aware of.

She made a hasty exit, only to find Sir Thorn waiting in the hallway for her. He took the tray of dishes before they overbalanced and toppled to the stone floor. He had surprised her and saved the day once again.

"Thank you, Sir Thorn." She tried not to sound breathless and failed. He made her nervous...in an exciting sort of way.

"Can I help you with these?" he asked, holding up the heavily laden tray.

"I wouldn't dream of keeping you. Don't you have to go in and talk strategy with my brother and Master Tristan?" She reached out to take it back from him, but he would not let go.

"I am at your disposal, milady. Lord Envard can wait. Tristan will keep him busy while I discuss matters with you. We tossed a coin for it and I won." His smile was sly, and very flattering. "Now, were you heading toward the kitchens, perhaps?" He motioned toward the hallway.

"Well...yes." She didn't really understand what was going on here between the two men.

"Then I will accompany you there, if I may and then perhaps we can talk, if you are agreeable." He was pleasant and almost gallant with his request. She couldn't say no.

So they walked together toward the kitchens, speaking of nothing in particular until Thorn commented on the dishes.

"These ceramics are quite fine. I have not seen their like outside the palace."

"They were my mother's," she admitted shyly. "One of the few things I have left from her."

Thorn's face grew concerned. "She was taken from you and Envard too young," he said in a kind voice.

"Oh, Envard's mother was our father's second wife. We are not full siblings. My mother died when I was born. Father remarried four years later and Envard was born about eight months after that. Perhaps that's why..." She trailed off, realizing she was about to say something indelicate. She should not speak openly about the distance between her and Envard. It wasn't seemly.

"I'm sorry. I didn't know Lord Harald had been married twice. My sympathies on the loss of your mother." His voice was quiet, seeming truly regretful and it touched her deeply.

"I never knew her, and Father did not speak of her often. She left a few things to me. The porcelain is one. Father never used it, but Envard ordered all his meals served on it the moment Father died." She bit back the anger at her brother's selfish insistence. She cringed every time he treated the precious plates roughly and he seemed to do it on purpose, just to needle her.

Thorn looked pained by her words, but let them pass as they entered the kitchen. He placed the tray gently on the countertop nearest the sink and the scullery maid blushed as he gave her a smile. She liked the way he treated the servants— like people, not like lower life forms. Her brother had been abusing the household staff since he was old enough to speak, though their father apparently never saw it.

"My mother was Princess Jala of the House of Jirand," Cara revealed. It felt good to speak of her mother. Envard had practically forbidden all talk of the woman who came before his own mother. It was freeing to speak of her openly and it warmed her heart just to say her name.

Even such a simple thing as speaking her mother's name was yet another thing Envard had denied her.

Chapter Eight

"You are of royal blood?" Thorn seemed shocked...and happy?

"Only on my mother's side. It's not something we talk about. I guess things would have been different had she lived."

Thorn's arm came around her shoulders and gave her a comforting squeeze. "Knowing this, I now understand a little more about our situation. It is no wonder you can hear dragons speak. You are part dragon yourself."

"Part dragon?" She really didn't understand. He'd walked her to a quiet corner of the large kitchen while they talked and pulled out a chair for her, seating her before he continued.

"All those of royal blood share the lineage of Draneth the Wise. You are all half-dragon and half-human, created that way to rule over both dragons and humans in our land. I can only guess that your mother would have taught you all about your heritage had you been given the chance to know her."

"There's a lot I don't know about her," Cara admitted.

"We will do our best to reconnect you with your cousins if you wish, Lady Cara. By rights, you are Princess Cara," he said with a grin, surprising her. "You are of the royal blood. Normal rules of inheritance do not count in such cases. All those descended of Draneth are considered royal."

"I didn't realize that." He'd given her a great deal to think about. Had Envard known? She thought he probably had. Maybe that's why he disliked her so much.

"Princess, there is much for us to speak about, but first, I want you to know how much I've always admired you. I was not free to speak before, but with the many changes that have occurred since yesterday, I begin to think the Mother of All is surely guiding our paths in this case. Shar and Rath think so too." He spoke in a quiet voice that calmed her, even as his nearness excited her. "I also must apologize for my behavior last night. I was very clumsy and I am sorry if I frightened you."

Cara knew her fair skin was glowing red with her blushes. She hadn't really been frightened by his advances last night. She knew he would never hurt her. She'd been confused. Needy. And a little shocked by the implications.

"Tristan and I had a long talk last night after you ran off," Thorn continued when she said nothing—not knowing how to answer. "He suggested a calmer approach, which is why I wanted to talk to you." He reached across the small table at which they sat and took one of her hands in his, surprising her, but not unpleasantly. "Lady Cara—Princess—I have admired you for a long time. I angled to get the patrols that would take me over your keep so I could see you, even if I felt at the time that I could never act on my feelings. I had hoped you'd noticed me too. Am I vain in thinking that perhaps you did?"

His teasing smile and the way his warm hand squeezed her fingers gently made her smile, even as her blush increased. She couldn't lie to the man. Not when he held her hand and looked so charming.

"I confess I did, Sir Thorn," she whispered. "But you never approached me," she dared to say.

"I felt I could not. Since the moment I agreed to be Sharlis's partner, I knew that whatever relationship I pursued it would not be a traditional one. Understand me—I have never regretted becoming a knight. It is my honor and my joy to share Sharlis's life and live in the Lair. But I have always had reservations about asking a woman—particularly one of your gentle

227

Bianca D'Arc

upbringing—to accept the lifestyle we must have. Not that there's anything wrong when three people share their lives and love binds their union. It's just that it can be a shock to a gently reared woman to contemplate such a marriage."

Cara decided it was time to find her backbone. "I confess it is a shock. And if you are asking me to consider it, you should say so straight out, Sir Thorn." There. That sounded better. She could see his eyes sparkle as if in approval and it gave her even more strength to speak her mind. "I was raised a lady, but you have seen for yourself that I am not quite the traditional keep lady. I fight alongside the men and acquit myself well. I am equally at home with a blade or a ladle in my hand. And I am not completely ignorant of the goings on between men and women. I admit that the thought of two men in my life instead of the single husband I was always led to believe I would have is both scary...and tantalizing. I'm not sure how it can work, but if the two men you are asking me to consider are yourself and Master Tristan..." She trailed off, the blush returning to heat her cheeks.

She lowered her eyes, but Thorn reached out to place a finger under her chin, raising her head playfully as he smiled at her. She met his gaze and all was right with the world. He didn't condemn her words or bold manner. Instead, his gaze glowed with approval and pride. It made her feel stronger.

"I am asking you to consider sharing your life with me. And with Tristan. If he agrees to be Rath's knight, he and I will be fighting partners. We will share our lives and our wife. It is my fondest wish that you be that wife, for I have loved you from afar too long. The idea that you could finally be mine makes me impatient for Tristan to give in and agree to Rath's claim."

"Sir Rath said the words of Claim to Tristan?" This was news to her.

She might not know a lot about dragons, but everyone in Draconia knew about how knights were made. The dragons

228

would speak words of Claim—though she didn't know what the actual words were—and the knight would agree, and a lifelong partnership would be made.

"Not the exact words." Thorn shook his head. "But he asked Tristan to consider it, spelling out all it would mean. I had hoped Tris would jump at the chance, but he is a cautious man. He asked for time and Rath agreed. I think a large part of his trepidation is you, Cara. He intimated to me last night that he would refuse if it meant you would be left here without a champion. I got the impression that your brother doesn't treat you well." Thorn's brows lowered in concern. "I had no idea, Cara. I did not see any evidence of it in all my visits, but I heard how Envard spoke to you this morning. Has he always treated you with such contempt?"

"We haven't really gotten along since we were children, but it only got bad after Father died," she admitted. It felt good to tell Thorn about it. She'd been so isolated at the keep since her father's passing.

Both of Thorn's warm hands clasped hers, surrounding them in his warmth.

"Cara, my dear, I am truly sorry for what you have suffered. I want you to think about coming away with me to the Border Lair, even if this doesn't work out between us. I want you to be safe and happy. As a princess of royal blood, you will always have a home among dragonfolk. You have a choice should you want to leave here, even if you don't want to marry us, and I will help you all I can. This I vow."

"Oh, Thorn." Her voice broke as emotion nearly overcame her. He was so earnest. He offered her a way out of the nightmare her brother intended for her future.

Thorn came around the corner of the small table and drew her into his arms, seating her on his lap as he took her chair. He held her close, her head tucked under his chin as he rocked her. Emotion threatened to overwhelm her for a long moment,

229

but she held it together. When she looked up at him, moving back slightly, time stretched as their eyes met and held.

She didn't know who moved first, but the kiss they shared was one of welcome, of hope and of deep, abiding passion. She loved the way his lips claimed hers, gently but with an authority she could not deny. He owned her in that moment of timeless beauty, claimed her and enthralled her. All with a single world-altering kiss.

"Damn." Tristan's amused voice drew her out of the fog of pleasure Thorn had created around them. "I've never been sorrier to lose a coin toss."

Cara was shocked by the heat in Tristan's gaze as he caught her on the lap of the knight. He seemed more amused and envious than anything else, which surprised her. He'd snapped at men at arms who dared glance at her with more than bland interest. And after last night's strange confrontation, she hadn't quite expected Tristan to be so accepting of finding her kissing Thorn.

Thorn seemed to become aware of their location and he stood, gently placing her back on her own chair.

"My apologies, Princess. I didn't mean to kiss you in such a public place. Forgive me."

Cara looked around and noticed the attention they were drawing from the few servants in the kitchen. Luckily, all were long-serving women she counted as friends. They would not speak of this where her brother might hear.

"It's all right. These women can be trusted with my secrets. I've known most of them since I was old enough to toddle into the kitchen to beg for treats." She smiled at the memory and noted that the cook was smiling back, delight on her old, lined face.

"Regardless..." Thorn offered her his hand, helping her to rise from her chair. "I would not have you be the subject of gossip. Let us adjourn this conversation to somewhere more private."

"Conversation," Tristan mused as they walked out the kitchen door, Thorn and Cara in front, Tristan bringing up the rear. "Is that what they call it in this land? I surely need to study your language more."

All three of them laughed as they entered the main hall. Thorn only slowed when they reached the giant door that led to the entryway.

"Where to?" Thorn asked.

She tried to think of a place all three of them could be seen entering without causing tongues to wag. She couldn't take them to her room. Someone would surely see and it might get back to her brother.

"Follow me," Tristan said, taking the lead out the door and into the courtyard, surprising her.

He led them to the armory, a locked room that held all the weapons. Nobody who saw her enter there would be surprised. She often worked on broken lacings and made minor repairs to things like chainmail and leatherwork. Everyone in the keep knew of her interest in the fighting arts.

Tristan closed and barred the door behind them after they'd entered, then turned to regard her with a penetrating stare. Thorn had left her standing by the long bench that ran the length of the room, then turned to light the lamps. There was no window in the armory and no other entrance. It was a secure room with walls lined with armor and weapons of every kind.

"Now, Lady Cara," Tristan began, stalking toward her on silent feet, holding her gaze all the while. "We have much to discuss. Your brother, as you no doubt know, has plans to marry you off as soon as possible to the very disagreeable Lord Vron of Hester."

"Lord Vron?" she asked with dismay. The man was old enough to be her father.

"He confirmed it to me just now. The discussions are already open and your brother is inclined to agree. But I have other plans," he said, surprising her yet again. "Has the knight told you of your options?"

"Thorn said I would be welcome in the Lair, either on my own merit or as...your wife," she said, uncertainty creeping into her voice. She hadn't had time to think about any of this. Her head was telling her to be cautious while her body was counseling her to throw caution to the wind and jump them both before they changed their minds.

Tristan halted before her, his golden eyes glowing with arousal. "If you think you can live your days as part of a triad, I will agree to be a knight. If you wish to remain single, I will follow wherever you go as your champion." He slid one arm around her waist and drew close, his gaze holding hers. "I will never leave you unprotected, Cara. Even if we are not together as lovers. But I tell you this now...if you agree to be with us, I will never let you go. I did it once. Never again. I have not the strength."

His forehead rested against hers as he held her close. Then she felt Thorn come up behind her, enveloping her in heat from behind as well as in front. It was the reverse of the night before and it felt every bit as exhilarating and dangerous as the night before. She was beginning to really like this kind of danger.

"Has he made love to you before, Princess?" Thorn whispered, making her shiver as his tongue licked around the outer shell of her ear.

"Yes," she moaned as Thorn's hands cupped her breasts, playing with her nipples through her clothing. She didn't know if she was answering his question or begging him for more. Probably both.

"I confess, I'm very jealous. And intrigued." He bit down gently on her earlobe, making her jump a little as hot sensations began to roll over her body.

"It was one magical night," Tristan said, his slightly accented voice making her tremble as he began untying her belt and unlacing her skirts. "But I didn't know she was the lady of the keep. I thought she was a warrior woman. I would not have touched her had I realized who she truly was, but I can never regret the greatest pleasure I have ever known." Tristan dropped to his knees as her skirts fell around her ankles.

He stroked the skin of her legs and her knees almost gave out when his skilled hands slid between them. She still wore her pantalets, but the soft fabric was thin and getting moist as her arousal kicked into high gear. As his fingers worked at the bows that held up the pantalets, Thorn was removing her corset and blouse. She allowed him to raise her arms and undress her like a doll. She wanted nothing more than to be naked with these two amazing, arousing men. If that made her a hussy, she didn't particularly care. She wanted them. Both.

Tristan did away with her pantalets and his fingers parted her folds. The next thing she knew, his mouth was on her clit, sucking and licking in a way guaranteed to make her knees buckle. But Thorn held her up, his arms surrounding her from behind, her bare breasts spilling out over his big hands. He seemed to enjoy her nipples, rolling them in just the right way, as if he were made to pleasure her and already knew how she liked to be touched.

A scandalous thought crossed her mind. Had the two men discussed this seduction in advance? Had Tristan told Thorn things about her body? Had they plotted and planned how they would work her?

If so, she was all in favor of their battle plan so far.

When her body shuddered in a tiny completion against Tristan's warm lips, the men laid her out on the room's long, wide bench. Tristan spread the mounds of fabric of her clothes under her so the surface of the wooden bench wasn't hard against her back. Considerate of him, she thought, but she didn't have time to say anything as Thorn spread her legs and knelt between them. He'd undressed and Cara's first glance at Thorn's slightly furred chest made her want to stroke him like a cat.

He had scars. Old and new. His body was built on the massive side, more muscular than she'd expected, with a sharply defined abdomen and a light dusting of hair that arrowed downward to a very impressive cock. A cock that was hard and waiting to give her pleasure. She wanted that cock and she wanted it now.

Cara lay back and spread her thighs even wider, inviting him in. She saw no reason to be coy when the instrument of her desire was ready and waiting. She knew what she wanted and she didn't want to wait.

Tristan had moved off to the side and she met his gaze for a moment, looking back at Thorn at the moment his cock slid home, taking her in one, long, amazing sweep. Oh, yes. He fit perfectly. Longer than Tristan and wider at the base, his cock curved slightly. She appreciated that little curve when he began to move and the head rubbed over a spot inside her that made her gasp.

Over and over, she felt the sensation that drove her wild and she clutched his shoulders while he pushed into her, making her breasts dance merrily as his pace increased. He grunted her name as he pistoned inside her, making her feel as if she were the only woman in his universe. But he was one of two men who inspired her. Cara looked over at Tristan when Thorn sank lower over her body, his teeth biting gently at the skin of her neck. No man had bitten her before and she found she liked it. A lot.

Tristan was naked, his thick cock in his hand as he watched Thorn fucking her. His golden eyes glowed with arousal and she understood in that moment that this triad could work. Really work. They'd have to work on the mechanics so all three found pleasure together—she still wasn't sure of the logistics on that—but there was no jealousy, no guilt. No anger or shame. Just pleasure and passion and a love that expanded inside her heart. The heart that held both men in it, never to be removed.

She stifled her scream of pleasure, holding Tristan's eyes as Thorn bit into her shoulder. They came together and it was a wild ride as he bucked inside her. She wrapped her legs around him, clutching him to her straining body as fireworks went off inside her pussy, their fire working through her whole body.

When they were both breathing steadier, Thorn sat up, careful to keep his cock tightly embedded inside her body. The glow of completion was rising into desire again as she felt him harden and lengthen, the head of his cock rubbing over that special place in her pussy as she caught her breath. Tristan hadn't come. He still stroked himself, watching all.

"Come over here," Thorn called to the other man, as if it were a prearranged signal they had worked out. Tristan stepped up, close to where Cara sat impaled on Thorn's cock. "Will you suck him off while I fuck you this time, Princess?" Thorn nearly growled in her ear. "I want to watch you take him in your mouth while I possess your pussy. Are you up for it?"

Thorn drew back to look into her eyes. She looked from Thorn to Tristan. The height of the bench positioned her at the perfect level. She was in exactly the right spot to turn her head and take Tristan's cock the way Thorn suggested.

Dare she?

Chapter Nine

Yes, she decided. Right at that moment, there was nothing she wanted more than to give both of these men pleasure.

She reached out to Tristan, pushing his hand away from his hard cock and grasping it. She gave it a few strokes as he stepped nearer and then she leaned out a short way to lick him from balls to head, taking her time while Thorn began to move under her. He would have to take care of the bottom half of this triad for both of them. She would see to Tristan while Thorn rocked them to completion.

Oh, yes. This could work.

They bounced and fucked and sucked together for long moments of intense pleasure and when they came, it was in unison. As it should be. Tristan let loose in her mouth and she swallowed every drop while Thorn shot into her from below, filling her pussy with his come. She shuddered and shook against them both, glad her cries of pleasure were stifled by Tristan's cock in her mouth. It wouldn't do for passersby to hear her scream and storm the armory at this particular moment.

No, this was a moment for the three of them to share alone. Just them. Learning each other and discovering the intricacies of each other's bodies and needs.

They spent hours in the armory. After they recovered a bit, they reversed places. Tristan took Cara from behind while Thorn thrust into her mouth in front. Thorn reached over her back, shocking her when he slid one finger inside her anus. The sensations released by that finger made her curious about how other things might feel and she began to understand how both men might take her at the same time.

Her suspicions were confirmed later, when she found breath to ask him about it. Thorn told her about many different ways they could all come together, and when the talk made her hot again, they tried out a few of them.

Thorn showed her a small bag of supplies—salve and soft cloths—they had to have stashed in the armory beforehand. That sealed their conspiracy in her mind.

"You two planned all this, didn't you? Don't try to deny it," she teased when Tristan retrieved a bag from a dark corner.

Thorn laughed while Tristan smiled a bit sheepishly.

"I got him drunk last night," Thorn confessed as he lazily stroked her breasts. "We talked about all the ways we could take you and he told me how you liked to be squeezed here." He pinched her nipple. "And here." His fingers teased her clit, tapping, then pushing in a rhythm that made her breath catch. "I stroked myself to sleep in my lonely bed dreaming of making love to you, Princess. And last night wasn't the first time. I've fantasized about you since the first time we met."

"You have?" She liked the sound of that. She'd thought of him often enough since that first meeting.

He nodded in response, taking a jar of salve from Tristan and turning her over so she was across his lap, ass up in the air. When he spread her cheeks, she looked back over her shoulder, intrigued and a little embarrassed by her position.

"What are you doing?" She gasped when he placed a large dollop of cold salve in the crevice of her ass. His fingers soon warmed the cream and her body as well, working the slippery substance into the small opening that grew wider and much warmer under his ministrations.

He slid one finger inside her and she moaned.

It felt surprisingly good.

Thorn nodded to Tristan and the Master at Arms sat on the bench, his hard cock close to her head. She knew, after the past hour, what he wanted. What they both wanted.

She opened her mouth and took him inside as Thorn added another finger in her ass, stretching her in a way that started out slightly uncomfortable, but soon became a desperate need for more. And he gave her more, stretching her beyond what she thought was possible, the cream seeming to dull some of the twinges as soon as they happened. Perhaps the salve had medicinal qualities? She'd have to check that out. Later. Much, much later.

Before too much longer, Thorn had slid his cock right up her ass and she didn't mind in the least. Far from it. It felt really good and when the men positioned her so that Tristan could join them, sliding into her pussy, the sensations were like nothing she could have ever expected.

It didn't take long for the first explosion of pleasure to overcome her senses. But it didn't stop there. No, the men kept at her until she was coming and coming, over and over. She lost count of the orgasms as they overtook her, stretching into one long, long climax that seemed to have no end.

Finally, it did end, when both men had come in her body, groaning as they joined her in that state of sated bliss.

They emerged from the armory late in the afternoon. The dragoness Sharlis had been enlisted as a lookout, communicating to them when the coast was clear. The men were adamant that Cara's reputation remain intact. No one but the dragons would know about their afternoon tryst.

After seeing her safely inside, Cara knew Tristan would go to Rath. Things were coming together. Tristan would become

Rath's knight and Cara would share their lives as their wife. They'd spent the afternoon making love and making plans as well.

She wasn't sure what Thorn was doing at the moment, but he'd asked her where to find the keep's archives before he'd left her in the hall with a chaste kiss. She was curious but didn't really have the energy to question him further. She had to clean up, change her gown and prepare for dinner in the great hall with the retainers. The outlying families had come to live in the keep for protection when the skirmishes started escalating. Nobody wanted to be caught alone on a farm with little protection when the enemy started herding skiths at them.

As a result, dinner had become a much larger affair than she was used to. It had been nice in the beginning, having folk around to talk to and help through tough times. Anything to break the uneasy silence that reigned between herself and her brother.

She wasn't sure, but Envard might demand to come down for dinner now that he was lucid, and she had to prepare for the inevitable confrontation. It could happen this very eve.

Sure enough, when she entered the great hall after bathing and changing into a fresh gown, Envard was already there, holding court as if he was the king himself. He liked lording it over everyone and making the retainers bow and scrape. That was something her father had never done and she knew she didn't imagine the dirty looks some of the older retainers gave Envard behind his back. They didn't like him but were powerless in the face of his inheritance. Only the king could remove him from the seat of power now, and King Roland had much more important things to worry about with war on the horizon.

Taking a deep breath, Cara took her seat beside her brother. Thorn and Tristan swept into the room only a moment later. Thorn sat next to Cara while Tristan took the chair on

Envard's other side. It was a bold move, but Envard didn't seem to realize the men had upset the normal seating plan as Tristan engaged him in conversation about the men at arms.

Thorn took Cara's hand under the table. "Are you ready? There are bound to be fireworks in this hall tonight." His smile reassured her that he would protect her from the worst of her brother's wrath as he squeezed her hand.

"Ready as I'll ever be, I suppose." She offered him a weak smile. She was not looking forward to what must be done.

"That's the spirit." Thorn winked at her before standing and going to the stained-glass window behind the dais on which they all sat. "It is a bit stuffy in here. Does this window open?" he seemed to ask rhetorically as he proceeded to open the window as wide as it would go.

The moment he stepped back from the wide opening, the female dragon's head slid through the window and craned downward, toward those sitting at the dais. Thorn patted her neck and made a show of surprise that didn't fool Cara one bit. They were up to something.

"It appears Lady Sharlis wants to join us," he stated with a teasing smile for Cara.

The dragon began making the rounds, starting with Thorn. She sniffed and licked her way over every person on the dais. Cara felt the tip of the dragon's tongue on her skin and jumped with a laughing squeak. It tickled.

"Good evening, Lady Sharlis," Cara said politely as the dragon made eye contact with her.

"Good evening, Princess. If I had tasted your skin before, I would have known you were of royal blood. Forgive me. It is a joyous thing for one of your line to join with my knight. The royal blood must be preserved."

Sharlis's words surprised Cara, but she tried not to show it. Only those the dragon intended to hear her words—those capable of it—heard her. Tristan's eyes widened as he looked from Cara to the dragon and back, but the moment was lost as Sharlis moved on to Envard.

He tried to duck away from her, but with his injury he was unable to move far without assistance. The dragon had her way, sniffing and licking his skin before moving on to Tristan. The Master at Arms welcomed her touch, greeting her as a friend, and then the dragoness lifted her head, framed by the ornate window opening. She looked at all assembled and then to her knight, Sir Thorn.

"Well, what is your verdict, milady?" Thorn asked theatrically. Cara had no idea what was going on.

"As you suspected, he is not of House Fadoral, nor is he related to Princess Cara in any way."

The dragon's words, were broadcast wide, so that anyone with the ability to hear dragons would know what she'd discovered. A few gasps from the large audience of retainers and men at arms caught Cara's attention and she realized that more than a few were able to understand the dragon's speech. There were witnesses other than Thorn, Tristan and Cara, which would help their case.

"I spent some hours this afternoon searching through the keep's archives," Thorn said conversationally. "I discovered a series of personal journals of Lord Harald and his late wives hidden among a group of exceedingly dusty estate ledgers. Two volumes in particular were of great interest." Thorn motioned to Tristan and the Master at Arms lifted two small journals from inside one of his many pockets.

"I have read these at Sir Thorn's request and found evidence, written in both the lord's and lady's hands, that Envard is not the legitimate heir to House Fadoral. Lord Harald's second wife, Lady Mariar was already pregnant when they wed. He took her to wife as the result of a series of agreements with her father, his old friend, Lord Tharliss of

Jenra. The lady's own words confirm it. Envard is the son of a visiting minstrel, not Lord Harald."

Shocked gasps came from the rest of the audience who had not heard the dragoness's pronouncement.

"Lies!" Envard cried out.

"Why would they make a record of such a damning secret?" Cara wanted to know. "And why would Father agree to such a marriage in the first place?"

"The lady's diary records her undying—if rather foolish—love for a wayward minstrel. She agreed to the marriage arranged by her father, Lord Tharliss, because it was made clear to her that she had no other recourse. Tharliss's men had chased the minstrel right out of the country," Thorn replied, holding up one of the journals. "She seemed to think the minstrel would return for her and wanted her son to know who his father was. Such were her reasons for writing the tale in her diary."

Thorn then held up the other journal. "Lord Harald agreed to the marriage out of infatuation with the young lady and greed. He speaks frankly in his private writings about being willing to overlook the child she already carried in exchange for a great deal of land and riches that came with the lady by way of Lord Tharliss. The dowry was much larger than it should have been. More than enough to make up for the inconvenient child. And who knows? Perhaps an older man would want to be thought virile enough to have a babe so soon after wedding a young miss. Such things are not unheard of."

Murmurs sounded throughout those assembled.

"My partner, Lady Sharlis, has also confirmed it. Those of you who heard her will tell the others what she said, I'm sure. And if you did hear her, I'd like to talk to you later. It is a rare gift to be able to speak with dragons. One that should be cultivated if at all possible," Thorn went on in a friendly voice.

"Dragons can taste and smell subtle differences in all beings that tell them who is related to whom. It is one of their lesser skills, part of their natural abilities." He patted Sharlis's neck with obvious affection.

"Did you know, Envard?" Cara asked in a small, hurt voice.

Her brother turned away without answering.

"He knew," Thorn said with disgust. "Both of these diaries were not found in the archives. Only empty spaces where they should have been shelved. I had to search for them. They were in Envard's room, hidden among his personal belongings." The murmurs grew louder at his revelation. "This evidence and Sharlis's findings will be brought to the king as soon as possible," Thorn added. "For now, by my authority as a knight of the realm, I order Envard taken into custody and held until the king can decide the matter."

Envard started to yell at that point and Tristan moved in with several men at arms to subdue him. He would not be quiet, so they gagged him and several of the bolder retainers began to cheer. It was clear they had not liked Envard's reign over their lands and people.

When Envard had been carted away, tied up and carried by the men at arms back to his room where he would be placed under house arrest, Tristan moved to stand beside Cara's chair. Thorn stood on her other side.

Tristan called for calm and received curious glances. "There is more, good people of Fadoral. The dragon, Sir Golgorath, has asked me to become his knight and I have accepted," Tristan announced. Smiles and cheers of congratulations greeted his words.

When the sound died down, Thorn stepped forward. "Sir Golgorath and Lady Sharlis are mates, which makes Sir Tristan my fighting partner," Thorn explained. "Together, we have asked Lady Cara to be our wife and she has agreed. It was this that prompted my search into the archives because something here never did seem right to me on my many visits to your keep. For one thing, Envard always intervened when I wanted to speak with Lady Cara. I have uncovered this evidence, but it is for the king to decide. Whatever happens now, Lady Cara will be safe, as our bride."

Cheers followed, along with some laughter and good-natured humor at the threesome's expense. These retainers had known Cara all her life and she liked the way they reverted to the way they had been during her father's rule. Their friendship was easy, their respect obvious, if not the bowing and scraping her brother had favored.

The meal that followed was a celebration. The first of many.

Thorn and Tristan, along with Rath and Sharlis, flew her back to the Border Lair the next day, where they started preparations for a traditional Lair wedding. They also held a ceremony at the keep so all their friends and retainers could attend. The king himself flew in to settle the matter of her brother and Cara learned the secret of the royal blood. The welcome she received from the king and his brother, the Prince of Spies, made her feel like family—which she was, by a very distant blood relation.

The king soon settled the question of inheritance. Envard was stripped of the title. The king gave Cara the title, which would pass down to her children, regardless of their gender. The king allowed the trio to choose where they would live—either in the Lair or at the keep—and they settled on a plan of dividing their time between the two. Fadoral needed guidance and leadership while the skirmishes continued. Having the dragons living there, if only part-time, was a good deterrent and defense against future attacks.

Thorn, Tristan and Cara grew closer and closer, and when it came time for their Lair wedding and the first of many dragon mating flights, they were more than ready. The pleasure, amplified by the dragons, was unlike anything they had experienced alone. It was...more. More heady. More triumphant. And more love than she had ever known.

Cara had everything she'd ever dreamed of, though she could never have anticipated sharing the love to two brave and noble men. They had become Prince-Consorts by marrying her and the people of the keep had started calling her Princess rather than just lady. It would take some getting used to, but she was glad to try.

She had gone from having only one brother to having a whole family of royal cousins as well as dragons descended from Rath and Sharlis. She even had in-laws. Thorn's parents were an older set of knights and their lady, who adopted Cara and Tristan with open hearts and good cheer. They visited often, as did Rath and Sharlis's dragon children and grandchildren, bringing many knights to their hall.

Construction had started to widen the entryway so that dragons could enter and join in the festivities in the great hall. And a large pit of sand had been excavated inside the courtyard in which the dragons could wallow. Plans were underway to expand and remodel the keep even further to make it easier for dragons to live there, and the workmen set to their jobs with glad enthusiasm. Dragons were good to have around if one lived in constant threat of enemy attack. Not only that, but winter was coming and dragons generated their own heat.

The men and dragons had given her so much joy, she blessed the day the Mother of All had brought them into her life. Even as the conflict on the border continued, happiness and love reigned once more at Fadoral keep.

About the Author

Bianca D'Arc has run a laboratory, climbed the corporate ladder in the shark-infested streets of Manhattan, studied and taught martial arts, and earned the right to put a whole bunch of letters after her name, but she's always enjoyed writing more than any of her other pursuits. She grew up and still lives on Long Island, where she keeps busy with an extensive garden, several aquariums full of very demanding fish, and writing her favorite genres of paranormal, fantasy and sci-fi romance.

Bianca loves to hear from readers and can be reached through Facebook, her Yahoo group or through the various links on her website.

Website:
http://biancadarc.com

Yahoo Group:
http://groups.yahoo.com/group/BiancaDArc/join

It's all about the story...

Romance

HORROR

Retro ROMANCE

www.samhainpublishing.com

CPSIA information can be obtained at www.ICGtesting.com
Printed in the USA
BVOW08s0820120913

331006BV00003B/5/P

9 781619 215481